SQUIDDING AROUND

Prank You Very Much

KEVIN SHERRY

WITH COLOR BY WES DZIOBA

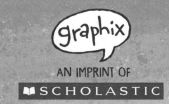

graphix

AN IMPRINT OF

SCHOLASTIC

To Erin Nutsugah,
a true catch and my reel love.

Library of Congress Cataloging-in-Publication Data Available

ISBN 978-1-338-75563-3 (hardcover)
ISBN 978-1-338-75562-6 (paperback)

10 9 8 7 6 5 4 3 2 1   22 23 24 25 26

Printed in China   62

First edition, February 2022
Edited by Jenne Abramowitz
Book designed by Steve Ponzo
Creative Director: Phil Falco
Publisher: David Saylor

CHAPTER 1

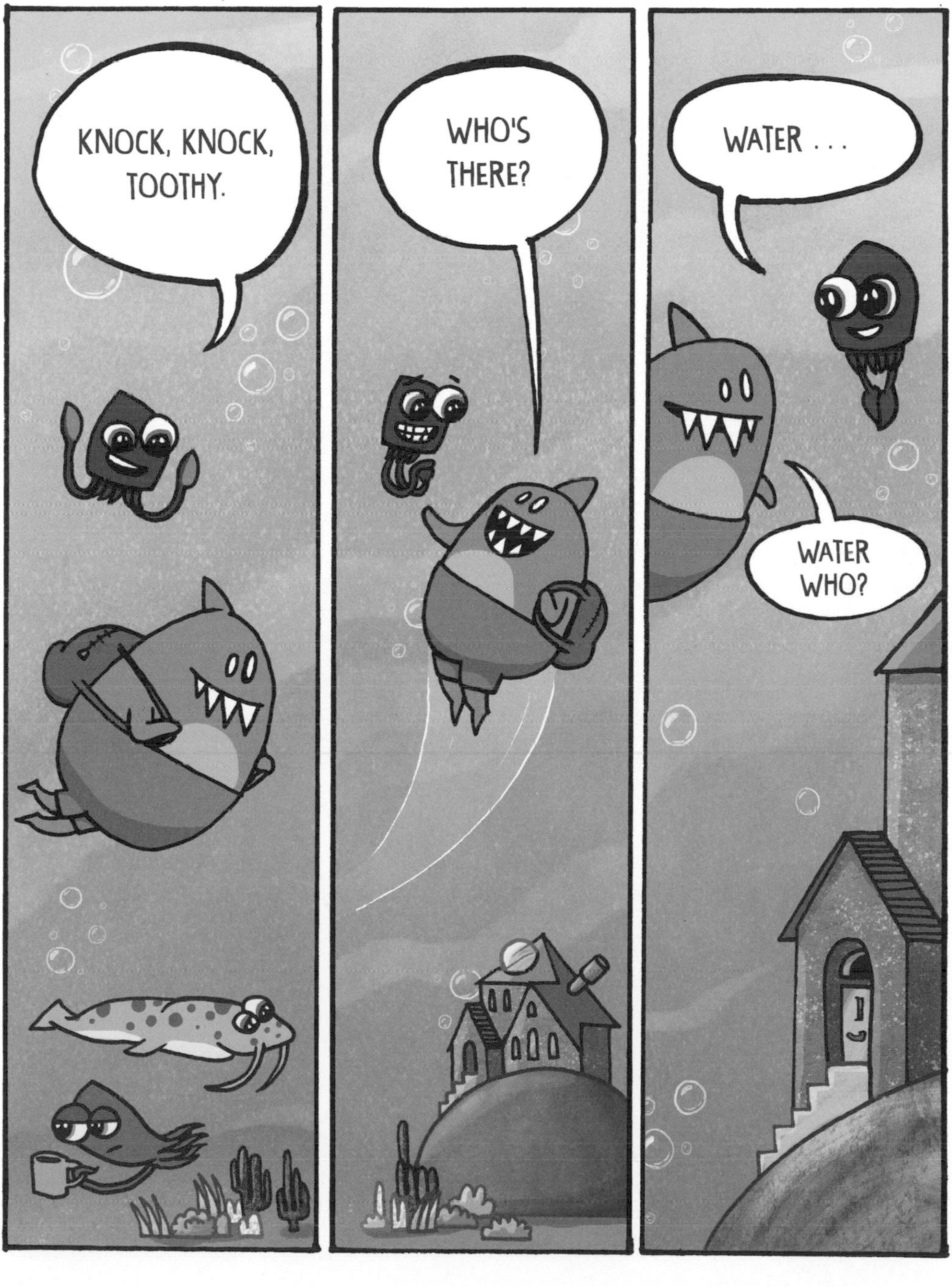
KNOCK, KNOCK, TOOTHY.
WHO'S THERE?
WATER . . .
WATER WHO?

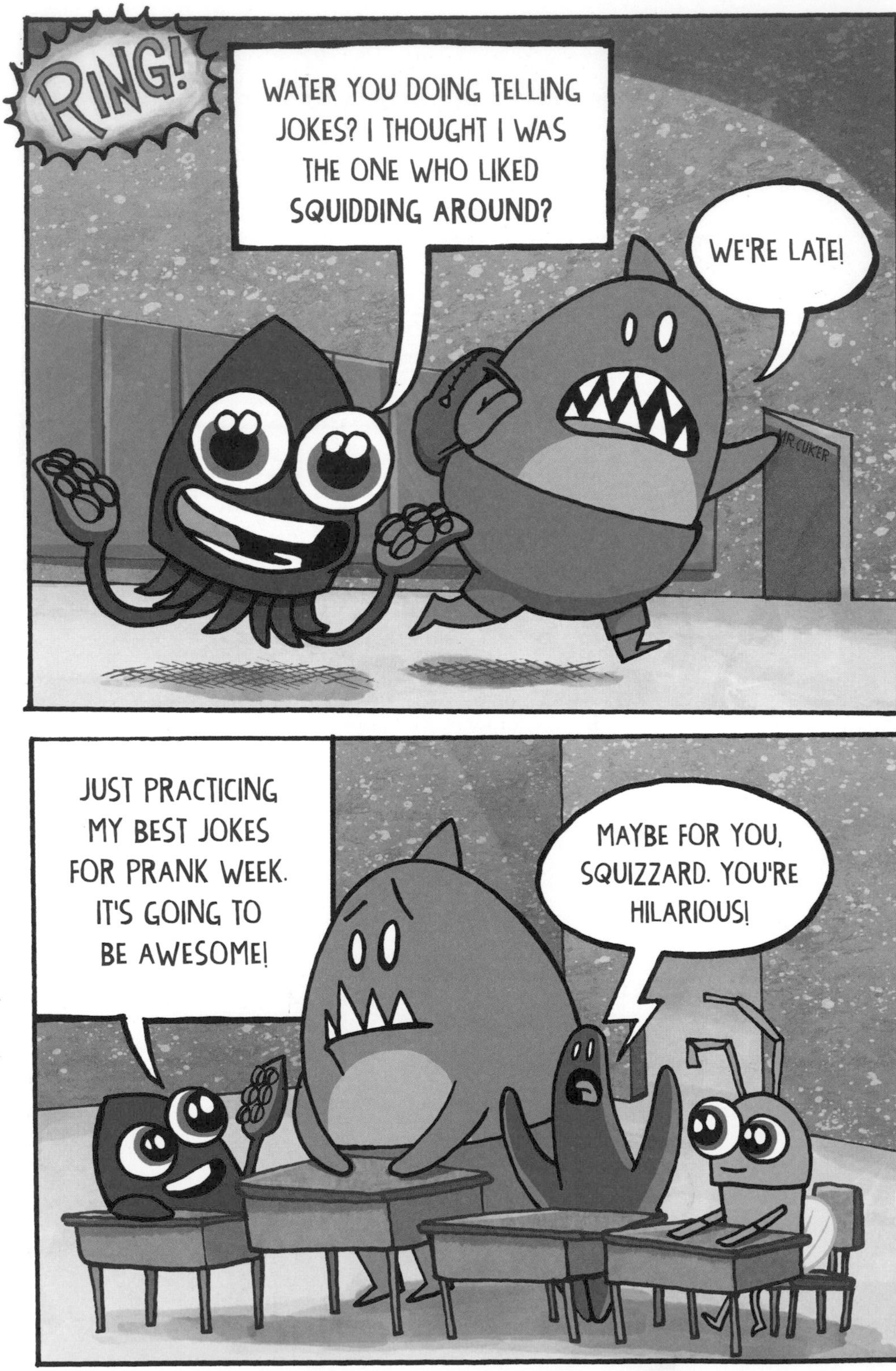
RING!
WATER YOU DOING TELLING JOKES? I THOUGHT I WAS THE ONE WHO LIKED SQUIDDING AROUND?
WE'RE LATE!
MR.CUKER
JUST PRACTICING MY BEST JOKES FOR PRANK WEEK. IT'S GOING TO BE AWESOME!
MAYBE FOR YOU, SQUIZZARD. YOU'RE HILARIOUS!

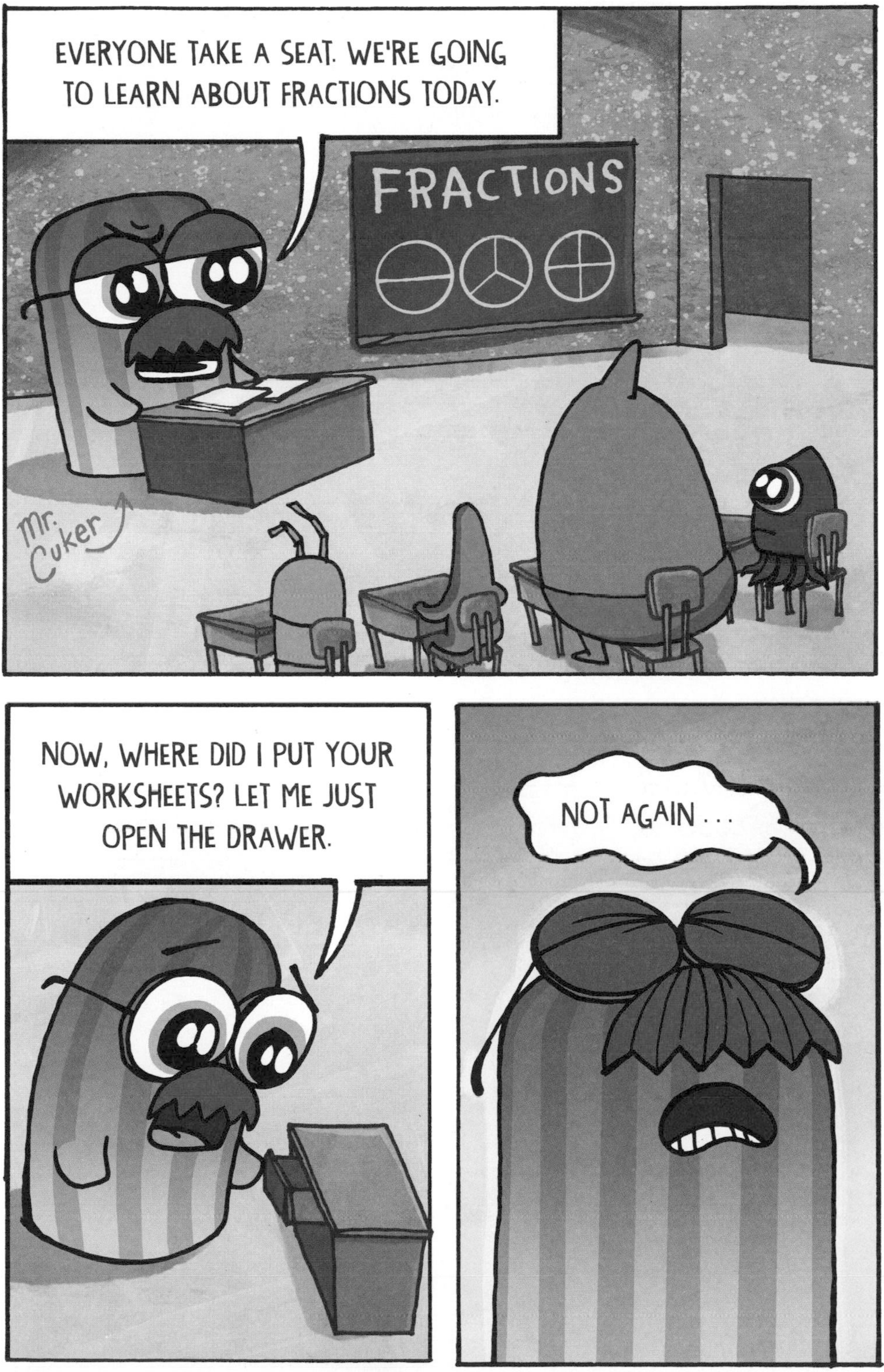
EVERYONE TAKE A SEAT. WE'RE GOING TO LEARN ABOUT FRACTIONS TODAY.
FRACTIONS
Mr. Cuker
NOW, WHERE DID I PUT YOUR WORKSHEETS? LET ME JUST OPEN THE DRAWER.
NOT AGAIN . . .

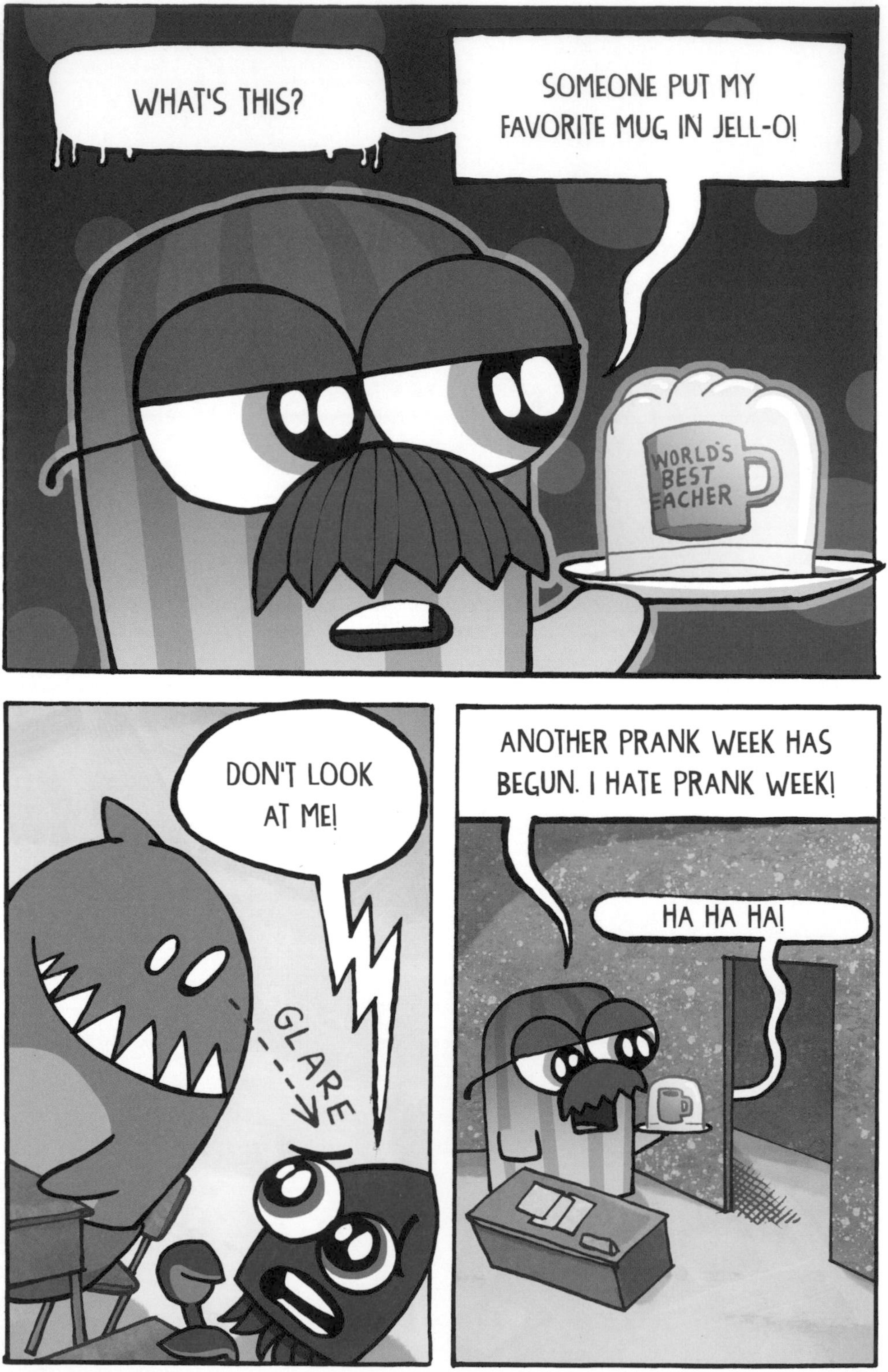
WHAT'S THIS?
SOMEONE PUT MY FAVORITE MUG IN JELL-O!
WORLD'S BEST EACHER
DON'T LOOK AT ME!
GLARE
ANOTHER PRANK WEEK HAS BEGUN. I HATE PRANK WEEK!
HA HA HA!

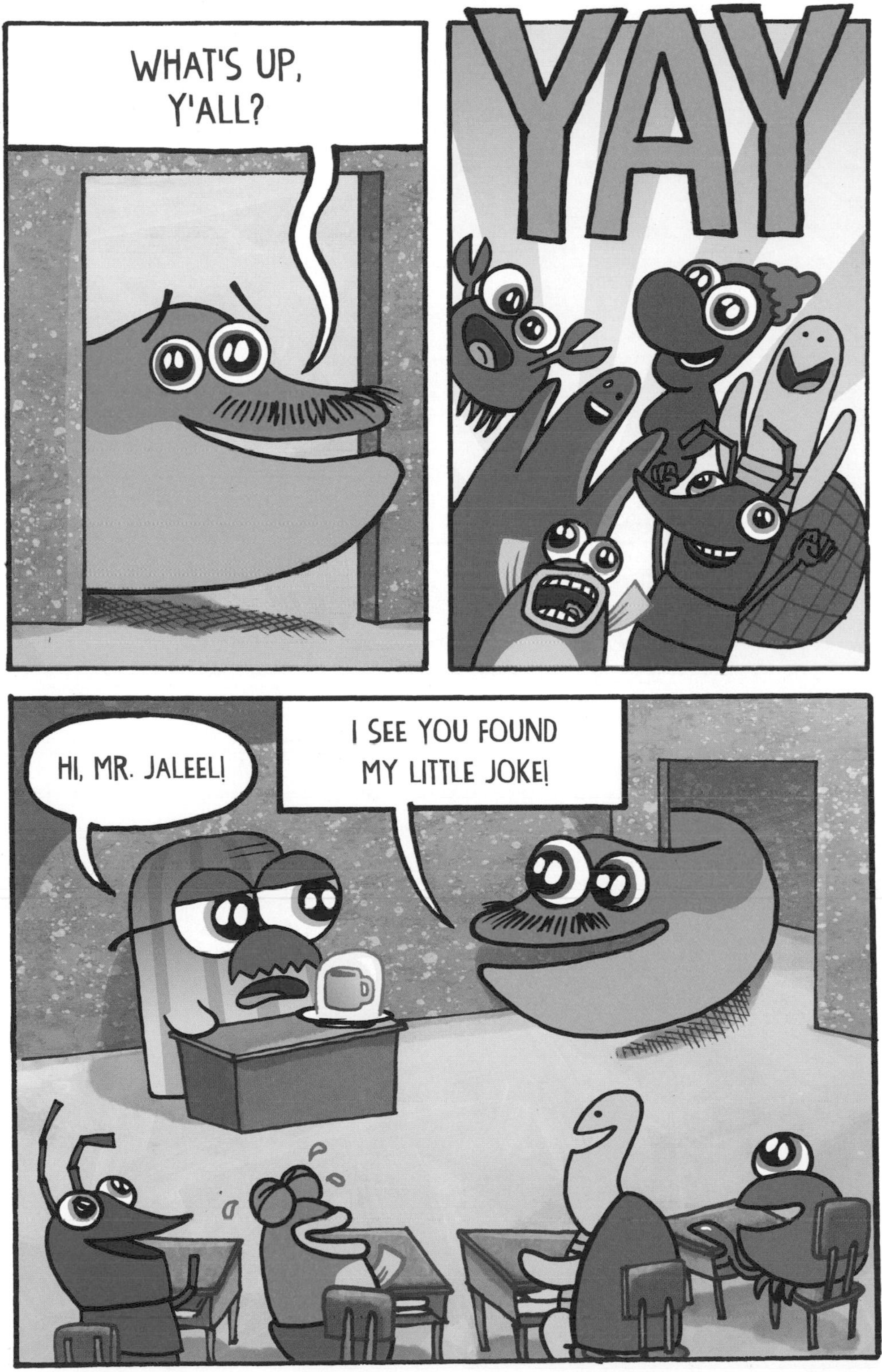
WHAT'S UP, Y'ALL?
YAY
HI, MR. JALEEL!
I SEE YOU FOUND MY LITTLE JOKE!

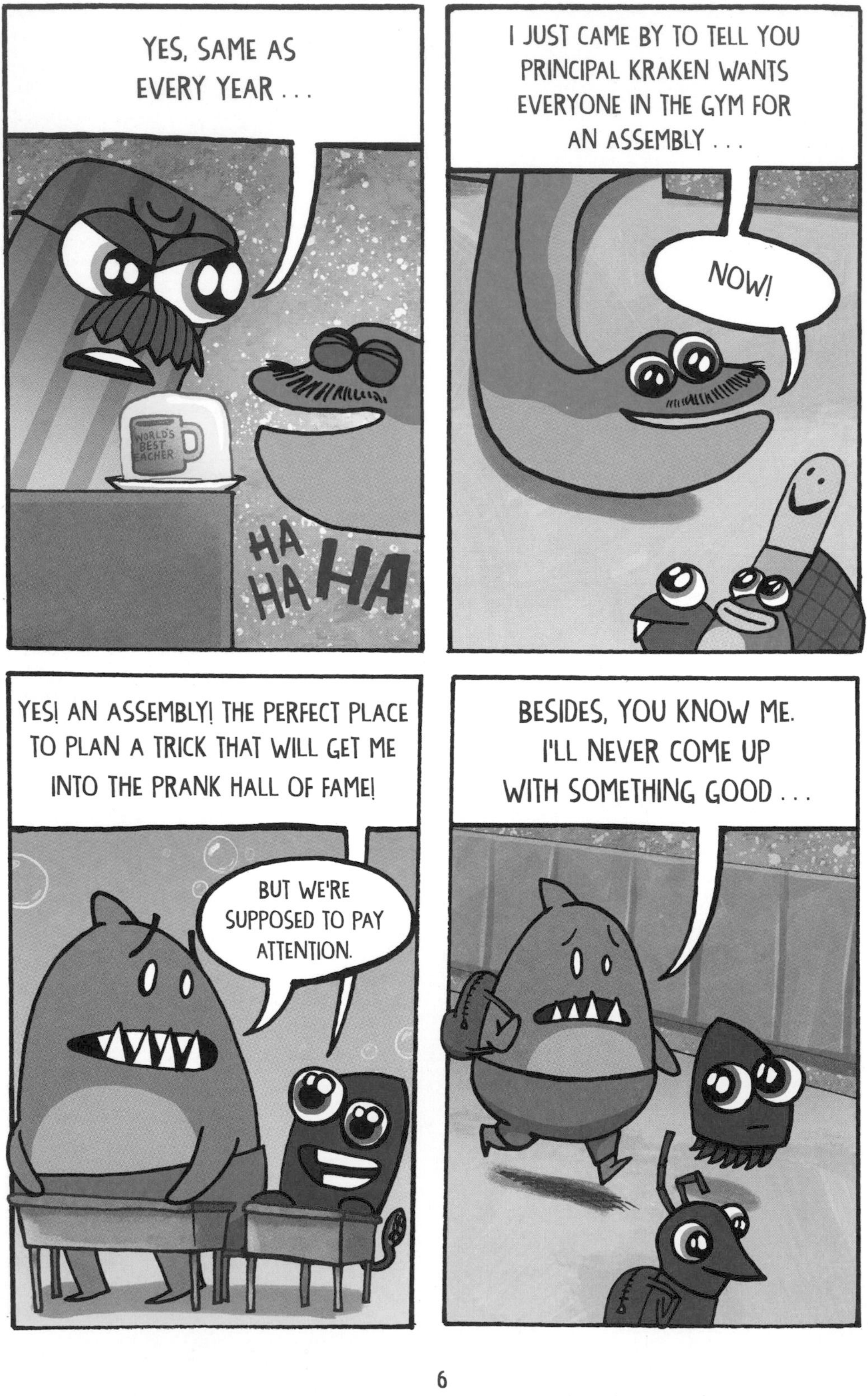
YES, SAME AS EVERY YEAR . . .
WORLD'S BEST EACHER
HA HA HA
I JUST CAME BY TO TELL YOU PRINCIPAL KRAKEN WANTS EVERYONE IN THE GYM FOR AN ASSEMBLY . . .
NOW!
YES! AN ASSEMBLY! THE PERFECT PLACE TO PLAN A TRICK THAT WILL GET ME INTO THE PRANK HALL OF FAME!
BUT WE'RE SUPPOSED TO PAY ATTENTION.
BESIDES, YOU KNOW ME. I'LL NEVER COME UP WITH SOMETHING GOOD . . .

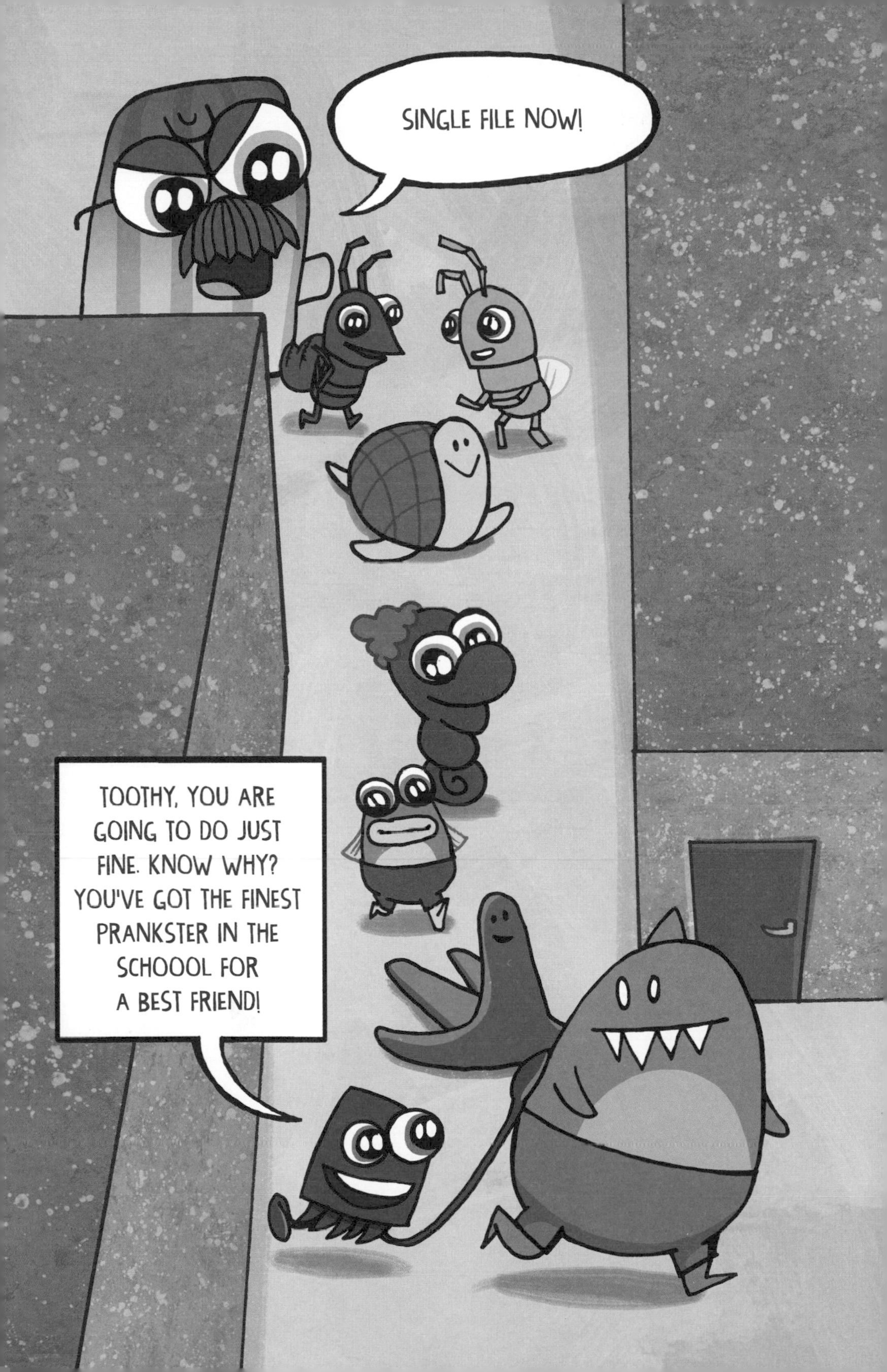
SINGLE FILE NOW!
TOOTHY, YOU ARE GOING TO DO JUST FINE. KNOW WHY? YOU'VE GOT THE FINEST PRANKSTER IN THE SCHOOOL FOR A BEST FRIEND!

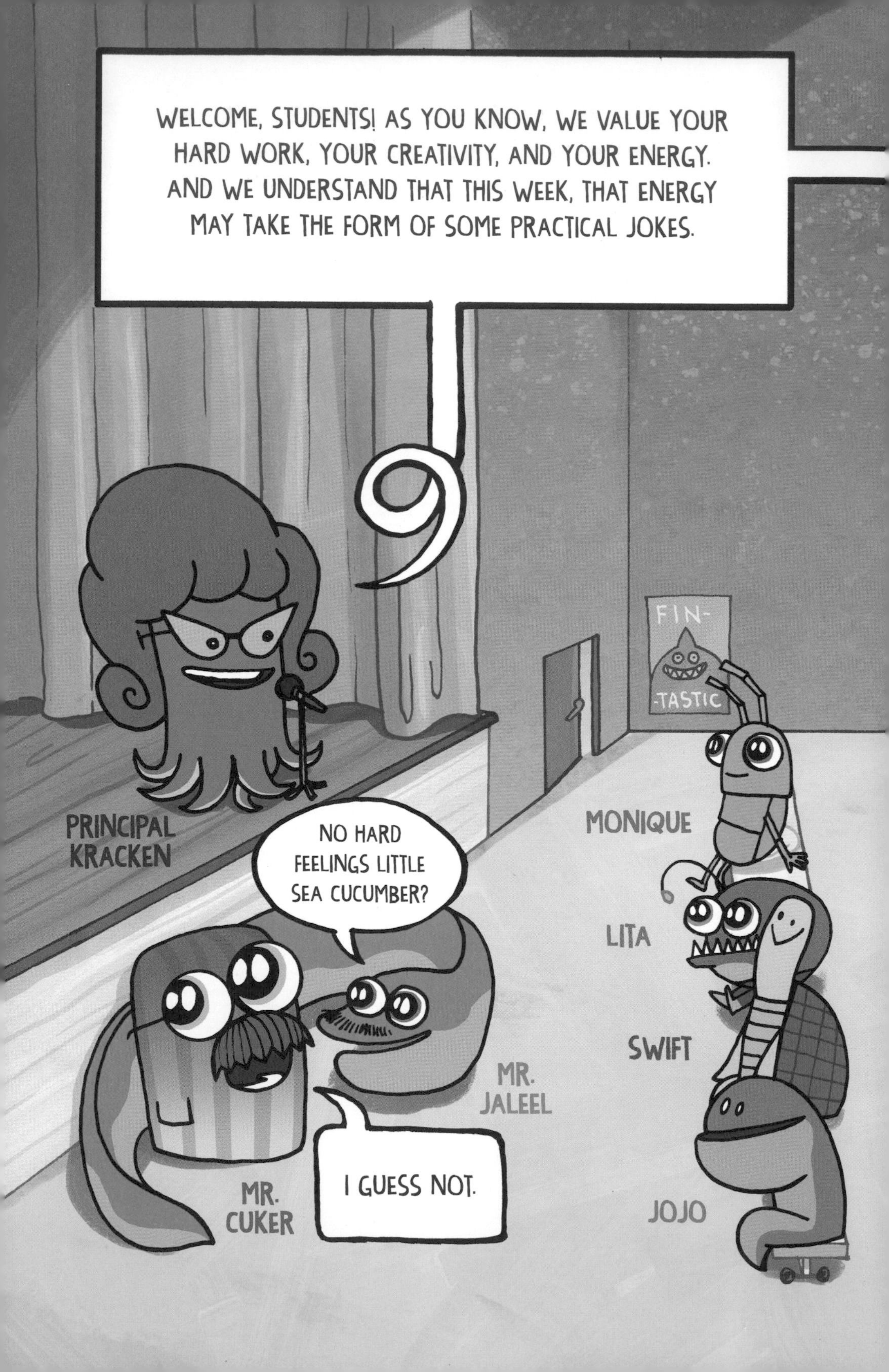
WELCOME, STUDENTS! AS YOU KNOW, WE VALUE YOUR HARD WORK, YOUR CREATIVITY, AND YOUR ENERGY. AND WE UNDERSTAND THAT THIS WEEK, THAT ENERGY MAY TAKE THE FORM OF SOME PRACTICAL JOKES.
FIN- -TASTIC
PRINCIPAL KRACKEN
MONIQUE
NO HARD FEELINGS LITTLE SEA CUCUMBER?
LITA
SWIFT
MR. JALEEL
I GUESS NOT.
MR. CUKER
JOJO

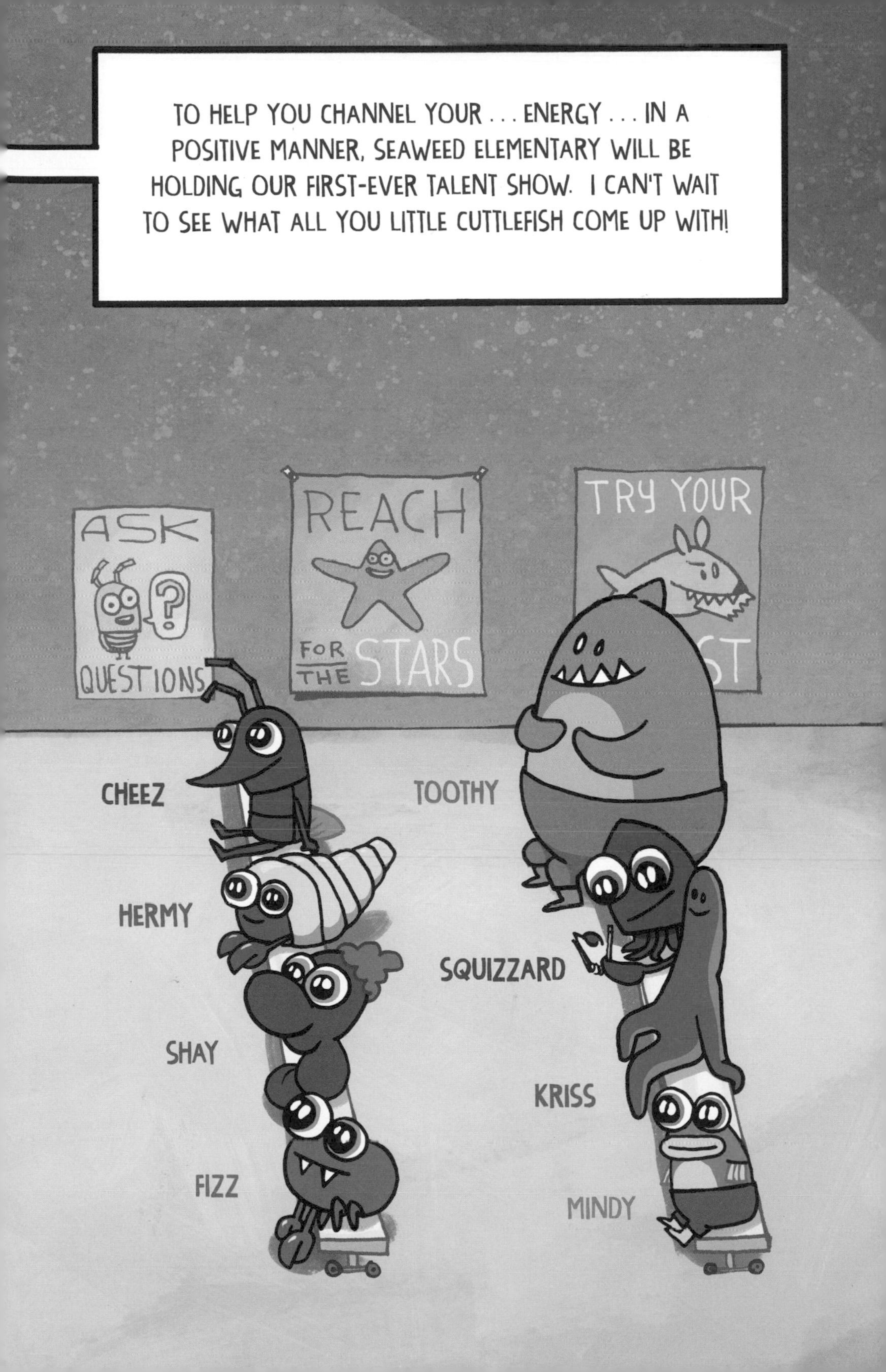
TO HELP YOU CHANNEL YOUR . . . ENERGY . . . IN A POSITIVE MANNER, SEAWEED ELEMENTARY WILL BE HOLDING OUR FIRST-EVER TALENT SHOW. I CAN'T WAIT TO SEE WHAT ALL YOU LITTLE CUTTLEFISH COME UP WITH!
ASK QUESTIONS
REACH FOR THE STARS
TRY YOUR
ST
CHEEZ
TOOTHY
HERMY
SQUIZZARD
SHAY
KRISS
FIZZ
MINDY

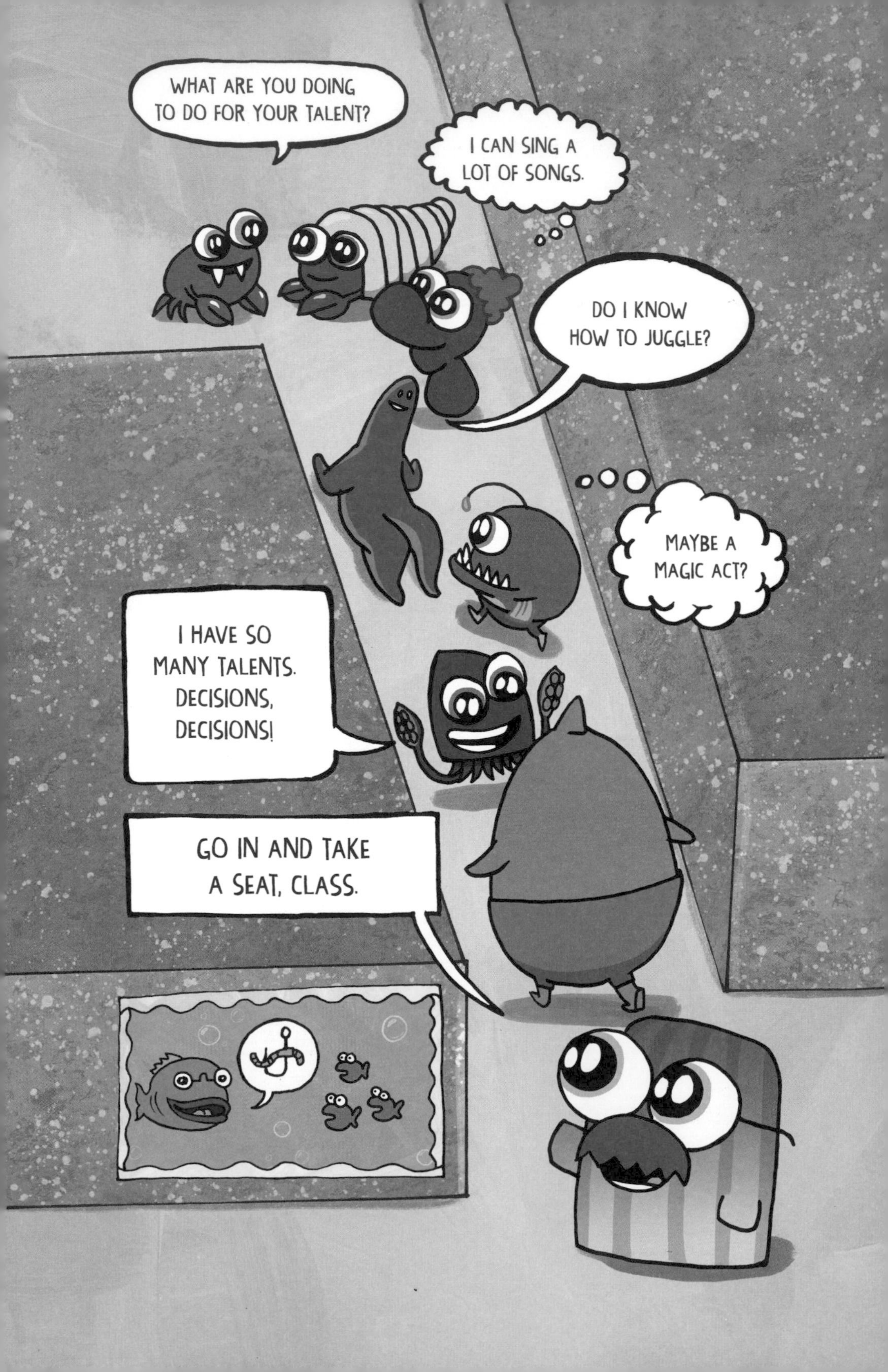
WHAT ARE YOU DOING TO DO FOR YOUR TALENT?
I CAN SING A LOT OF SONGS.
DO I KNOW HOW TO JUGGLE?
MAYBE A MAGIC ACT?
I HAVE SO MANY TALENTS. DECISIONS, DECISIONS!
GO IN AND TAKE A SEAT, CLASS.

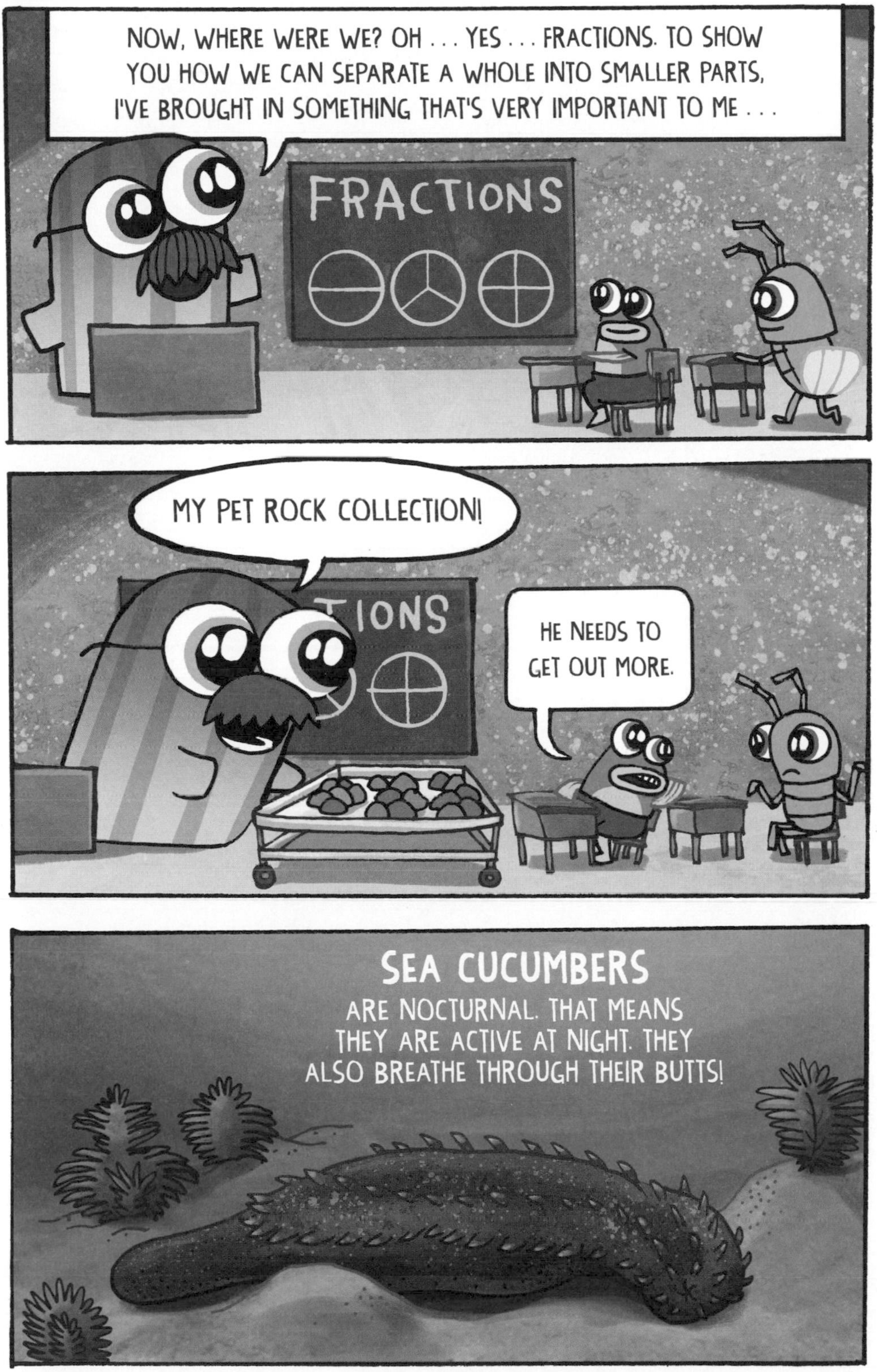
NOW, WHERE WERE WE? OH . . . YES . . . FRACTIONS. TO SHOW YOU HOW WE CAN SEPARATE A WHOLE INTO SMALLER PARTS, I'VE BROUGHT IN SOMETHING THAT'S VERY IMPORTANT TO ME . . .
FRACTIONS
MY PET ROCK COLLECTION!
HE NEEDS TO GET OUT MORE.
SEA CUCUMBERS
ARE NOCTURNAL. THAT MEANS THEY ARE ACTIVE AT NIGHT. THEY ALSO BREATHE THROUGH THEIR BUTTS!

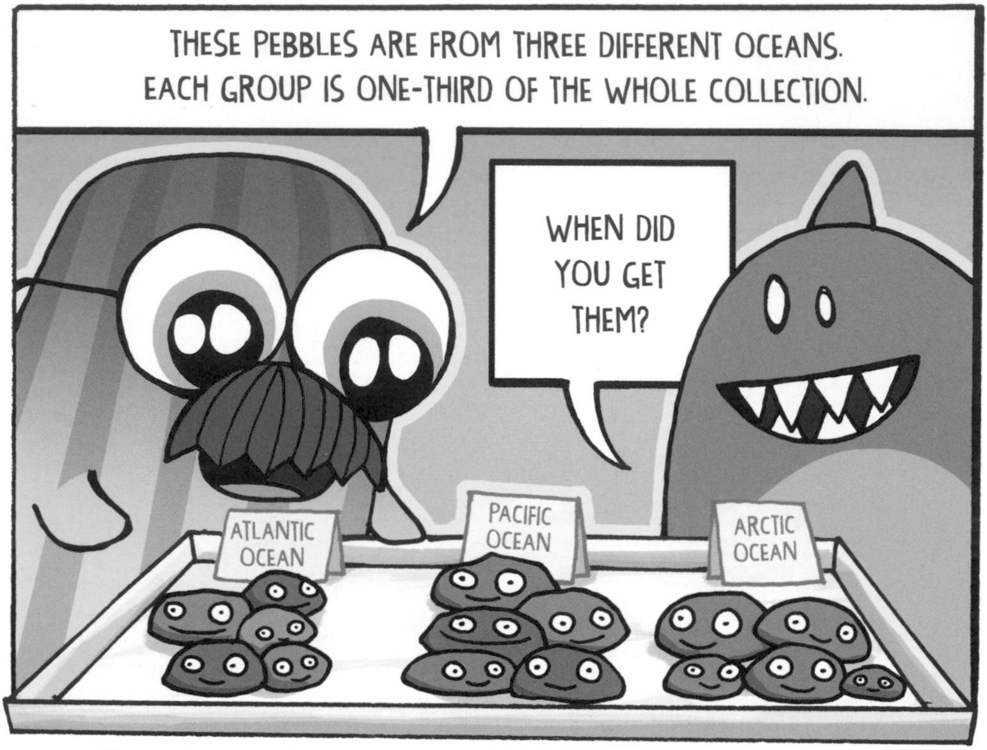
THESE PEBBLES ARE FROM THREE DIFFERENT OCEANS.
EACH GROUP IS ONE-THIRD OF THE WHOLE COLLECTION.
WHEN DID YOU GET THEM?
ATLANTIC OCEAN
PACIFIC OCEAN
ARCTIC OCEAN

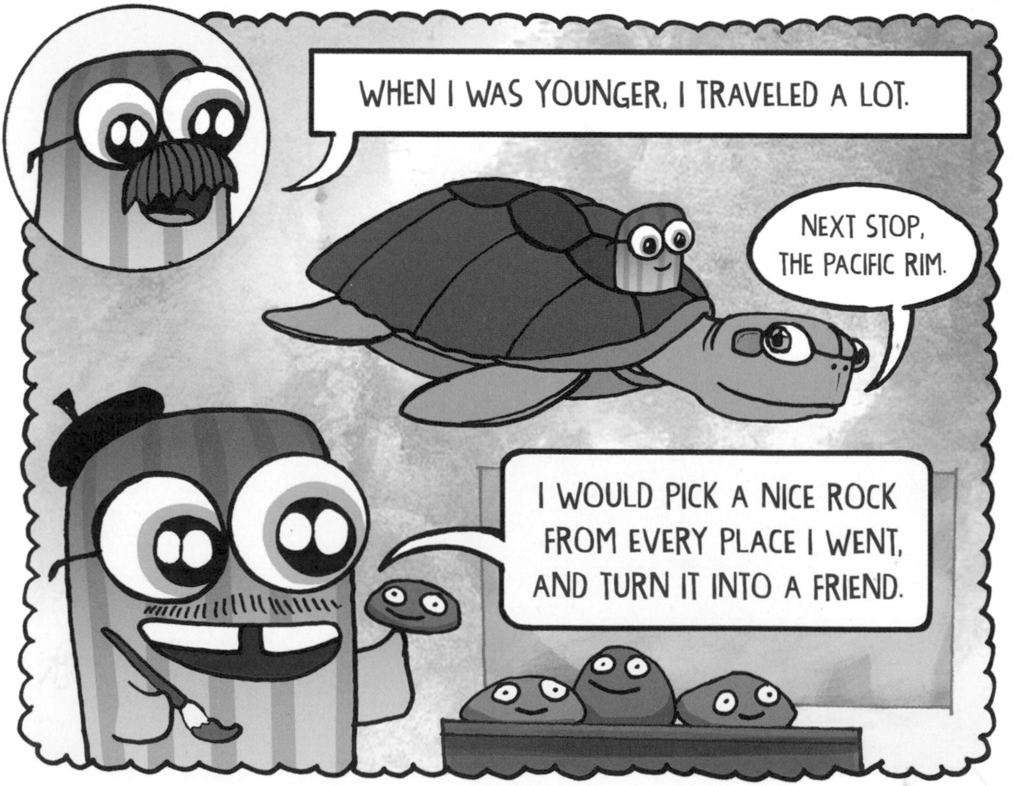
WHEN I WAS YOUNGER, I TRAVELED A LOT.
NEXT STOP, THE PACIFIC RIM.
I WOULD PICK A NICE ROCK FROM EVERY PLACE I WENT, AND TURN IT INTO A FRIEND.

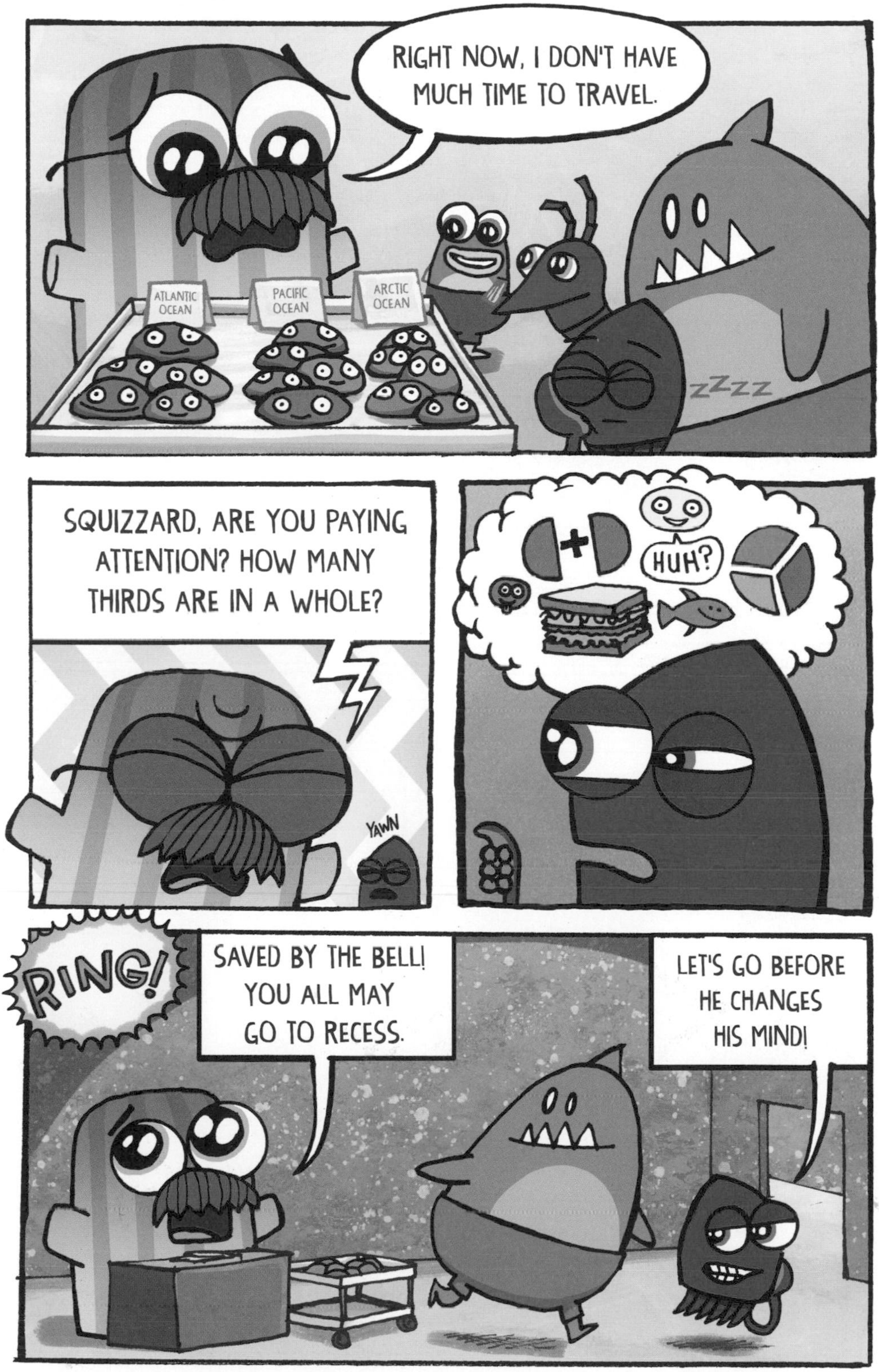
RIGHT NOW, I DON'T HAVE MUCH TIME TO TRAVEL.
ATLANTIC OCEAN
PACIFIC OCEAN
ARCTIC OCEAN
ZZZZ
SQUIZZARD, ARE YOU PAYING ATTENTION? HOW MANY THIRDS ARE IN A WHOLE?
YAWN
HUH?
RING!
SAVED BY THE BELL! YOU ALL MAY GO TO RECESS.
LET'S GO BEFORE HE CHANGES HIS MIND!

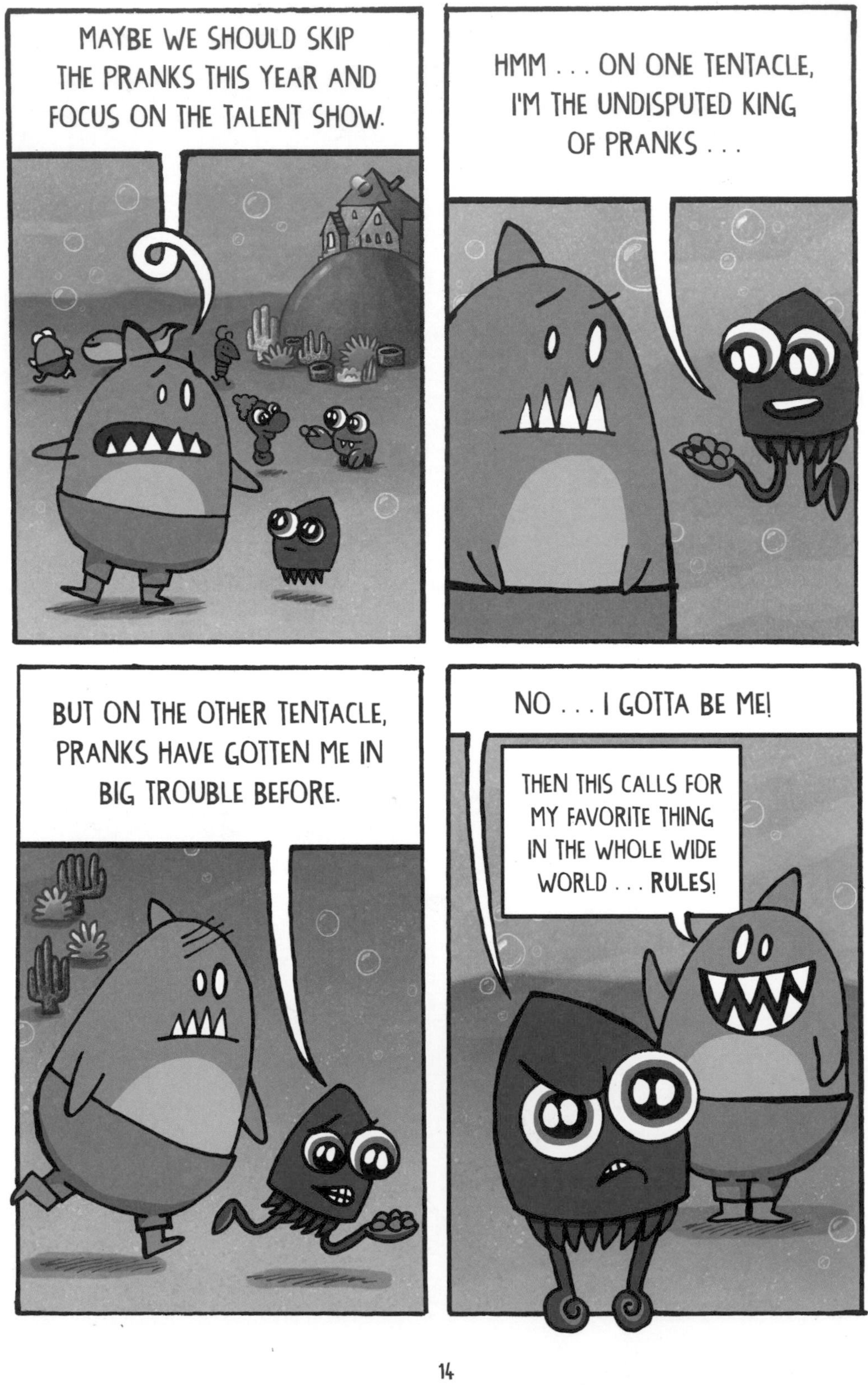
MAYBE WE SHOULD SKIP THE PRANKS THIS YEAR AND FOCUS ON THE TALENT SHOW.
HMM . . . ON ONE TENTACLE, I'M THE UNDISPUTED KING OF PRANKS . . .
BUT ON THE OTHER TENTACLE, PRANKS HAVE GOTTEN ME IN BIG TROUBLE BEFORE.
NO . . . I GOTTA BE ME!
THEN THIS CALLS FOR MY FAVORITE THING IN THE WHOLE WIDE WORLD . . . **RULES**!

NO HURT FEELINGS.	NO BODILY HARM.	NO BREAKING ANYTHING.	NO MAKING FUN.	BE CREATIVE.

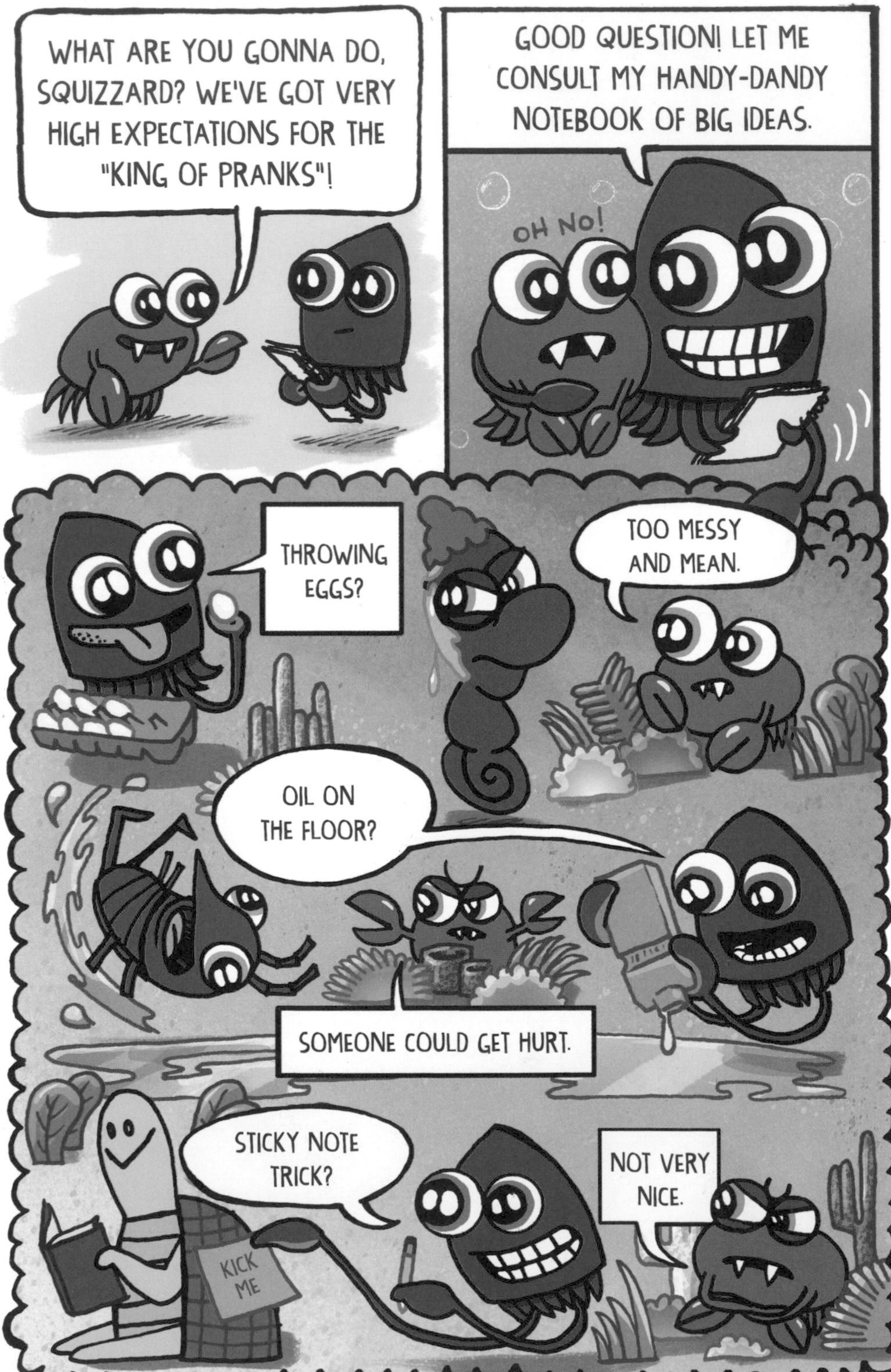
WHAT ARE YOU GONNA DO, SQUIZZARD? WE'VE GOT VERY HIGH EXPECTATIONS FOR THE "KING OF PRANKS"!
GOOD QUESTION! LET ME CONSULT MY HANDY-DANDY NOTEBOOK OF BIG IDEAS.
OH NO!
THROWING EGGS?
TOO MESSY AND MEAN.
OIL ON THE FLOOR?
SOMEONE COULD GET HURT.
STICKY NOTE TRICK?
KICK ME
NOT VERY NICE.

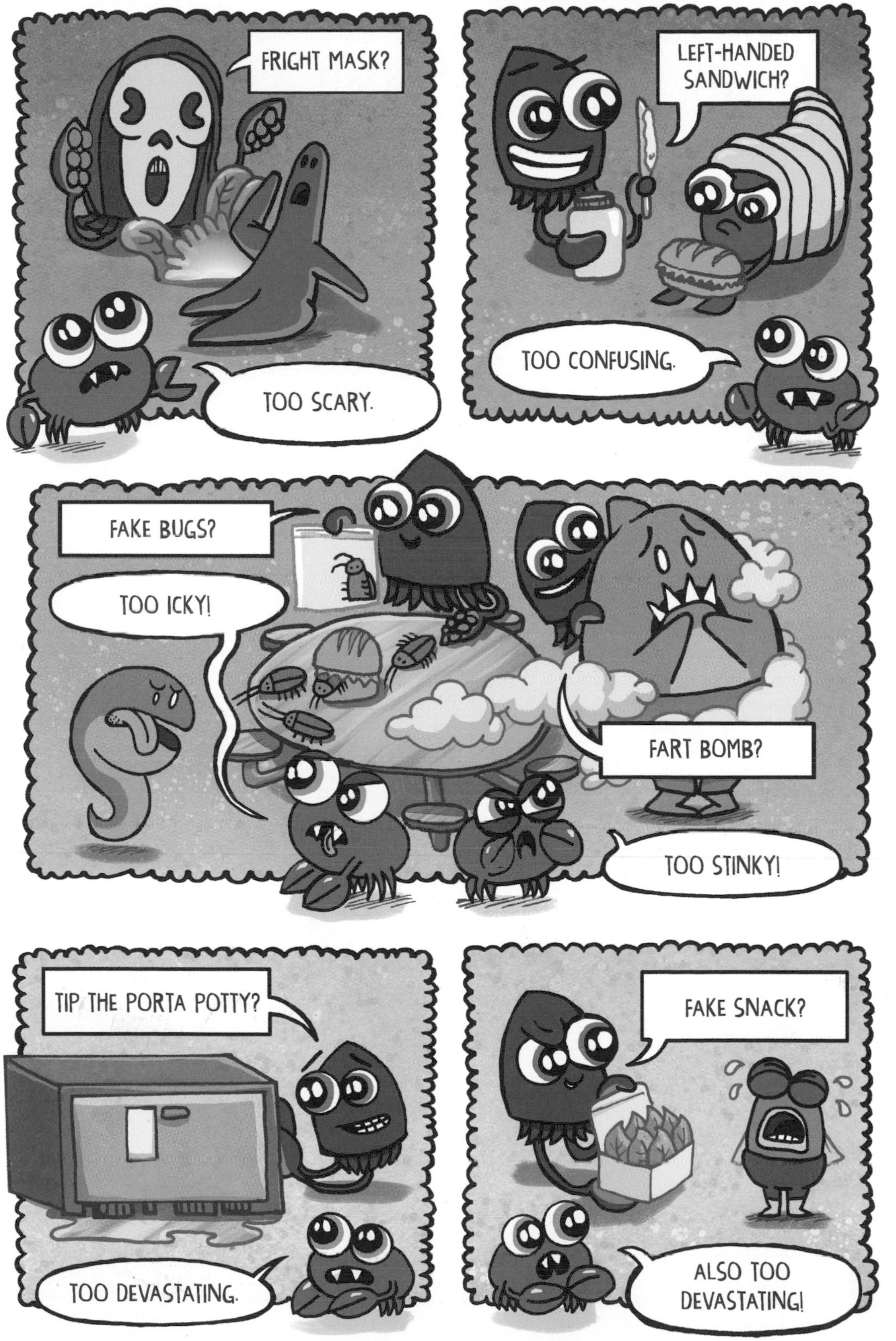
FRIGHT MASK?
TOO SCARY.
LEFT-HANDED SANDWICH?
TOO CONFUSING.
FAKE BUGS?
TOO ICKY!
FART BOMB?
TOO STINKY!
TIP THE PORTA POTTY?
TOO DEVASTATING.
FAKE SNACK?
ALSO TOO DEVASTATING!

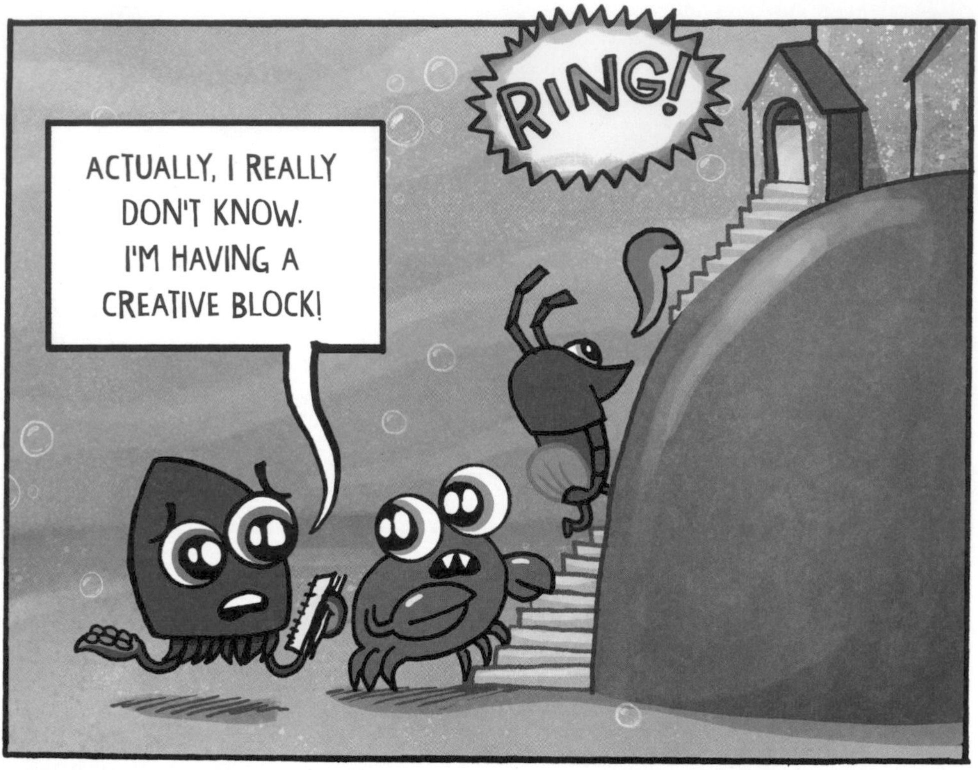
ACTUALLY, I REALLY DON'T KNOW. I'M HAVING A CREATIVE BLOCK!
RING!

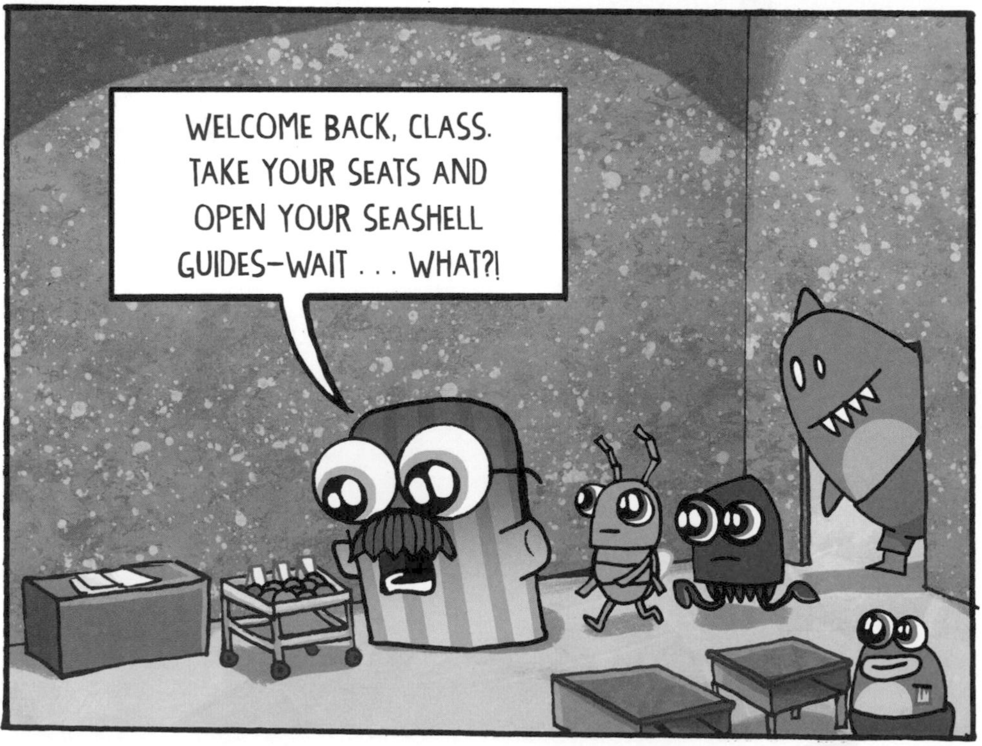
WELCOME BACK, CLASS. TAKE YOUR SEATS AND OPEN YOUR SEASHELL GUIDES—WAIT . . . WHAT?!

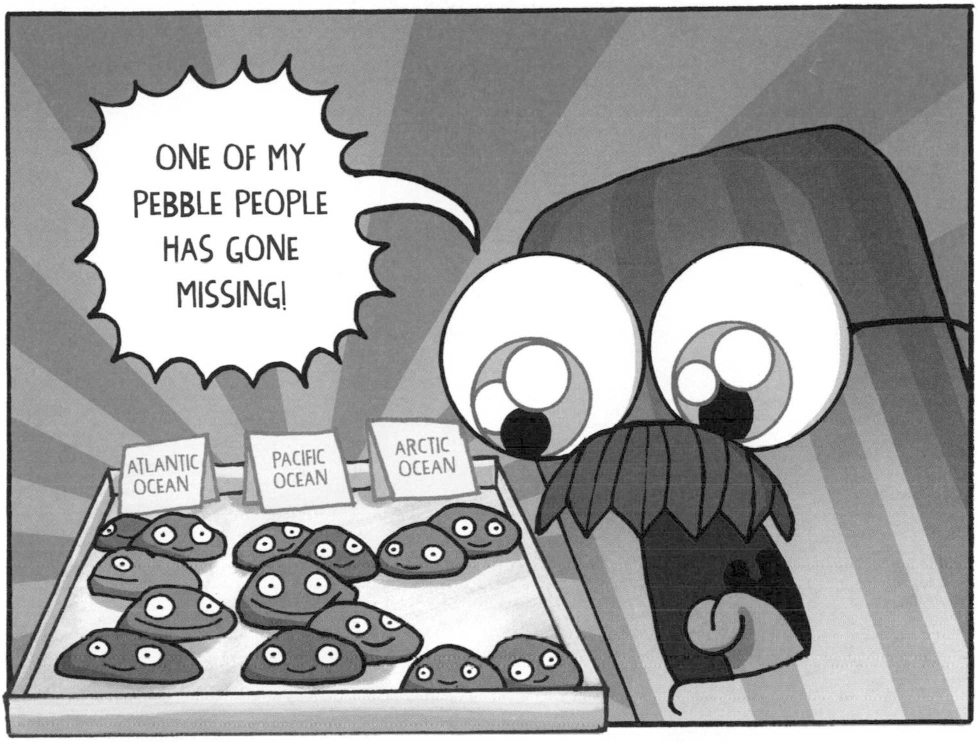
ONE OF MY PEBBLE PEOPLE HAS GONE MISSING!
ATLANTIC OCEAN
PACIFIC OCEAN
ARCTIC OCEAN

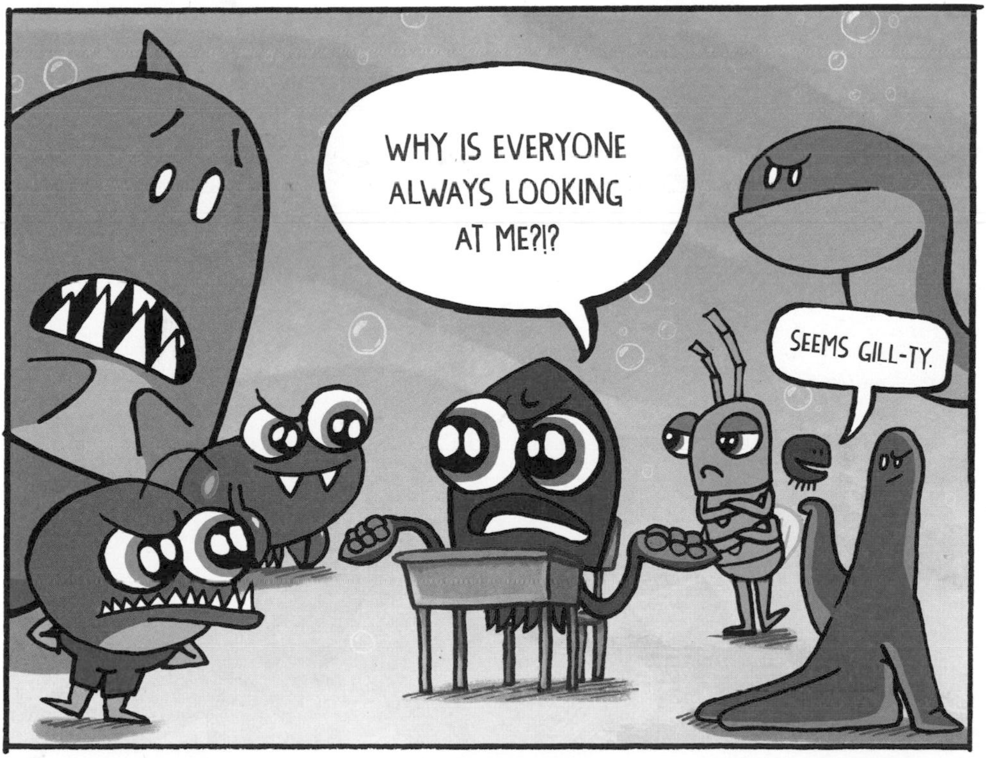
WHY IS EVERYONE ALWAYS LOOKING AT ME?!?
SEEMS GILL-TY.

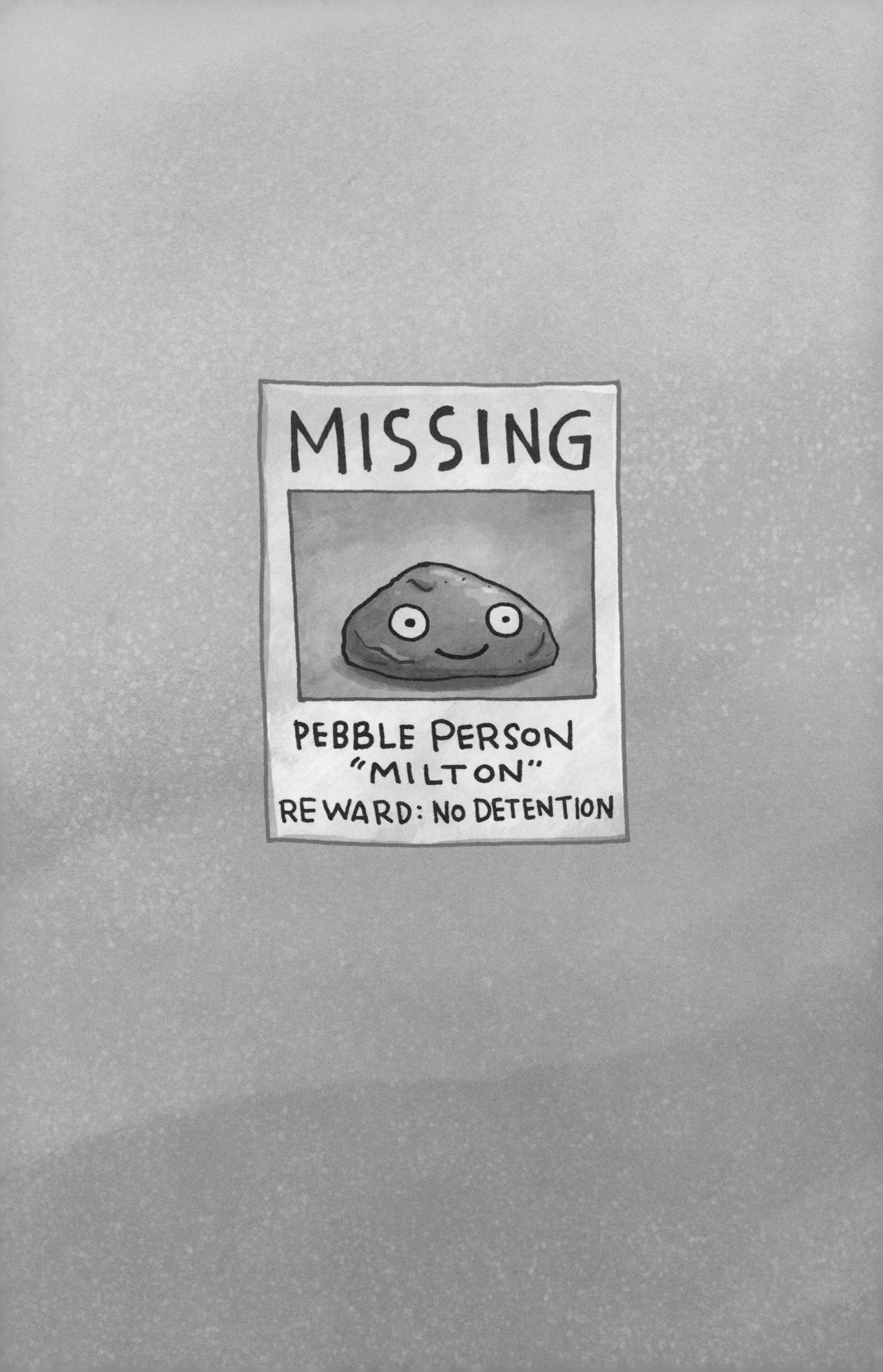
MISSING
PEBBLE PERSON
"MILTON"
REWARD: No DETENTION

CHAPTER 2

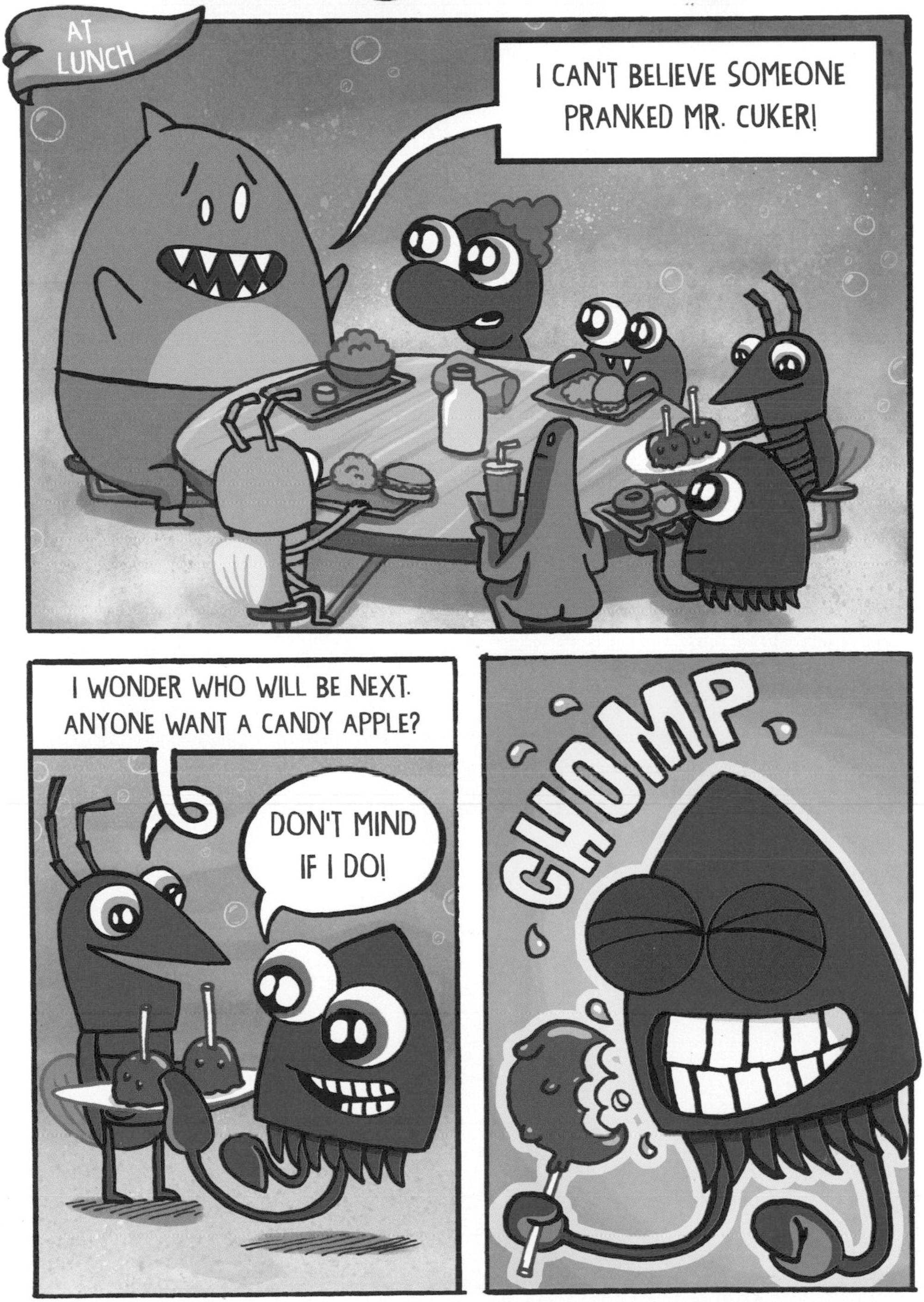
AT LUNCH
I CAN'T BELIEVE SOMEONE PRANKED MR. CUKER!
I WONDER WHO WILL BE NEXT. ANYONE WANT A CANDY APPLE?
DON'T MIND IF I DO!
CHOMP

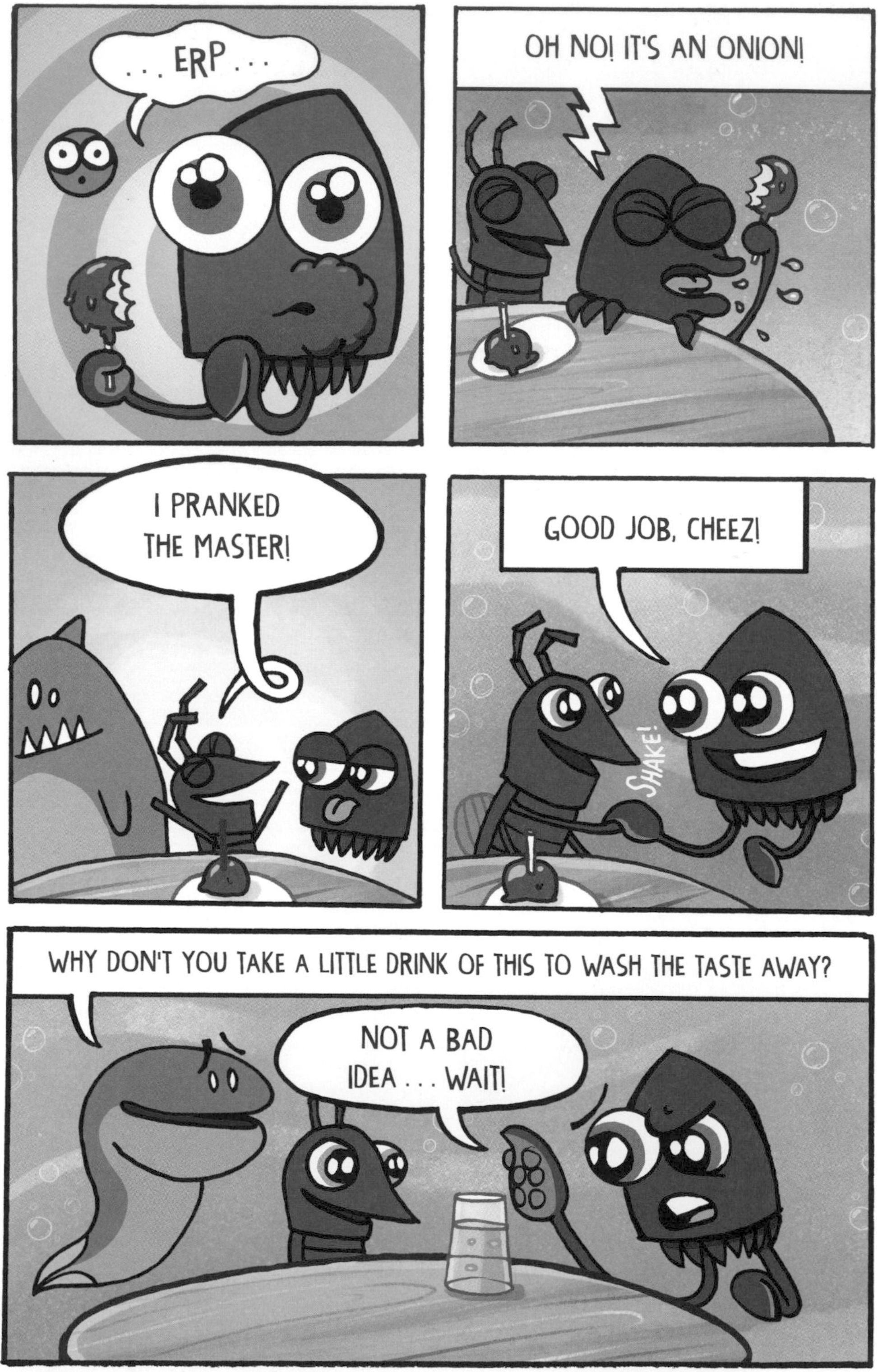
. . . ERP . . .
OH NO! IT'S AN ONION!
I PRANKED THE MASTER!
GOOD JOB, CHEEZ!
SHAKE!
WHY DON'T YOU TAKE A LITTLE DRINK OF THIS TO WASH THE TASTE AWAY?
NOT A BAD IDEA . . . WAIT!

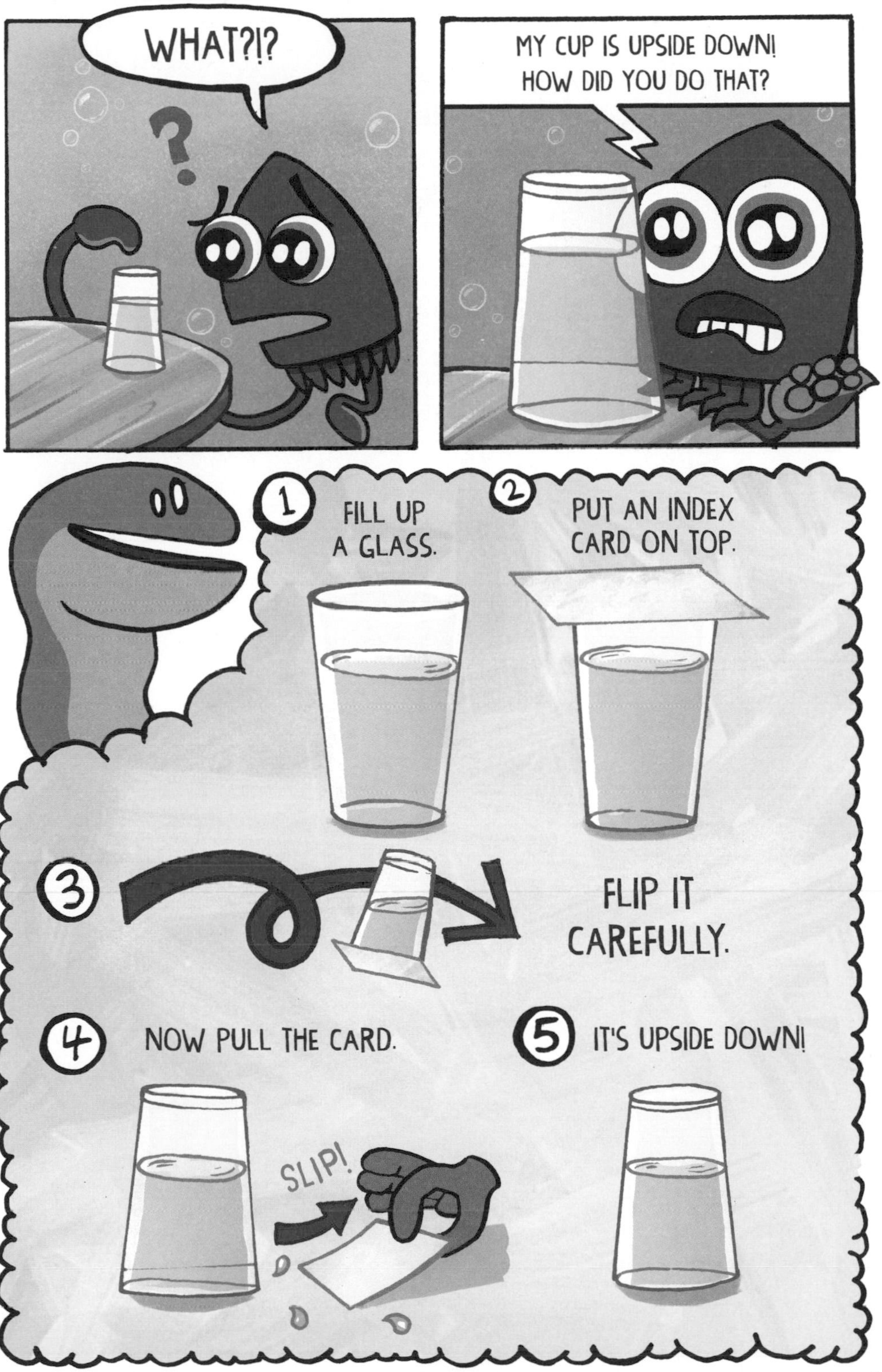
WHAT?!?
MY CUP IS UPSIDE DOWN! HOW DID YOU DO THAT?
1 FILL UP A GLASS.
2 PUT AN INDEX CARD ON TOP.
3 FLIP IT CAREFULLY.
4 NOW PULL THE CARD.
SLIP!
5 IT'S UPSIDE DOWN!

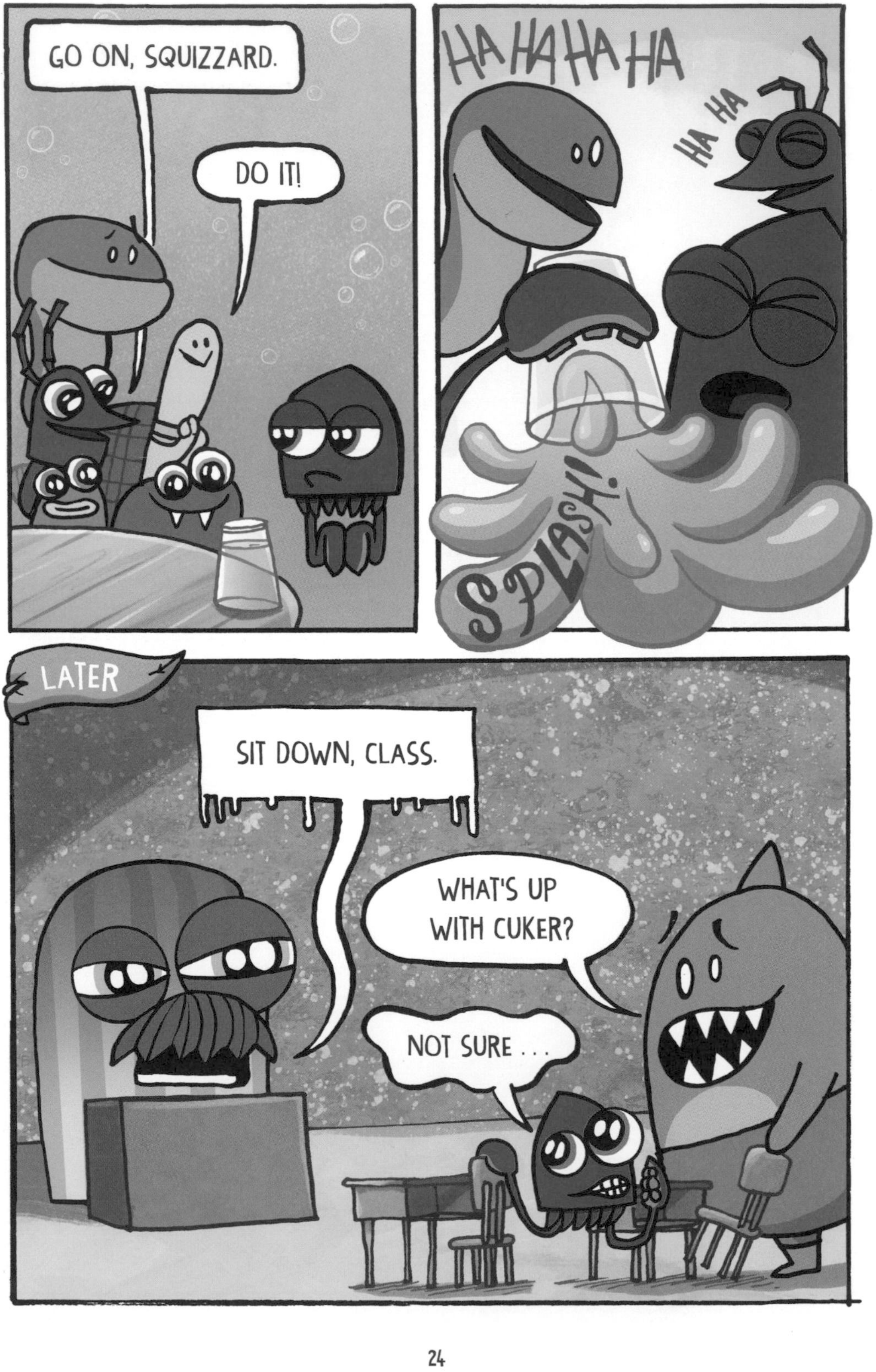
GO ON, SQUIZZARD.
DO IT!
HA HA HA HA HA
HA HA
SPLASH!
LATER
SIT DOWN, CLASS.
WHAT'S UP WITH CUKER?
NOT SURE . . .

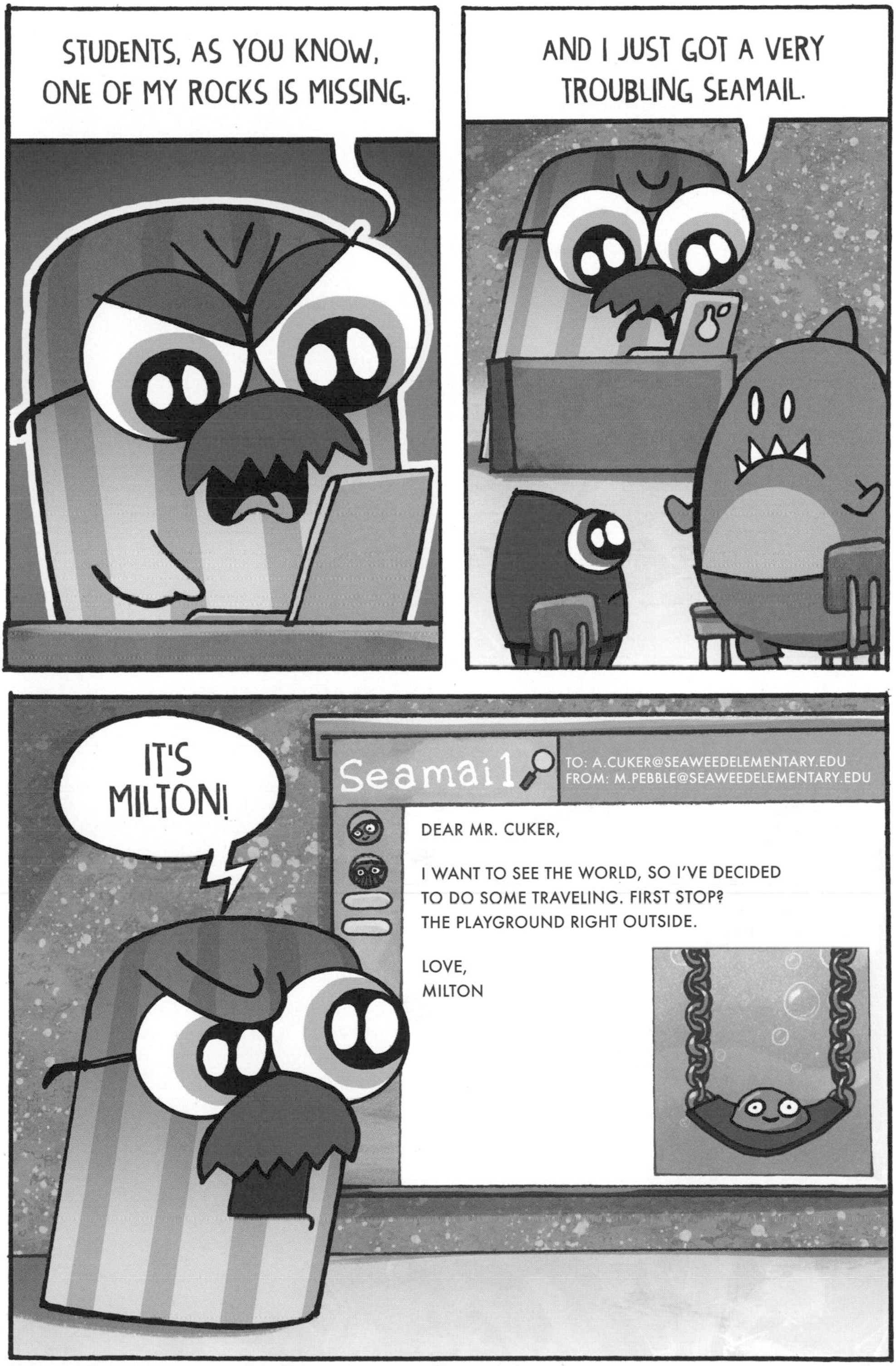
STUDENTS, AS YOU KNOW, ONE OF MY ROCKS IS MISSING.
AND I JUST GOT A VERY TROUBLING SEAMAIL.
IT'S MILTON!
Seamail
TO: A.CUKER@SEAWEEDELEMENTARY.EDU
FROM: M.PEBBLE@SEAWEEDELEMENTARY.EDU
DEAR MR. CUKER,
I WANT TO SEE THE WORLD, SO I'VE DECIDED TO DO SOME TRAVELING. FIRST STOP? THE PLAYGROUND RIGHT OUTSIDE.
LOVE,
MILTON

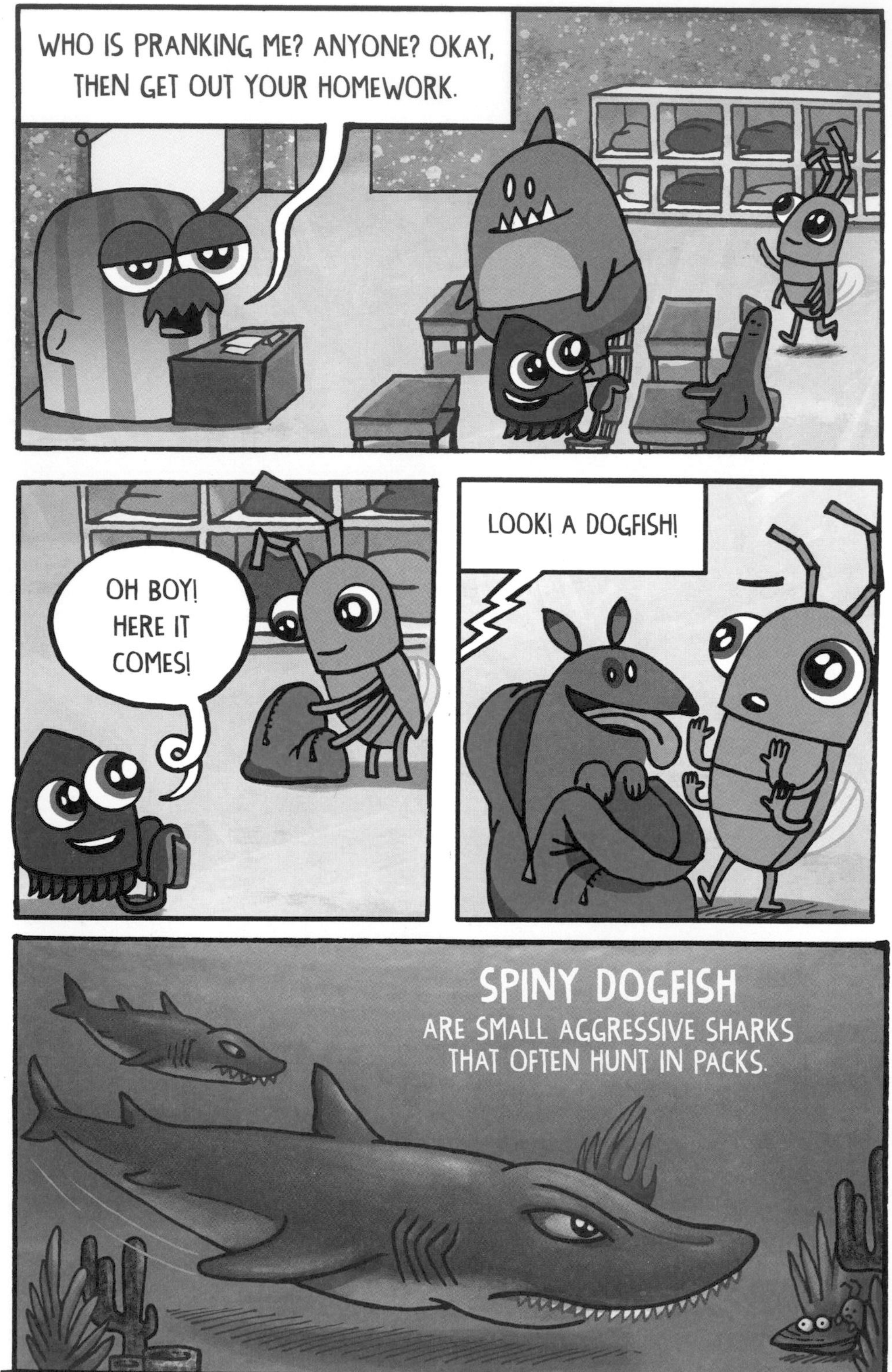
WHO IS PRANKING ME? ANYONE? OKAY, THEN GET OUT YOUR HOMEWORK.
OH BOY! HERE IT COMES!
LOOK! A DOGFISH!
SPINY DOGFISH
ARE SMALL AGGRESSIVE SHARKS THAT OFTEN HUNT IN PACKS.

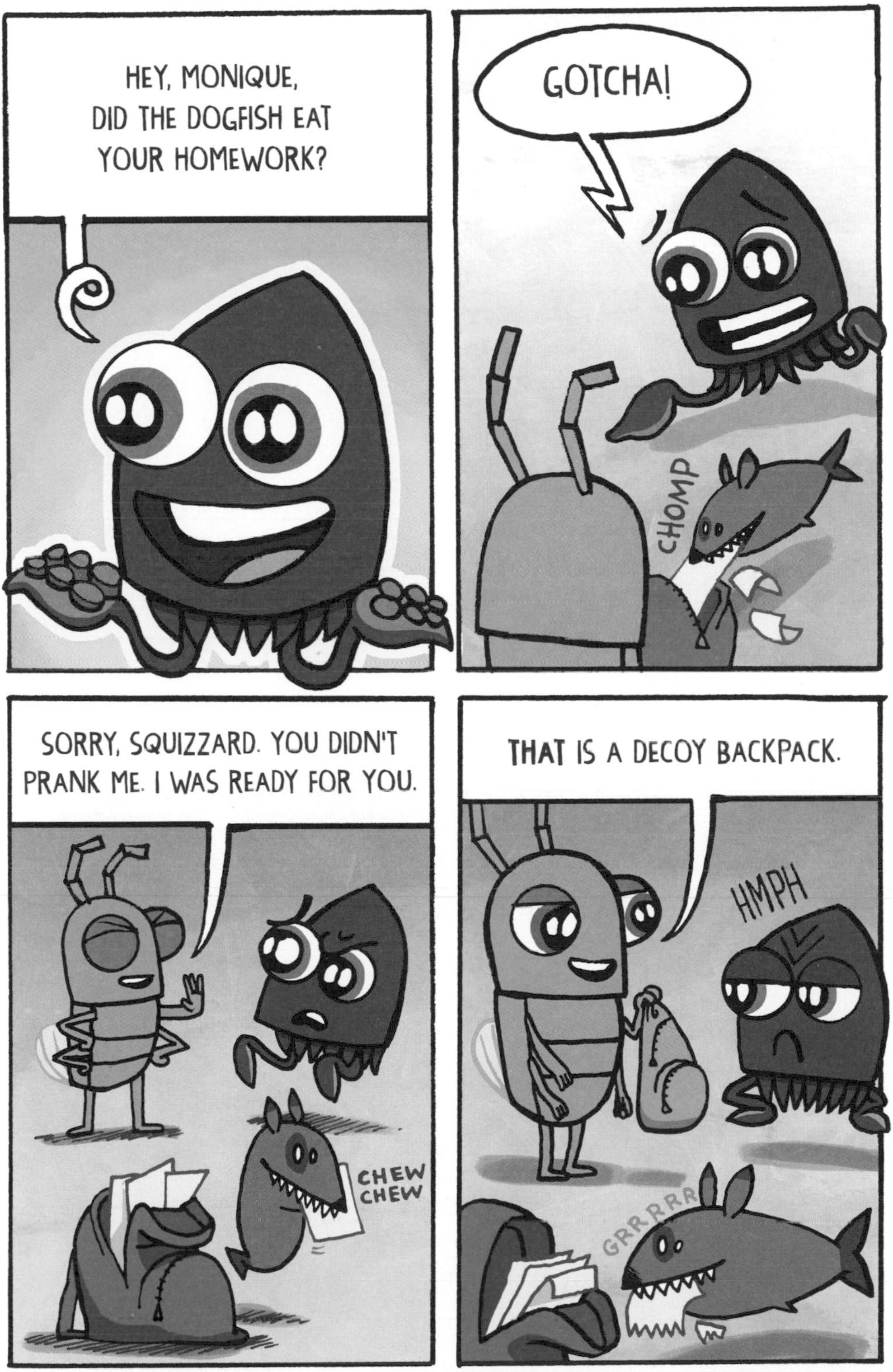
HEY, MONIQUE, DID THE DOGFISH EAT YOUR HOMEWORK?
GOTCHA!
CHOMP
SORRY, SQUIZZARD. YOU DIDN'T PRANK ME. I WAS READY FOR YOU.
CHEW CHEW
THAT IS A DECOY BACKPACK.
HMPH
GRRRRR

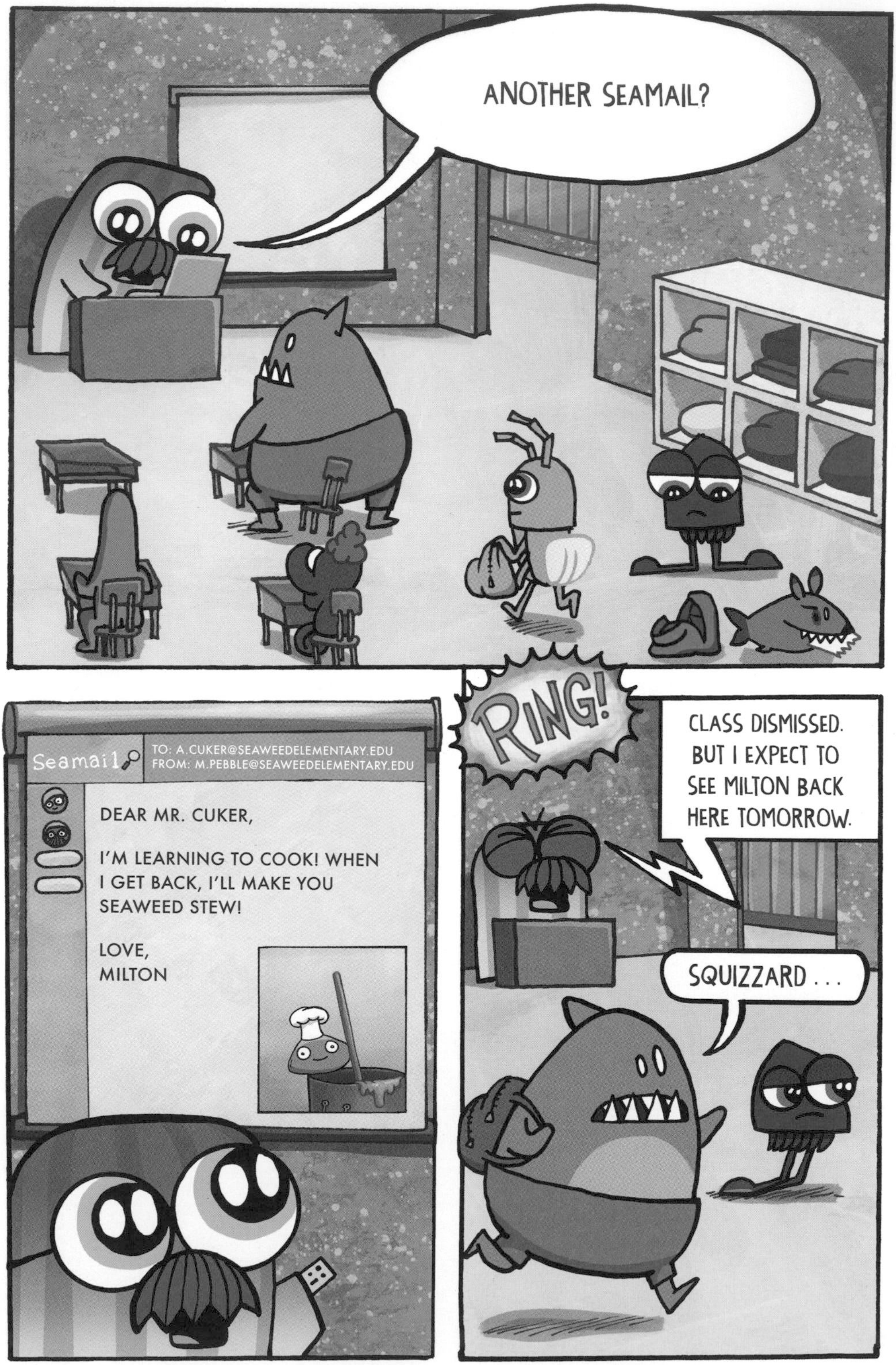
ANOTHER SEAMAIL?
Seamail
TO: A.CUKER@SEAWEEDELEMENTARY.EDU
FROM: M.PEBBLE@SEAWEEDELEMENTARY.EDU
DEAR MR. CUKER,
I'M LEARNING TO COOK! WHEN I GET BACK, I'LL MAKE YOU SEAWEED STEW!
LOVE,
MILTON
RING!
CLASS DISMISSED. BUT I EXPECT TO SEE MILTON BACK HERE TOMORROW.
SQUIZZARD . . .

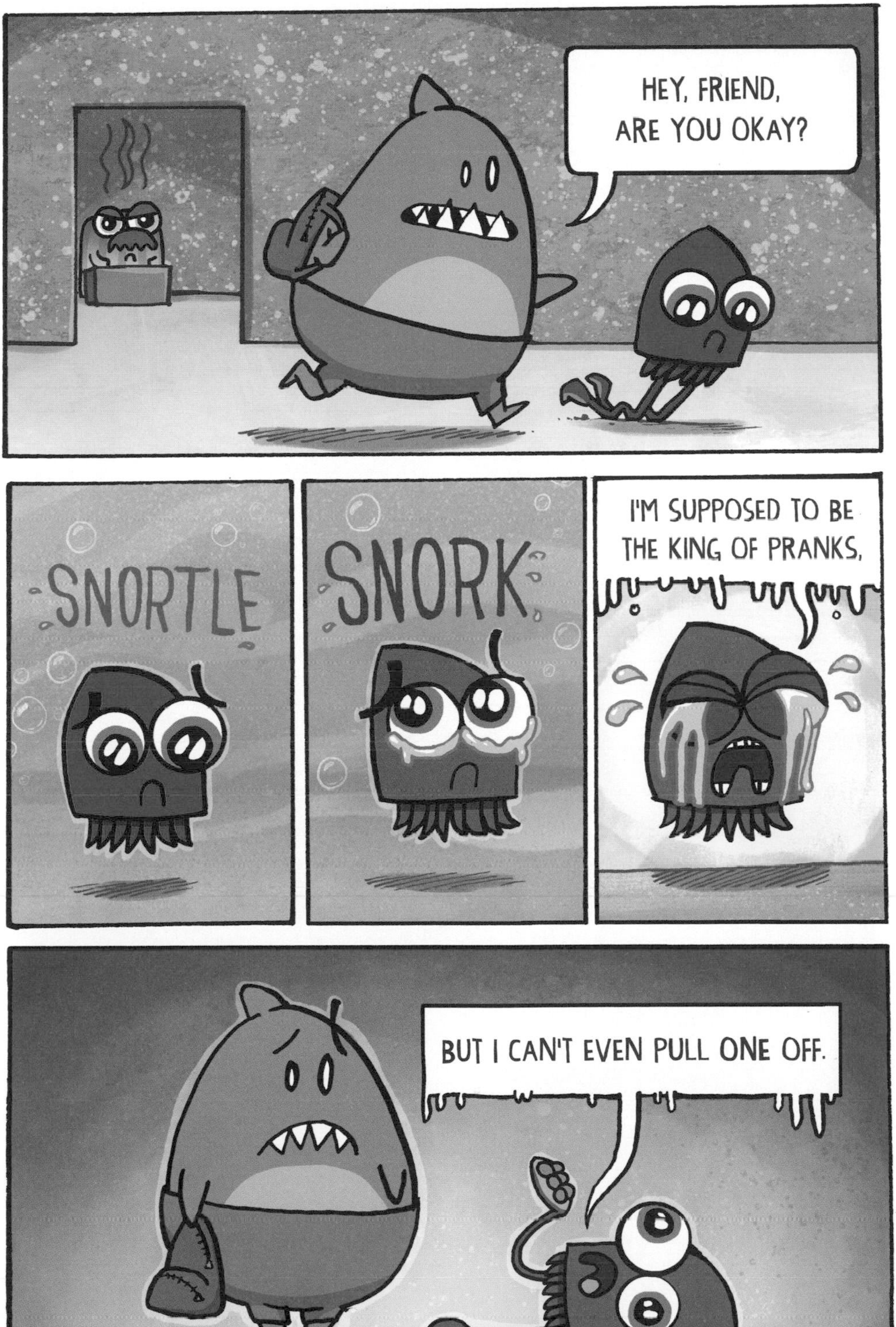
HEY, FRIEND, ARE YOU OKAY?
SNORTLE
SNORK
I'M SUPPOSED TO BE THE KING OF PRANKS,
BUT I CAN'T EVEN PULL ONE OFF.

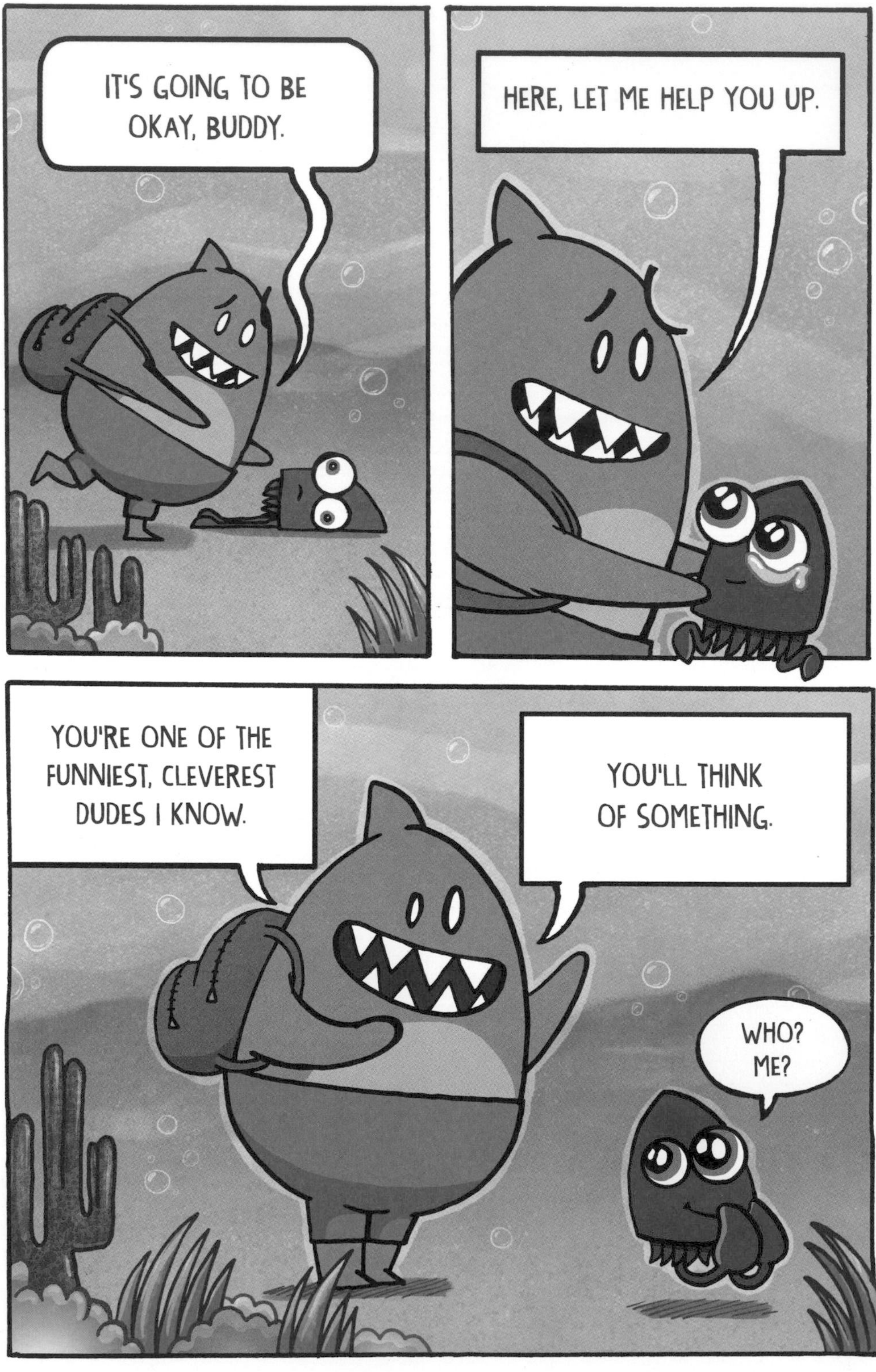
IT'S GOING TO BE OKAY, BUDDY.
HERE, LET ME HELP YOU UP.
YOU'RE ONE OF THE FUNNIEST, CLEVEREST DUDES I KNOW.
YOU'LL THINK OF SOMETHING.
WHO? ME?

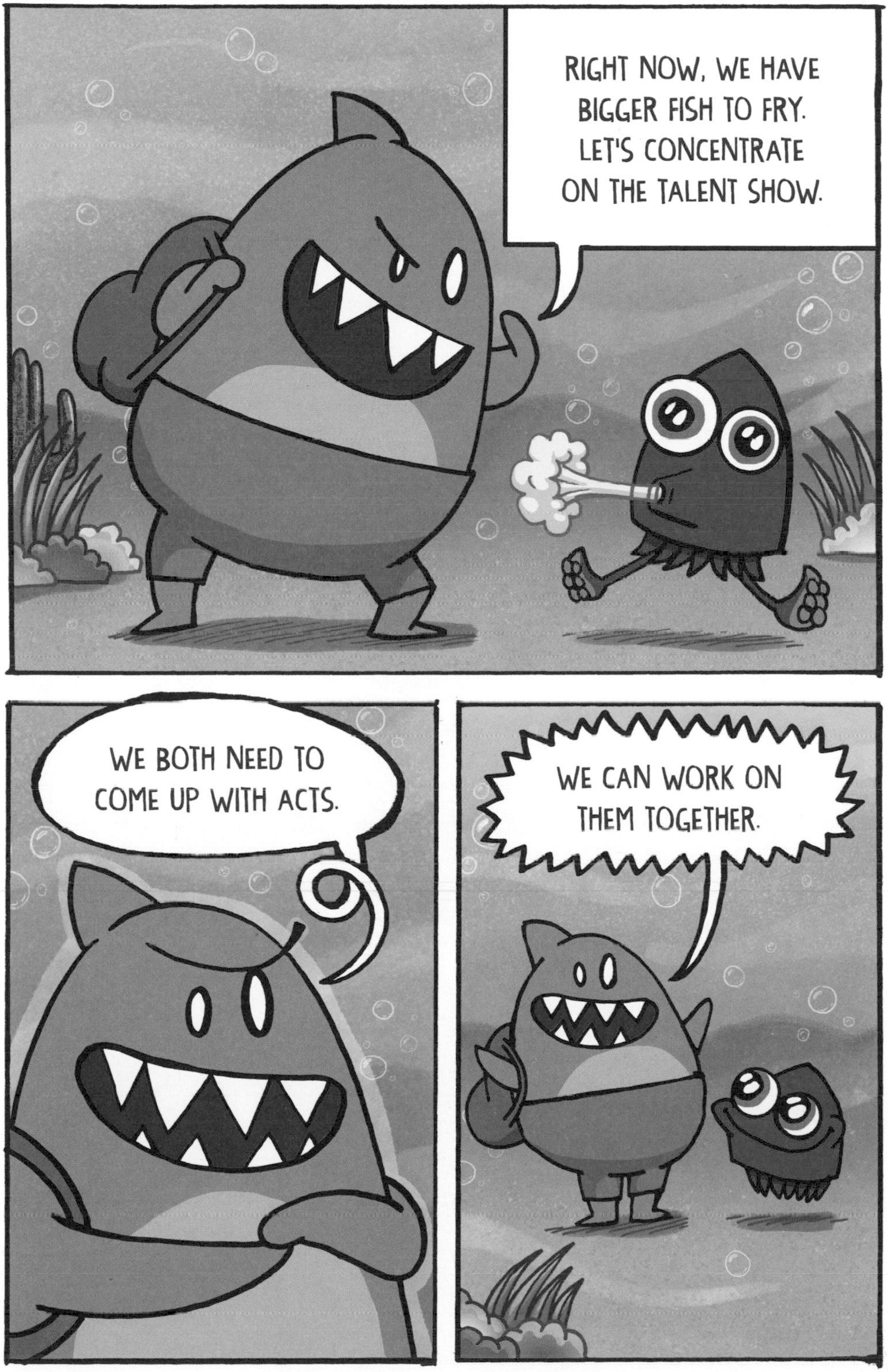
RIGHT NOW, WE HAVE BIGGER FISH TO FRY. LET'S CONCENTRATE ON THE TALENT SHOW.
WE BOTH NEED TO COME UP WITH ACTS.
WE CAN WORK ON THEM TOGETHER.

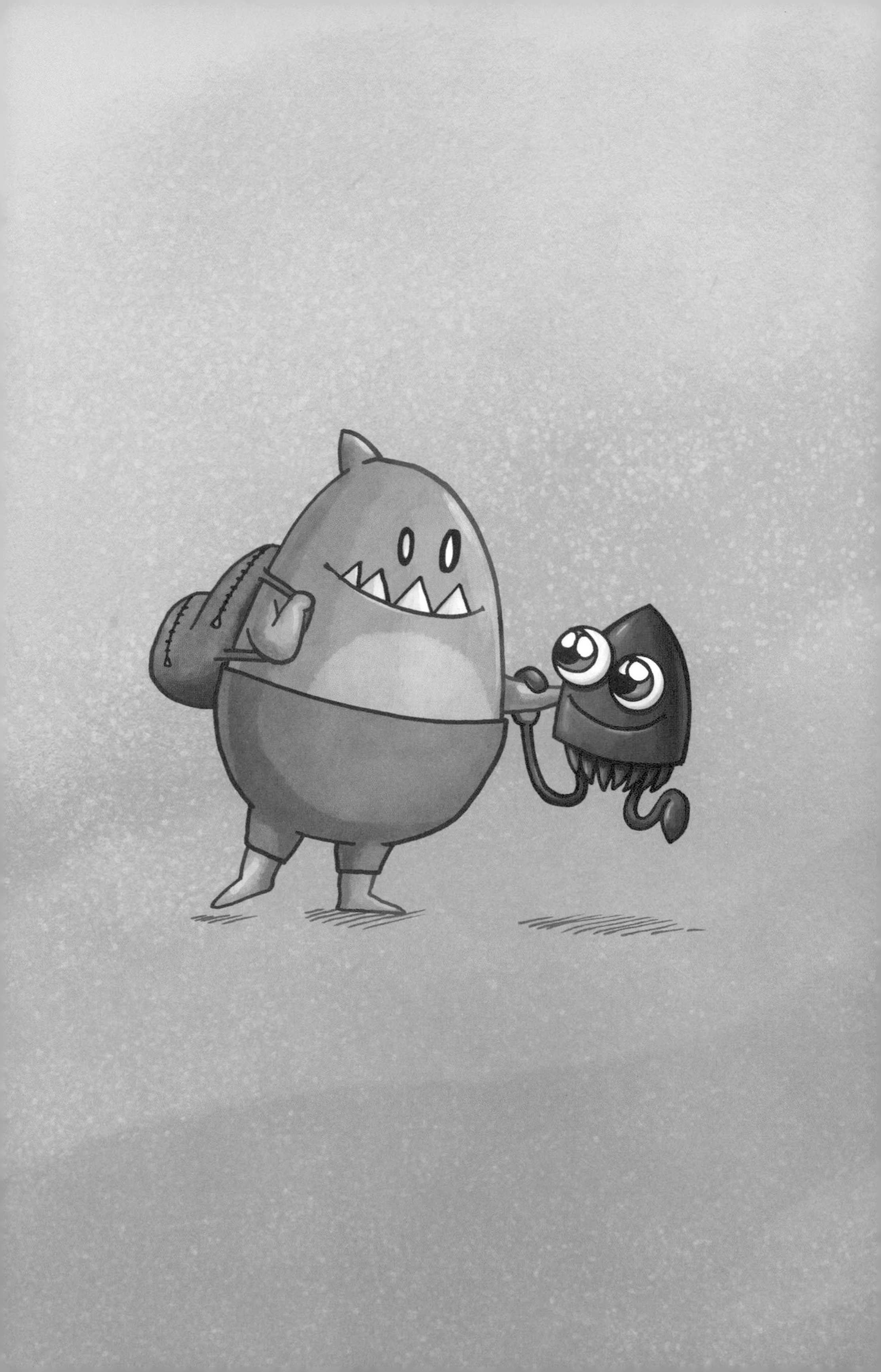

CHAPTER 3

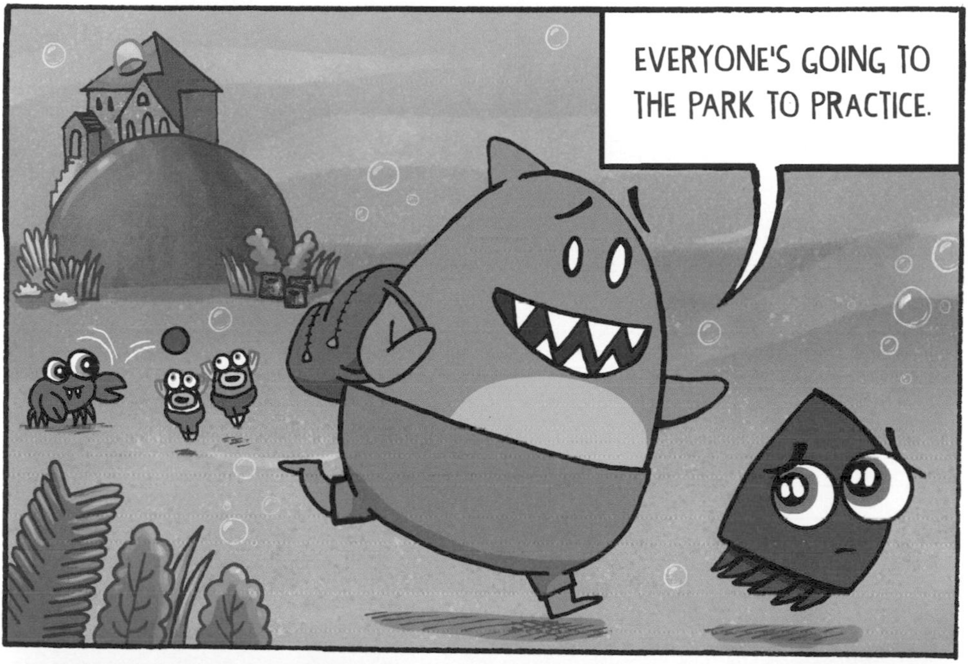
EVERYONE'S GOING TO THE PARK TO PRACTICE.

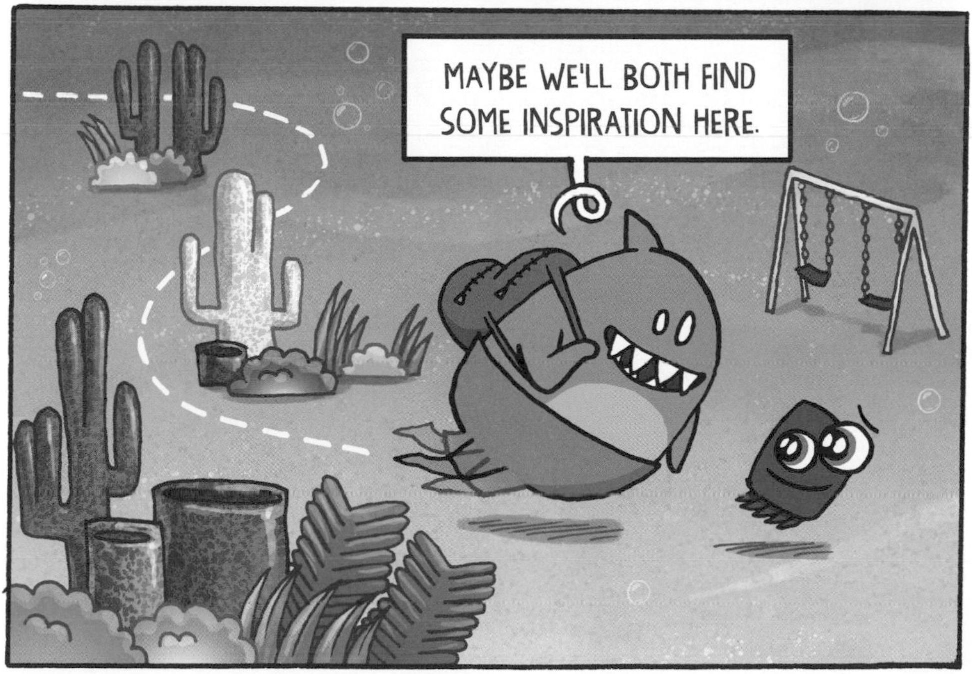
MAYBE WE'LL BOTH FIND SOME INSPIRATION HERE.

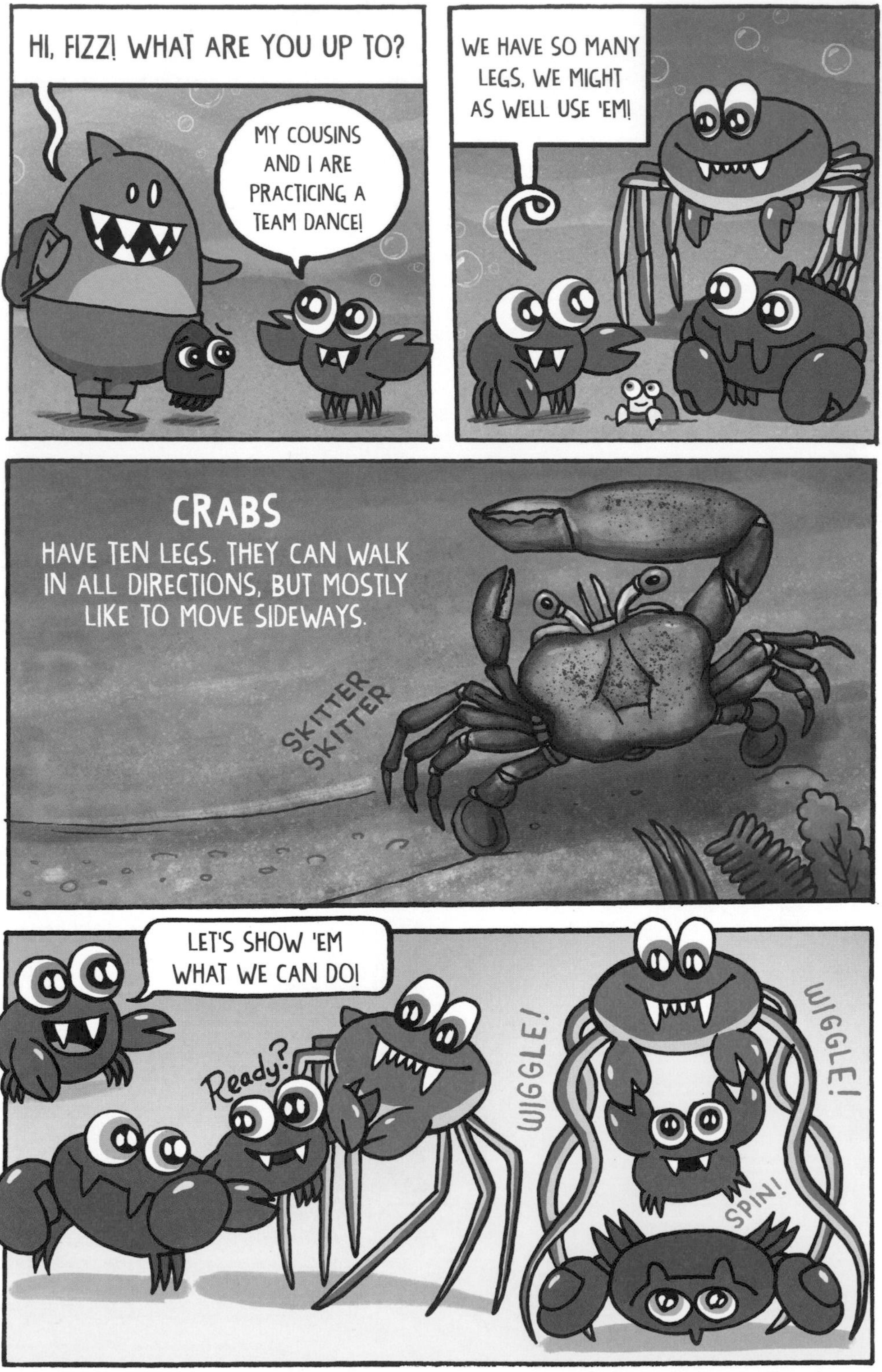
HI, FIZZ! WHAT ARE YOU UP TO?
MY COUSINS AND I ARE PRACTICING A TEAM DANCE!
WE HAVE SO MANY LEGS, WE MIGHT AS WELL USE 'EM!
CRABS
HAVE TEN LEGS. THEY CAN WALK IN ALL DIRECTIONS, BUT MOSTLY LIKE TO MOVE SIDEWAYS.
SKITTER SKITTER
LET'S SHOW 'EM WHAT WE CAN DO!
Ready?
WIGGLE!
WIGGLE!
SPIN!

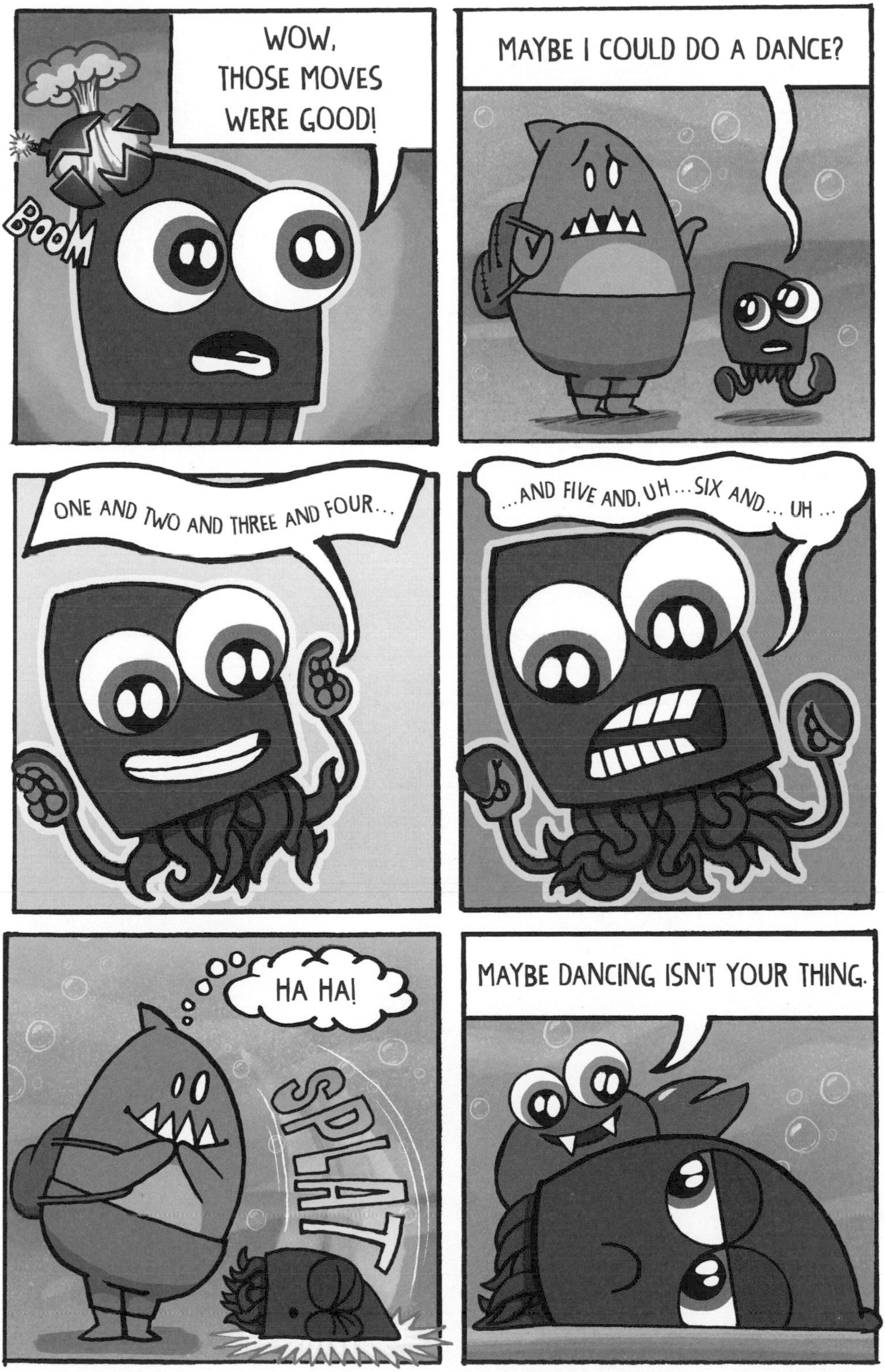

BOOM
WOW, THOSE MOVES WERE GOOD!
MAYBE I COULD DO A DANCE?
ONE AND TWO AND THREE AND FOUR...
...AND FIVE AND, UH...SIX AND... UH ...
HA HA!
SPLAT
MAYBE DANCING ISN'T YOUR THING.

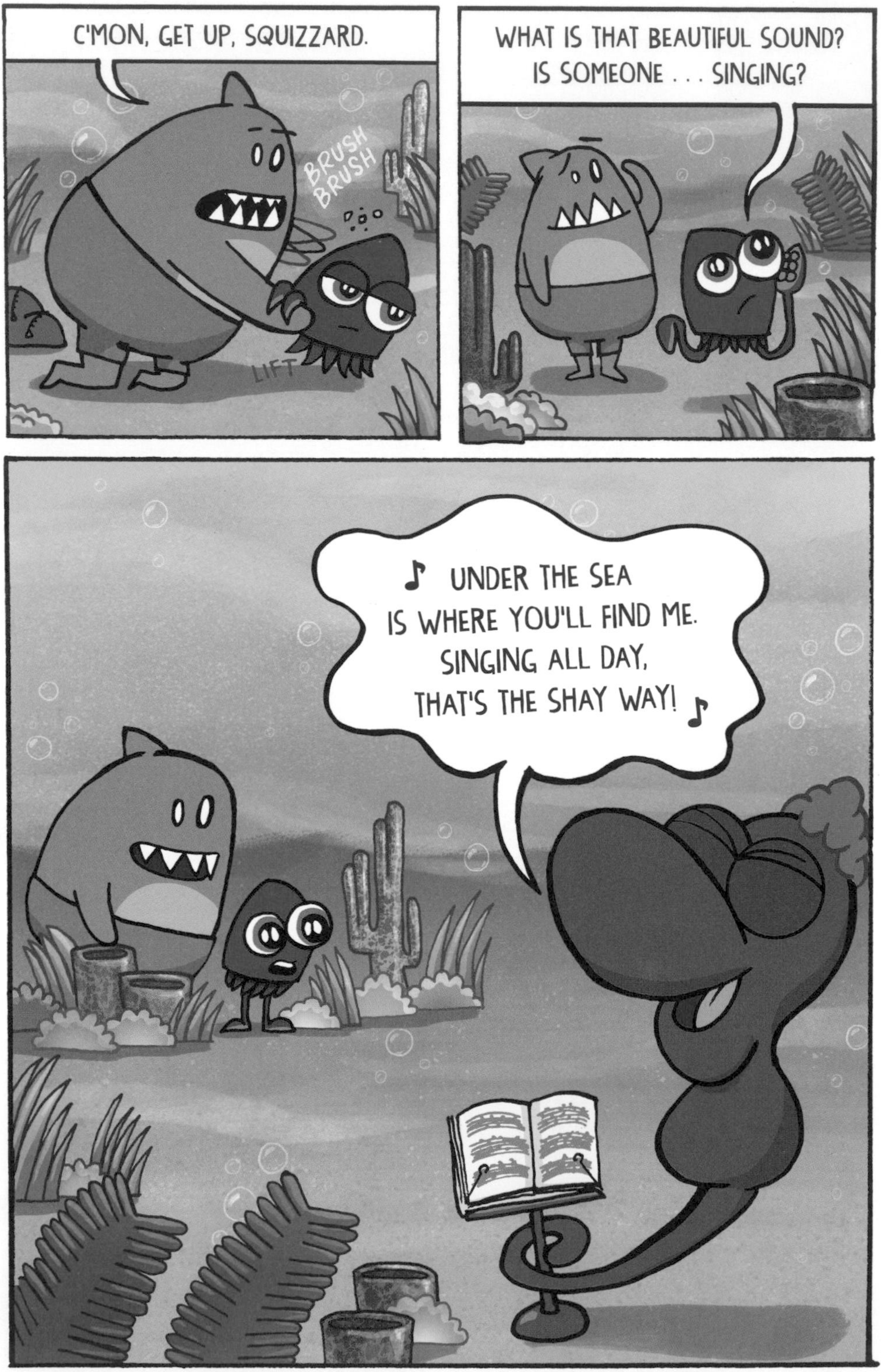
C'MON, GET UP, SQUIZZARD.
BRUSH BRUSH
LIFT
WHAT IS THAT BEAUTIFUL SOUND? IS SOMEONE . . . SINGING?
♪ UNDER THE SEA IS WHERE YOU'LL FIND ME. SINGING ALL DAY, THAT'S THE SHAY WAY! ♪

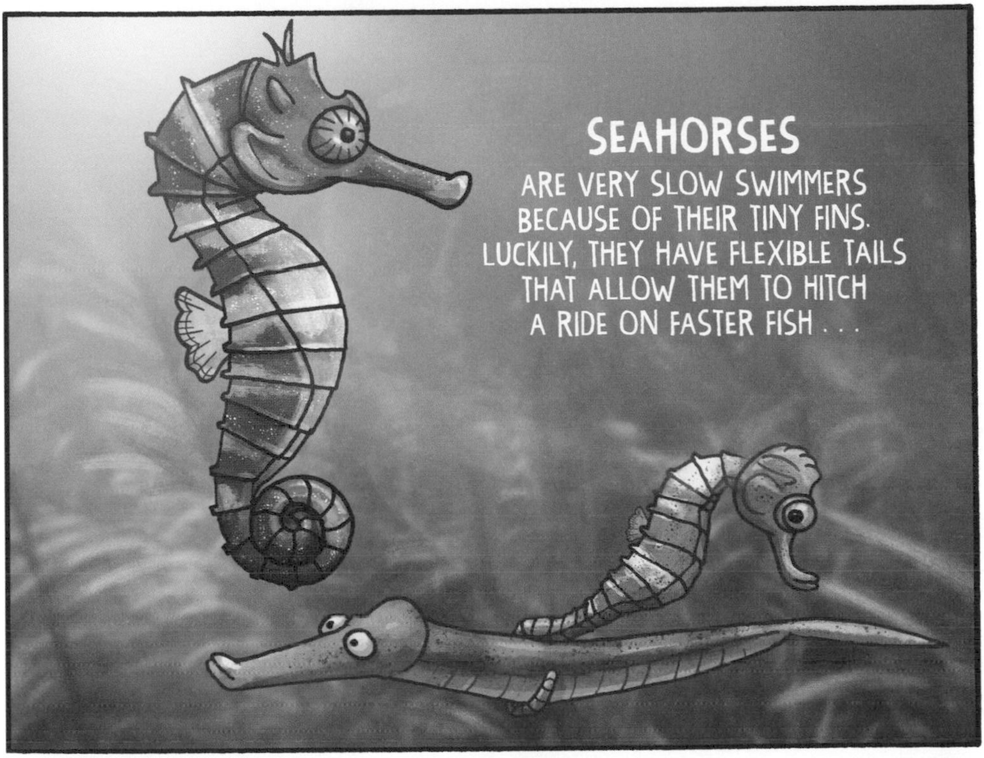
SEAHORSES
ARE VERY SLOW SWIMMERS BECAUSE OF THEIR TINY FINS. LUCKILY, THEY HAVE FLEXIBLE TAILS THAT ALLOW THEM TO HITCH A RIDE ON FASTER FISH . . .

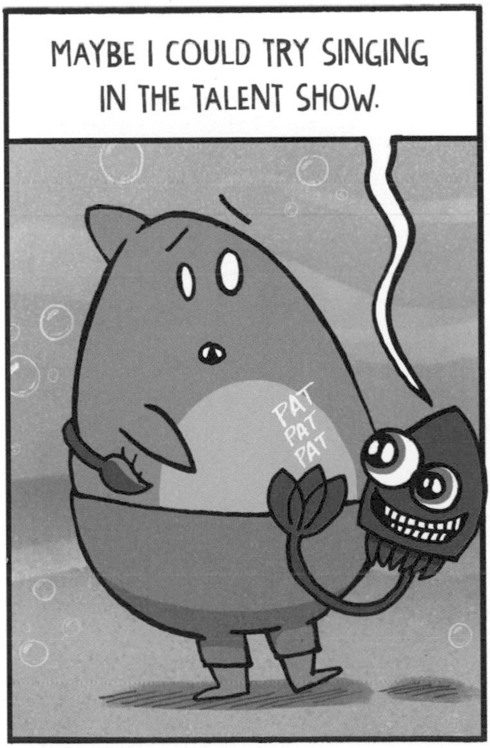
MAYBE I COULD TRY SINGING IN THE TALENT SHOW.
PAT PAT PAT

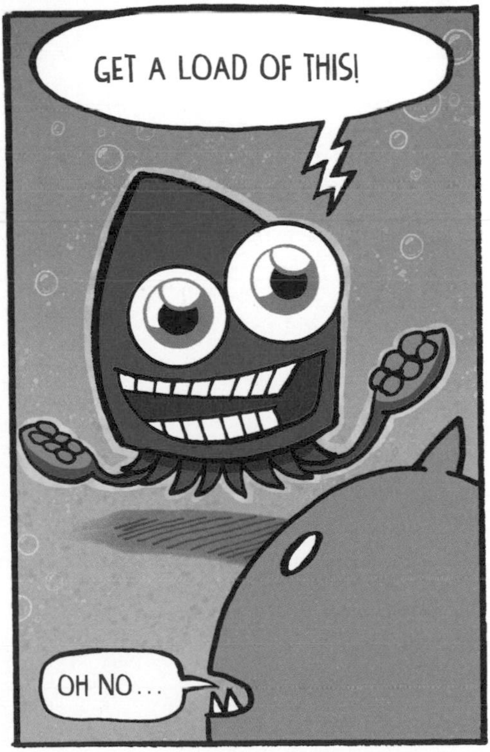
GET A LOAD OF THIS!
OH NO . . .

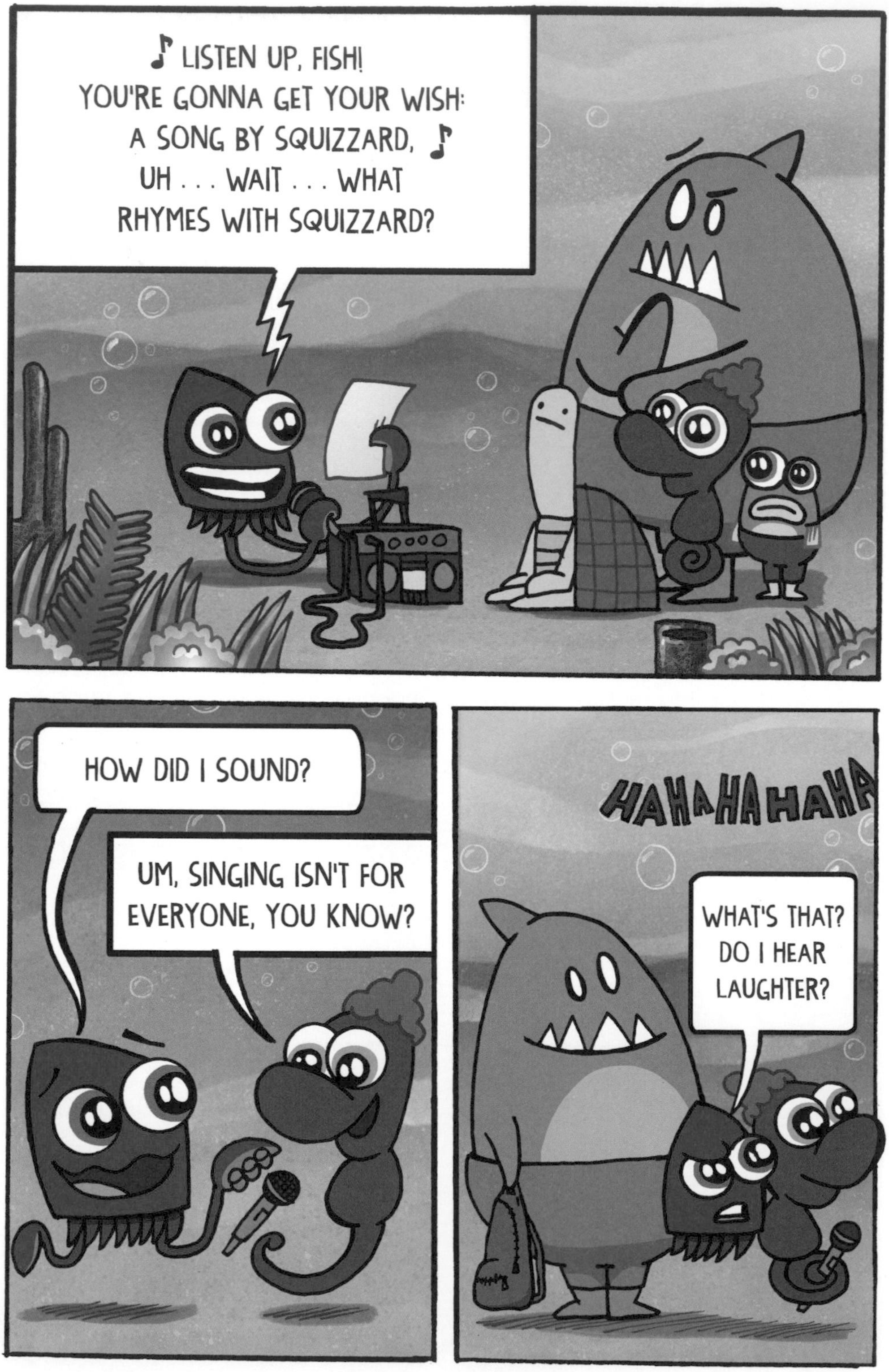
♪ LISTEN UP, FISH! YOU'RE GONNA GET YOUR WISH: A SONG BY SQUIZZARD, ♪ UH . . . WAIT . . . WHAT RHYMES WITH SQUIZZARD?
HOW DID I SOUND?
UM, SINGING ISN'T FOR EVERYONE, YOU KNOW?
HAHAHAHAHAHA
WHAT'S THAT? DO I HEAR LAUGHTER?

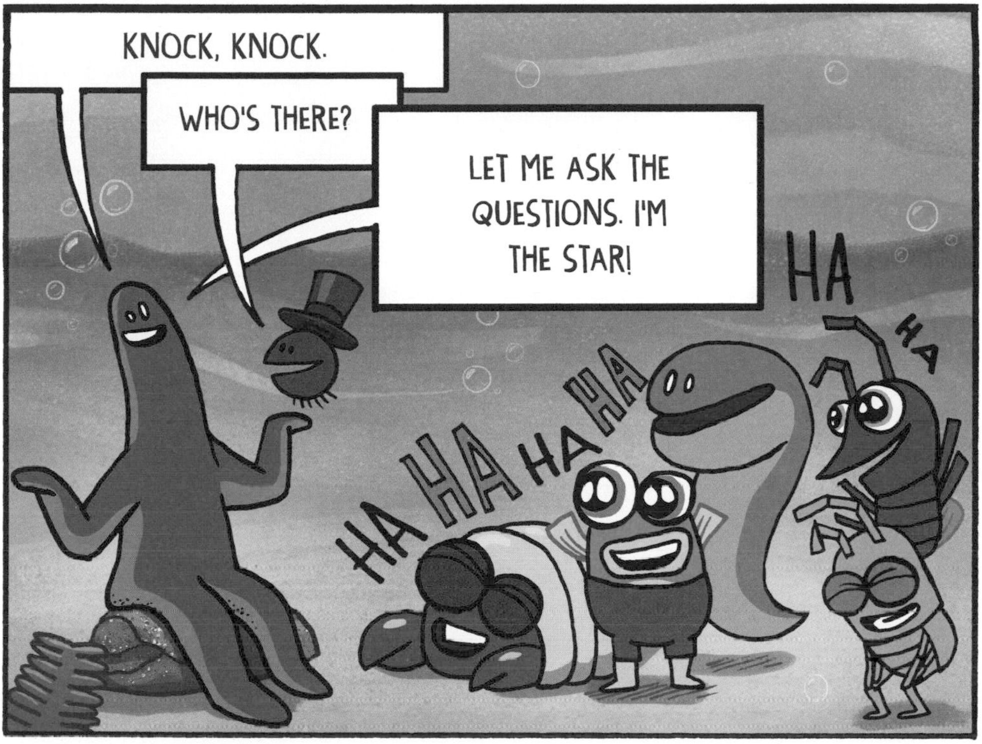
KNOCK, KNOCK.
WHO'S THERE?
LET ME ASK THE QUESTIONS. I'M THE STAR!
HA
HA
HA HA HA HA HA

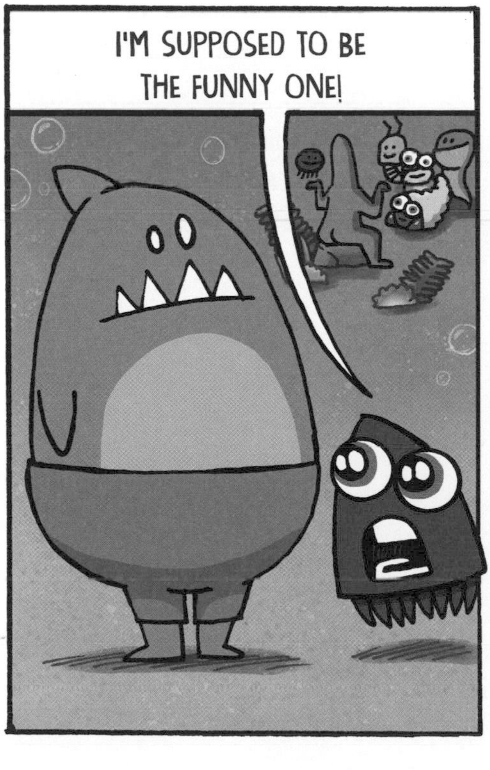
I'M SUPPOSED TO BE THE FUNNY ONE!

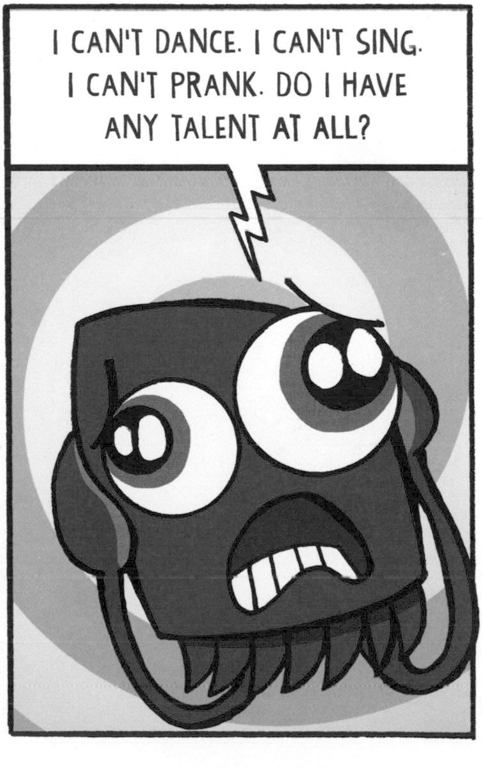
I CAN'T DANCE. I CAN'T SING. I CAN'T PRANK. DO I HAVE ANY TALENT AT ALL?

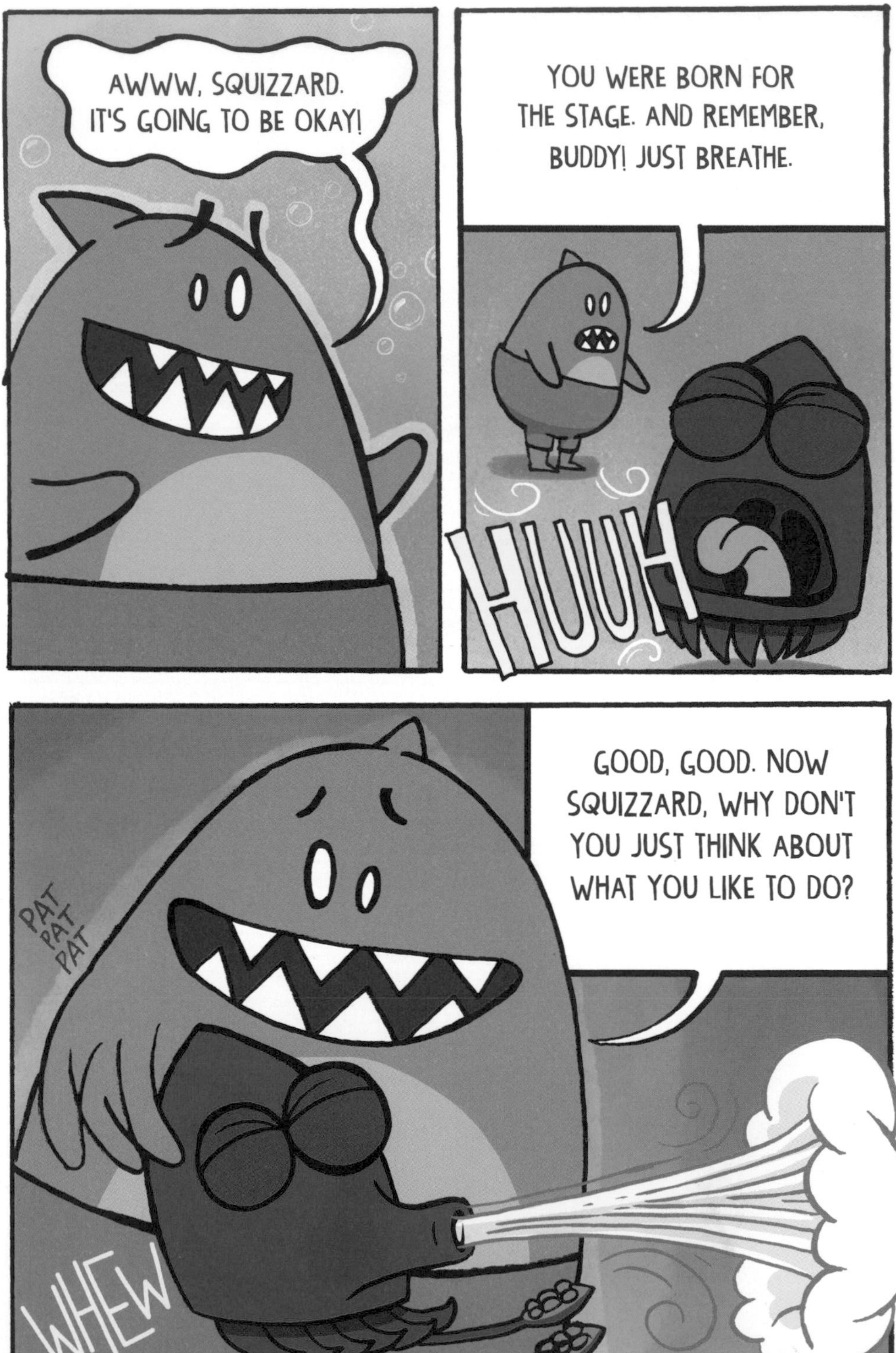
AWWW, SQUIZZARD. IT'S GOING TO BE OKAY!
YOU WERE BORN FOR THE STAGE. AND REMEMBER, BUDDY! JUST BREATHE.
HUUH
GOOD, GOOD. NOW SQUIZZARD, WHY DON'T YOU JUST THINK ABOUT WHAT YOU LIKE TO DO?
PAT PAT PAT
WHEW

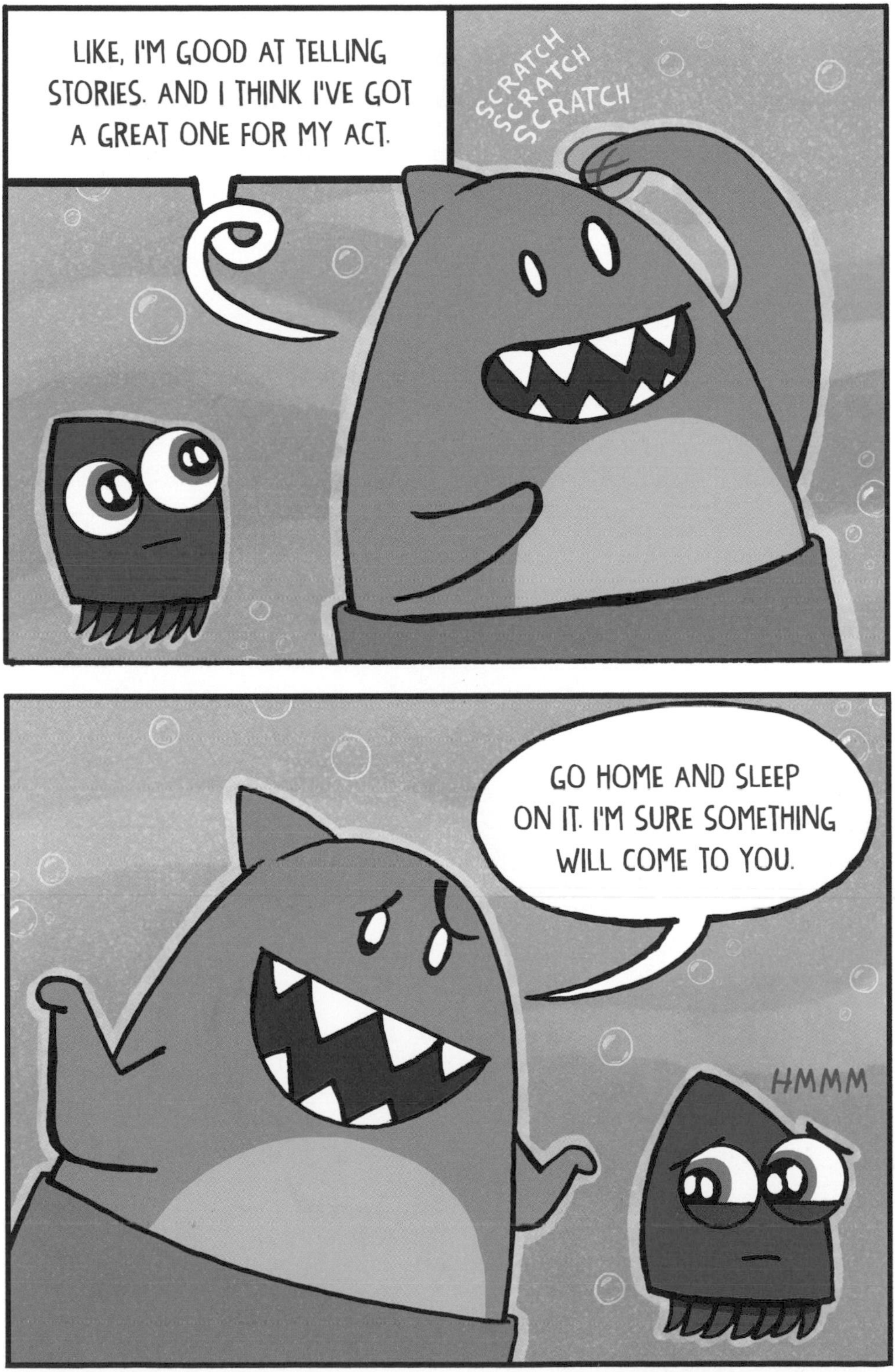
LIKE, I'M GOOD AT TELLING STORIES. AND I THINK I'VE GOT A GREAT ONE FOR MY ACT.
SCRATCH SCRATCH SCRATCH
GO HOME AND SLEEP ON IT. I'M SURE SOMETHING WILL COME TO YOU.
HMMM

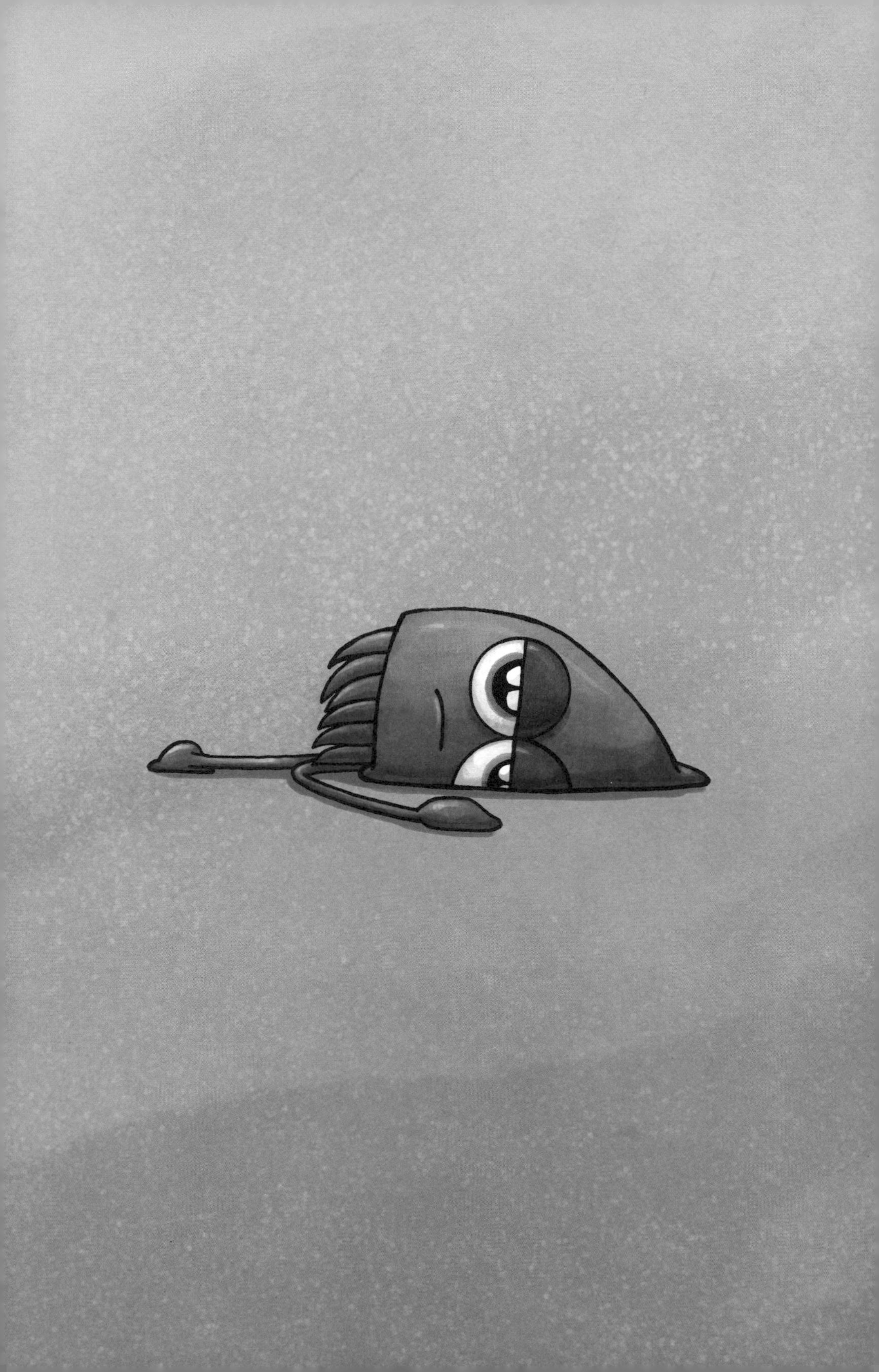

CHAPTER 4

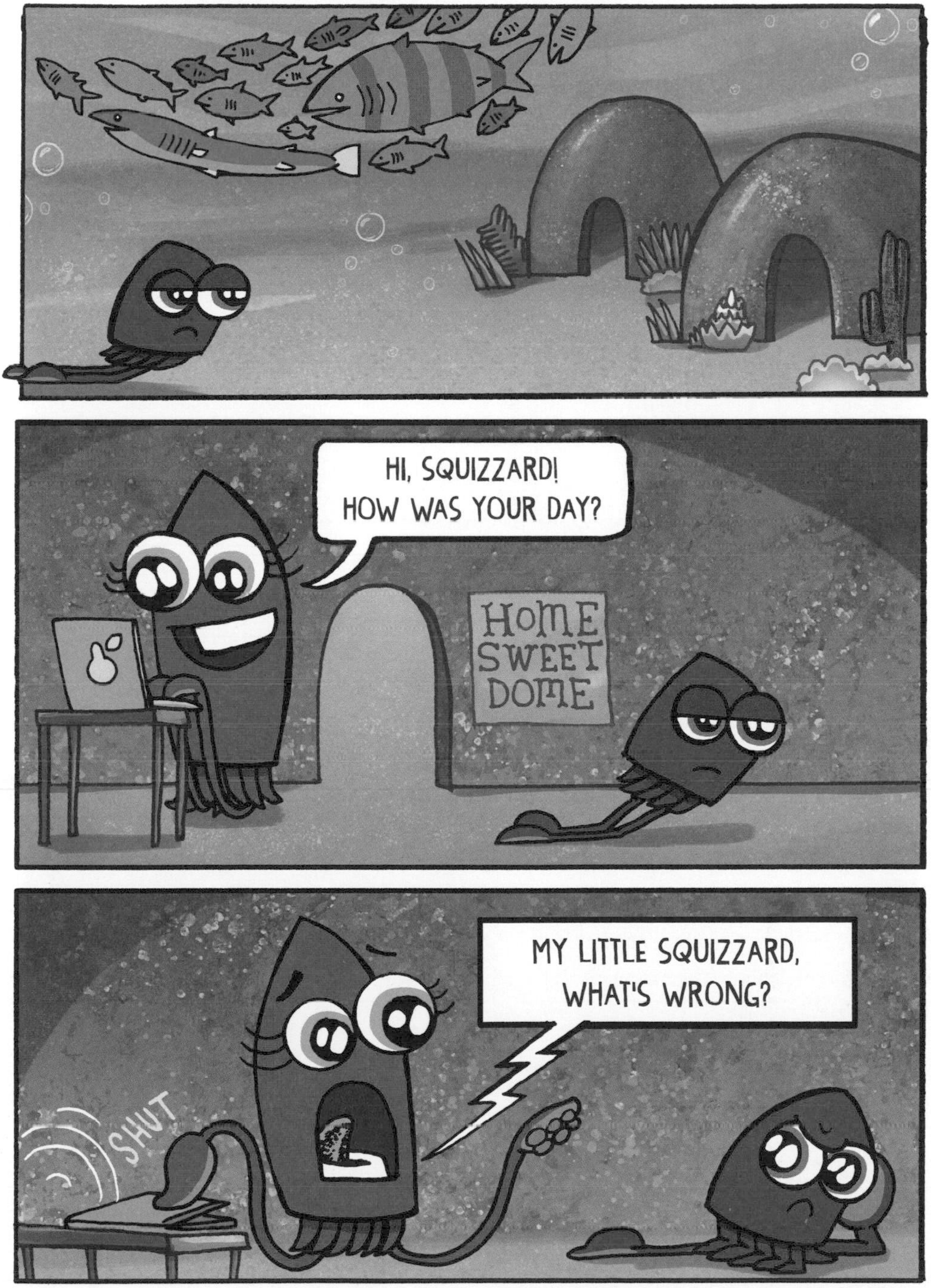
HI, SQUIZZARD!
HOW WAS YOUR DAY?
HOME SWEET DOME
SHUT
MY LITTLE SQUIZZARD,
WHAT'S WRONG?

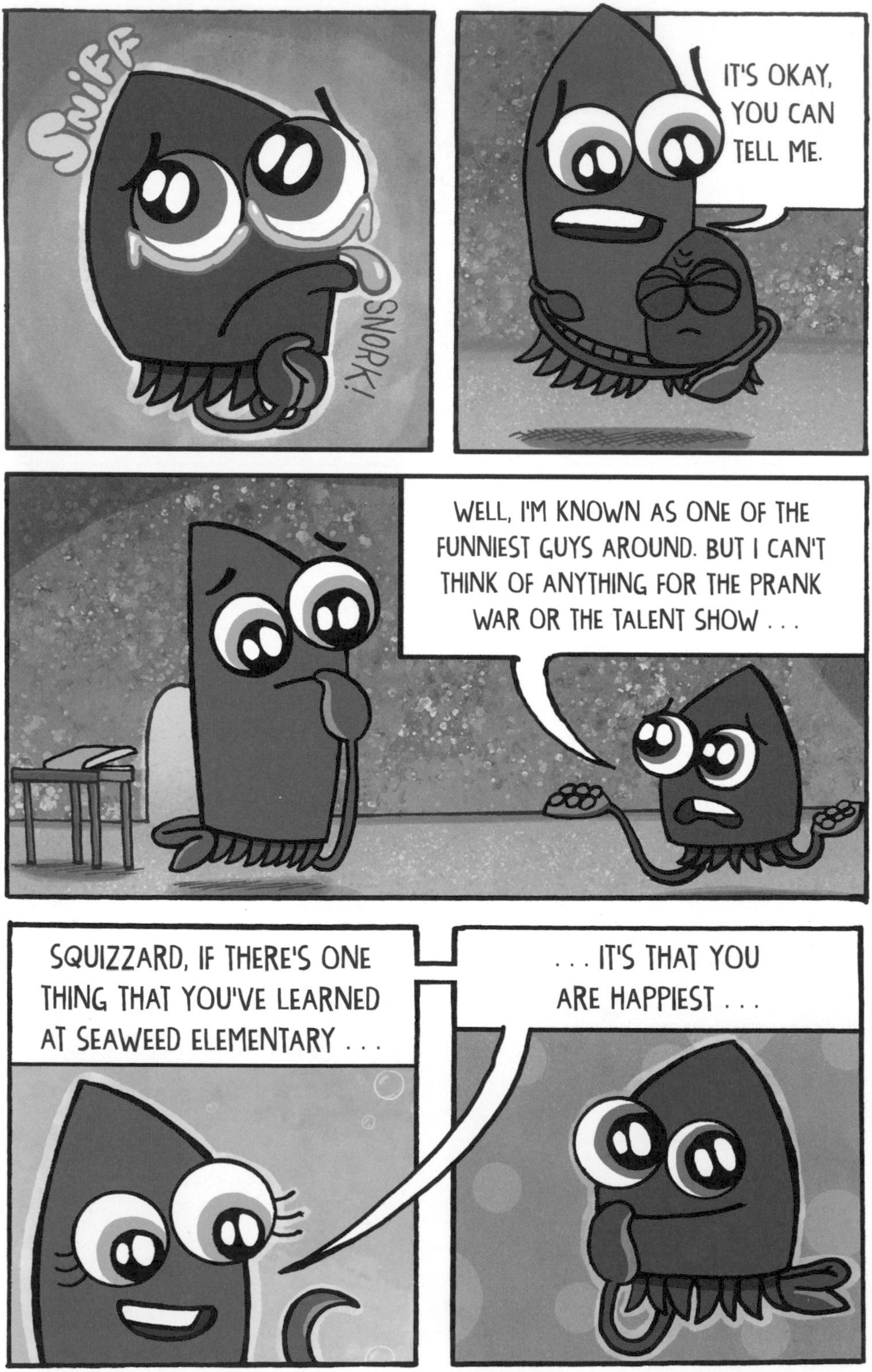
SNIFF
SNORK!
IT'S OKAY, YOU CAN TELL ME.
WELL, I'M KNOWN AS ONE OF THE FUNNIEST GUYS AROUND. BUT I CAN'T THINK OF ANYTHING FOR THE PRANK WAR OR THE TALENT SHOW . . .
SQUIZZARD, IF THERE'S ONE THING THAT YOU'VE LEARNED AT SEAWEED ELEMENTARY . . .
. . . IT'S THAT YOU ARE HAPPIEST . . .

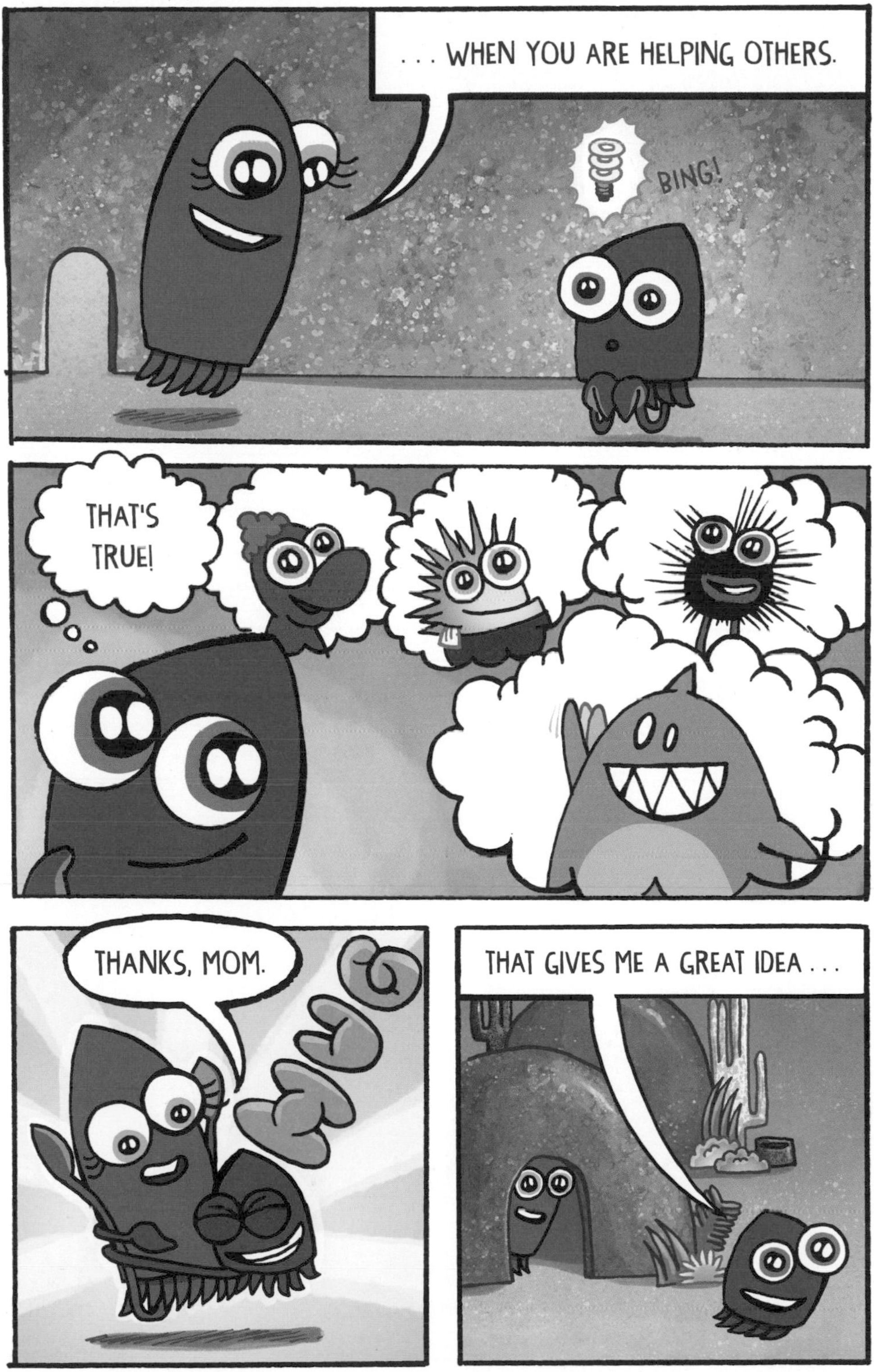
. . . WHEN YOU ARE HELPING OTHERS.
BING!
THAT'S TRUE!
THANKS, MOM.
THAT GIVES ME A GREAT IDEA . . .

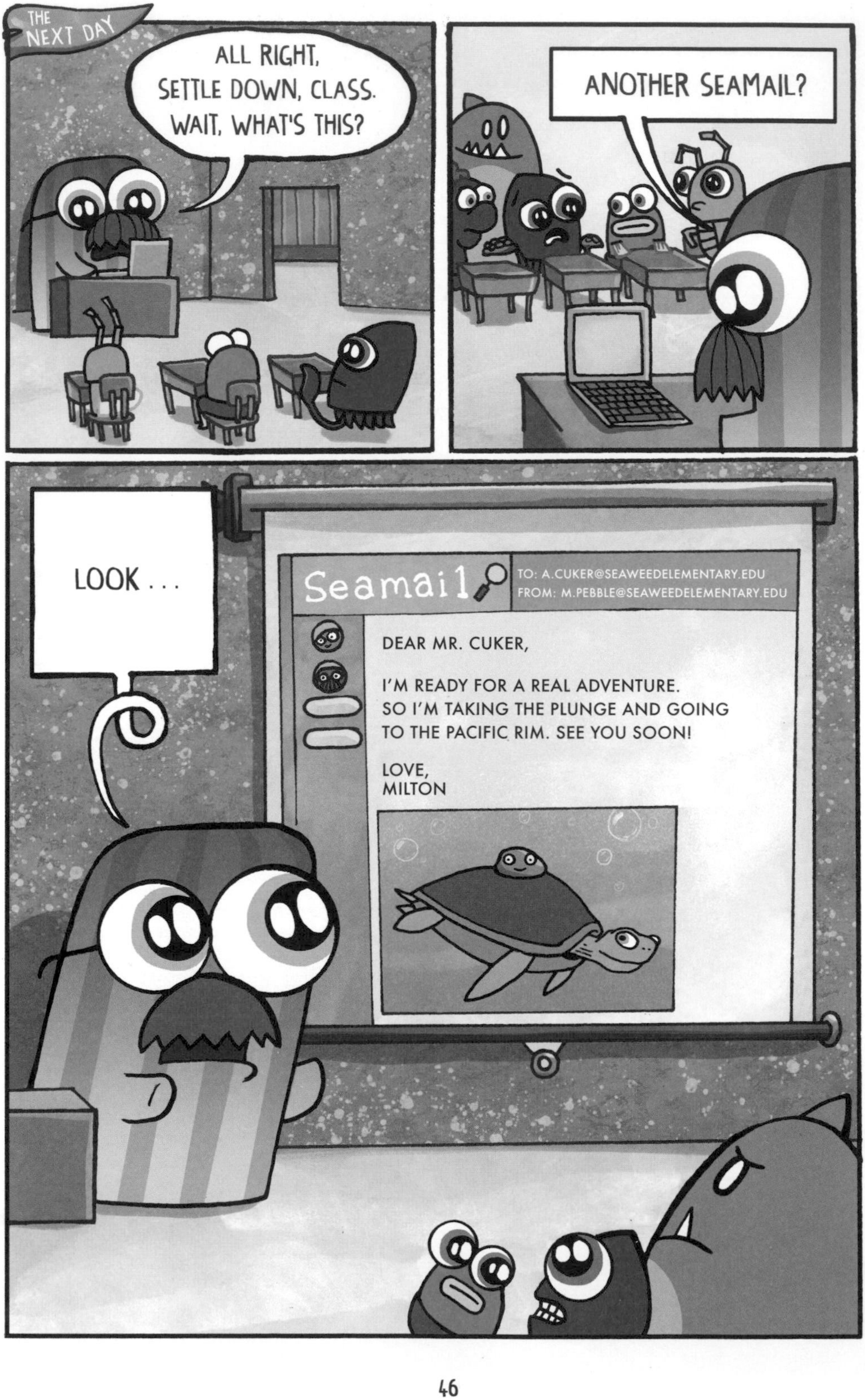
THE NEXT DAY
ALL RIGHT, SETTLE DOWN, CLASS. WAIT, WHAT'S THIS?
ANOTHER SEAMAIL?
LOOK . . .
Seamail
TO: A.CUKER@SEAWEEDELEMENTARY.EDU
FROM: M.PEBBLE@SEAWEEDELEMENTARY.EDU
DEAR MR. CUKER,
I'M READY FOR A REAL ADVENTURE. SO I'M TAKING THE PLUNGE AND GOING TO THE PACIFIC RIM. SEE YOU SOON!
LOVE,
MILTON

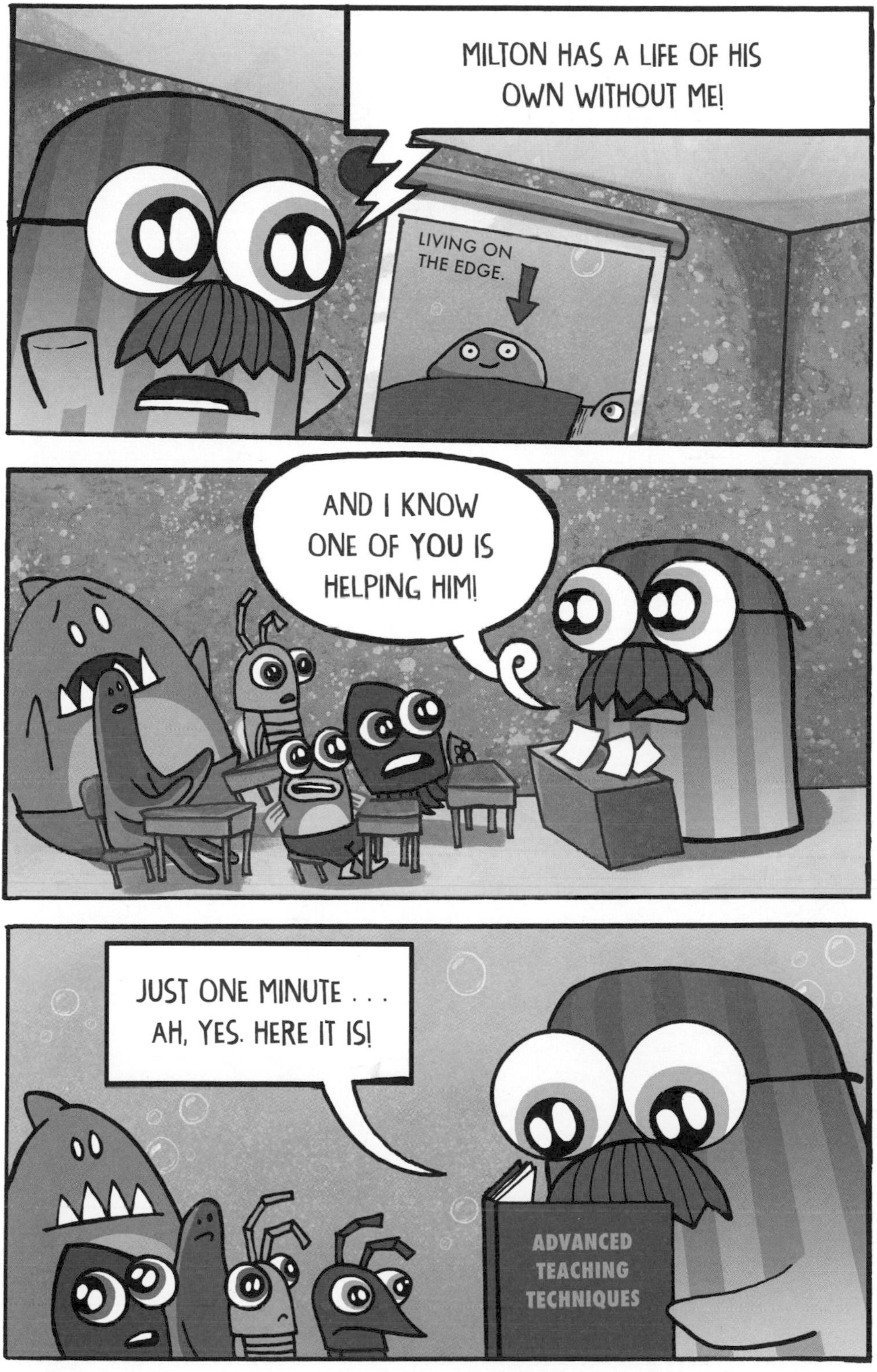
MILTON HAS A LIFE OF HIS OWN WITHOUT ME!
LIVING ON THE EDGE.
AND I KNOW ONE OF YOU IS HELPING HIM!
JUST ONE MINUTE . . . AH, YES. HERE IT IS!
ADVANCED TEACHING TECHNIQUES

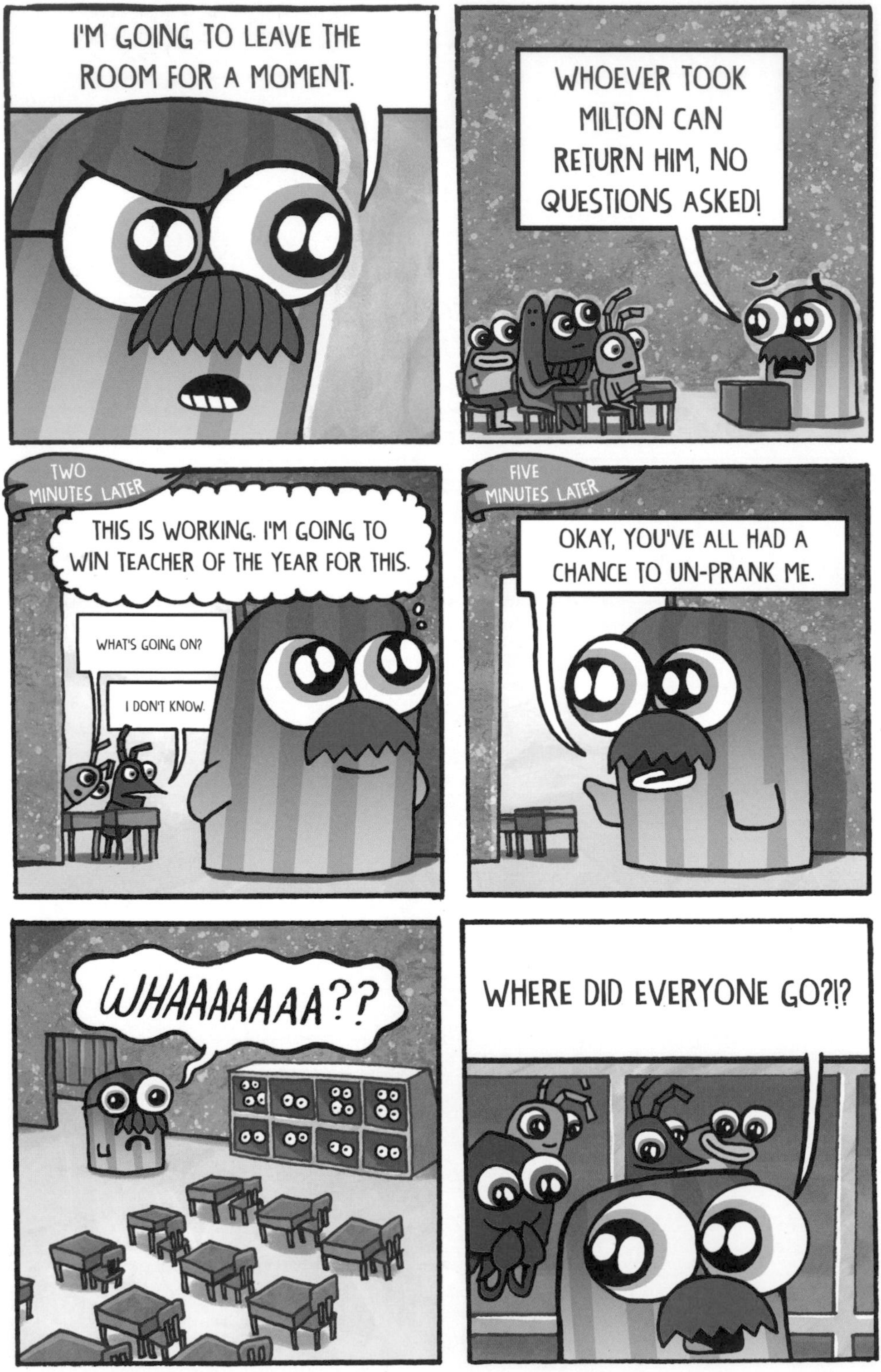
I'M GOING TO LEAVE THE ROOM FOR A MOMENT.
WHOEVER TOOK MILTON CAN RETURN HIM, NO QUESTIONS ASKED!
TWO MINUTES LATER
THIS IS WORKING. I'M GOING TO WIN TEACHER OF THE YEAR FOR THIS.
WHAT'S GOING ON?
I DON'T KNOW.
FIVE MINUTES LATER
OKAY, YOU'VE ALL HAD A CHANCE TO UN-PRANK ME.
WHAAAAAAAA??
WHERE DID EVERYONE GO?!?

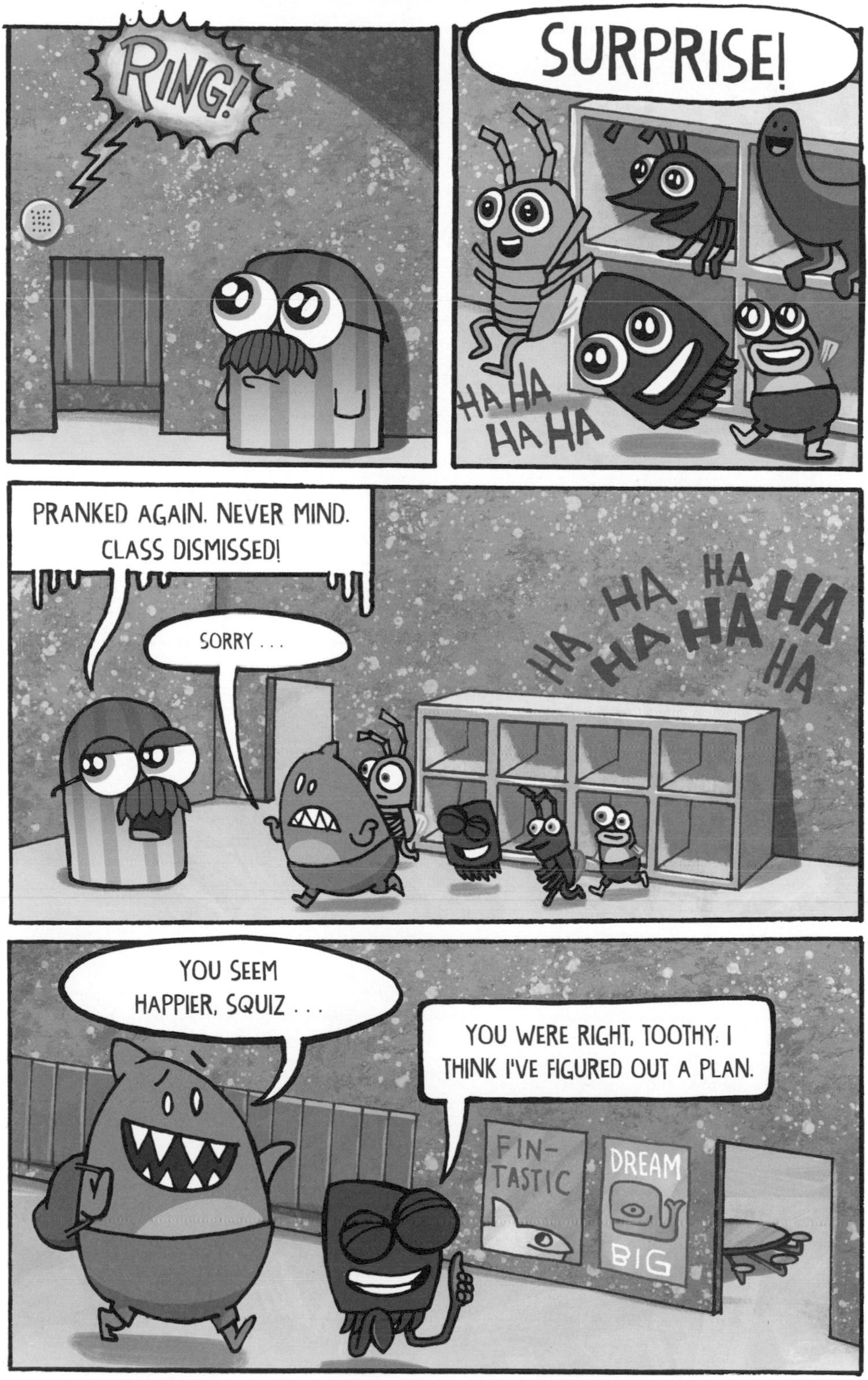
RING!
SURPRISE!
HA HA
HA HA
PRANKED AGAIN. NEVER MIND.
CLASS DISMISSED!
SORRY . . .
HA HA HA HA HA HA HA HA
YOU SEEM
HAPPIER, SQUIZ . . .
YOU WERE RIGHT, TOOTHY. I
THINK I'VE FIGURED OUT A PLAN.
FIN-
TASTIC
DREAM
BIG

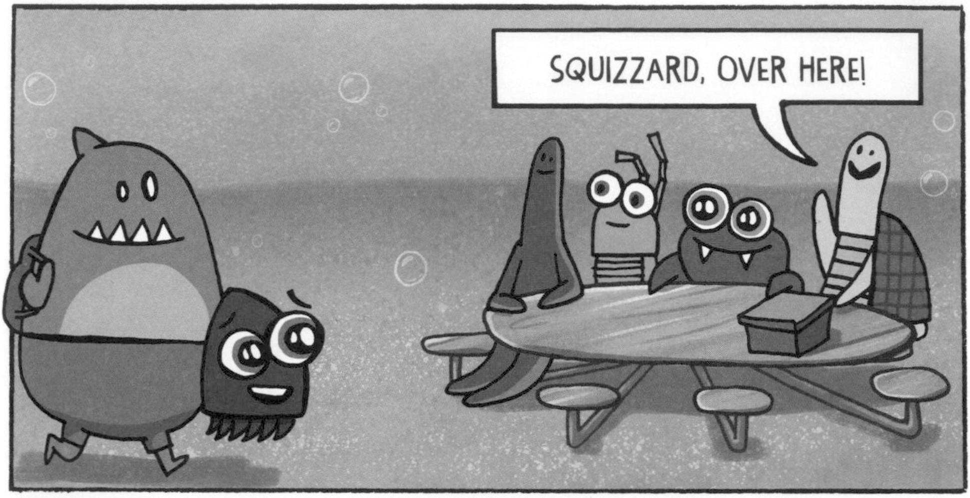
SQUIZZARD, OVER HERE!

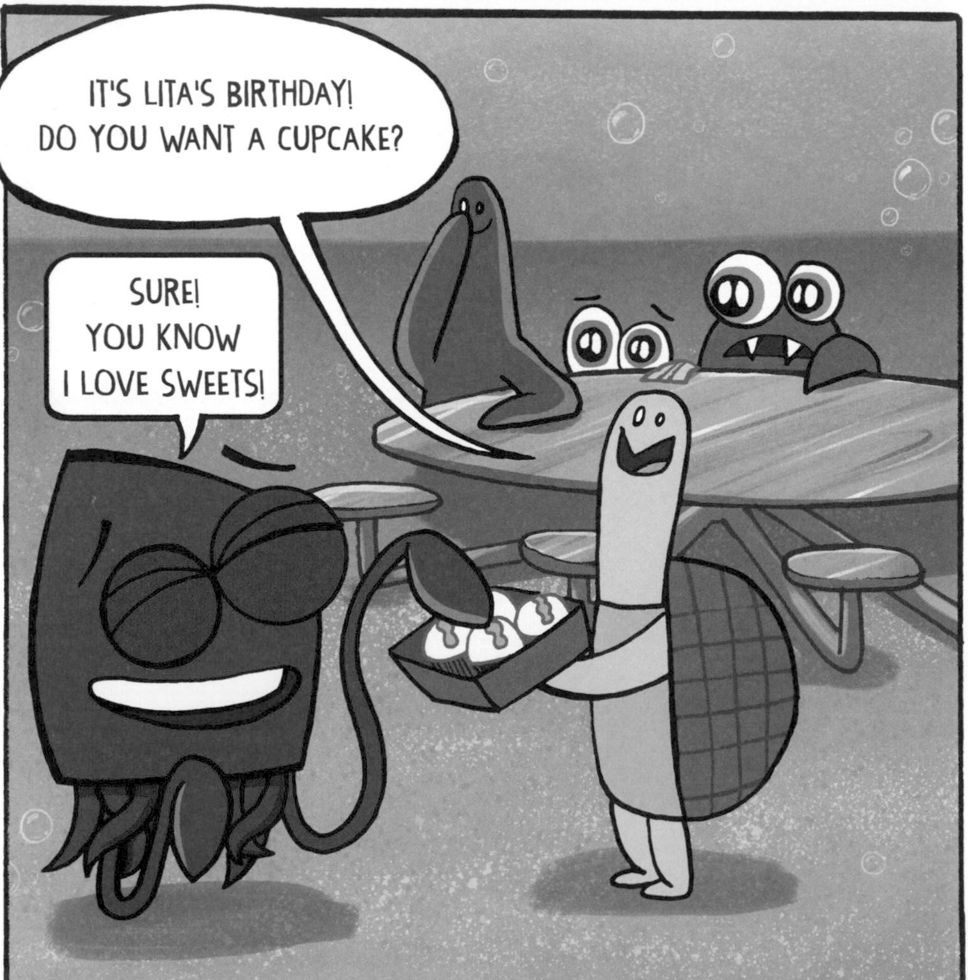
IT'S LITA'S BIRTHDAY! DO YOU WANT A CUPCAKE?
SURE! YOU KNOW I LOVE SWEETS!

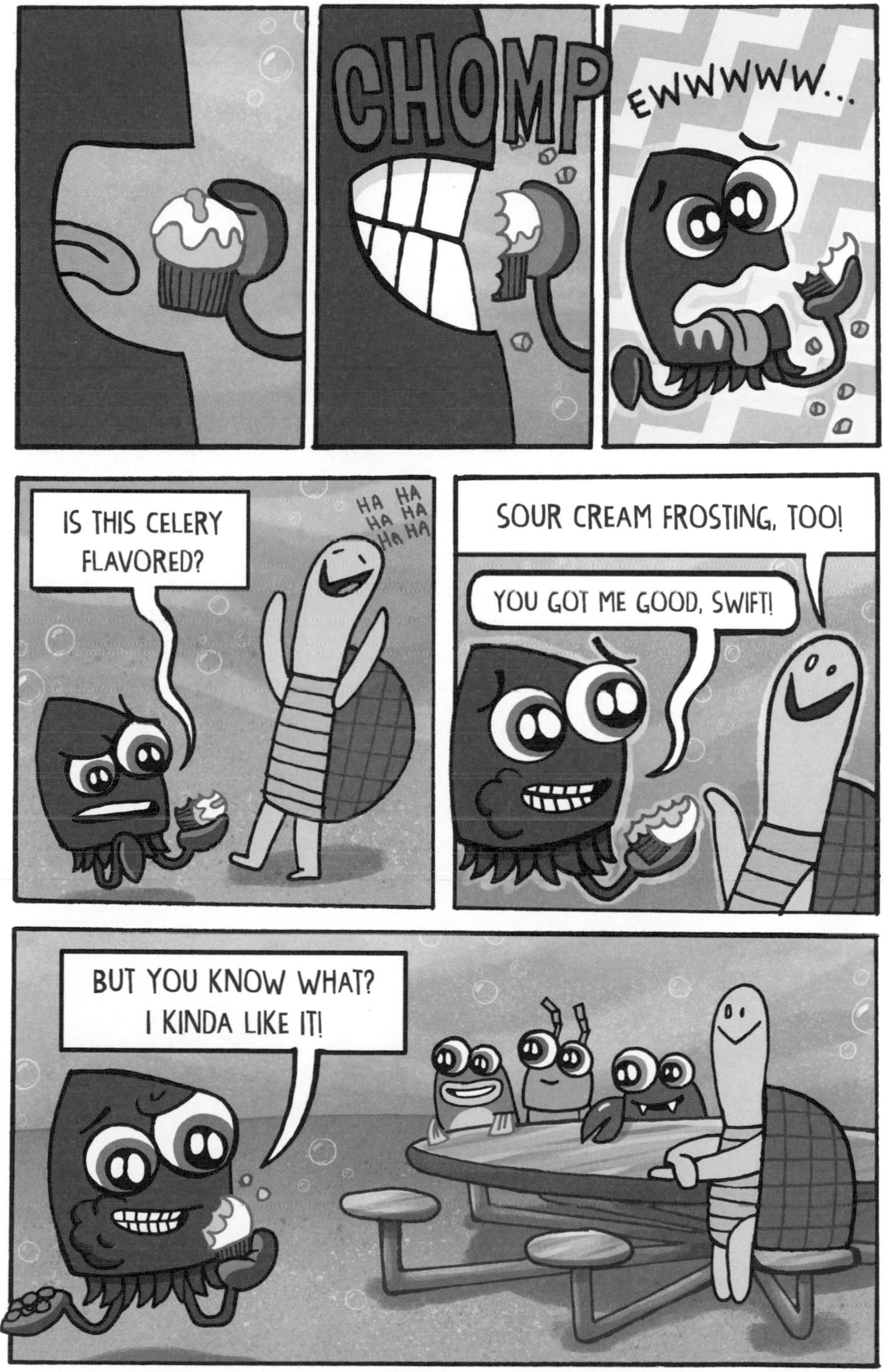
CHOMP
EWWWWW...
IS THIS CELERY FLAVORED?
HA HA HA HA HA HA
SOUR CREAM FROSTING, TOO!
YOU GOT ME GOOD, SWIFT!
BUT YOU KNOW WHAT? I KINDA LIKE IT!

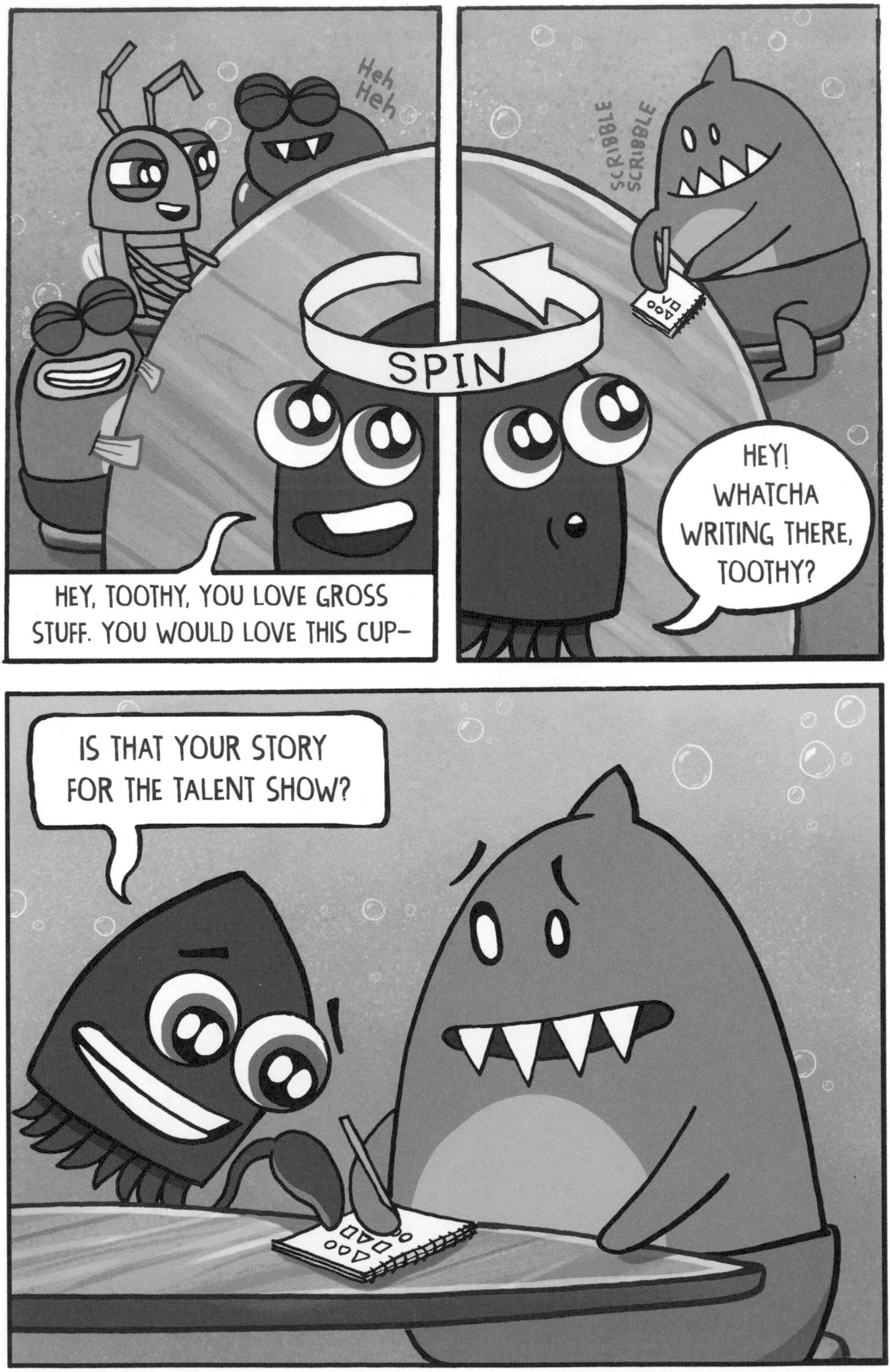
Heh
Heh
SPIN
HEY, TOOTHY, YOU LOVE GROSS STUFF. YOU WOULD LOVE THIS CUP-
SCRIBBLE
SCRIBBLE
HEY! WHATCHA WRITING THERE, TOOTHY?
IS THAT YOUR STORY FOR THE TALENT SHOW?

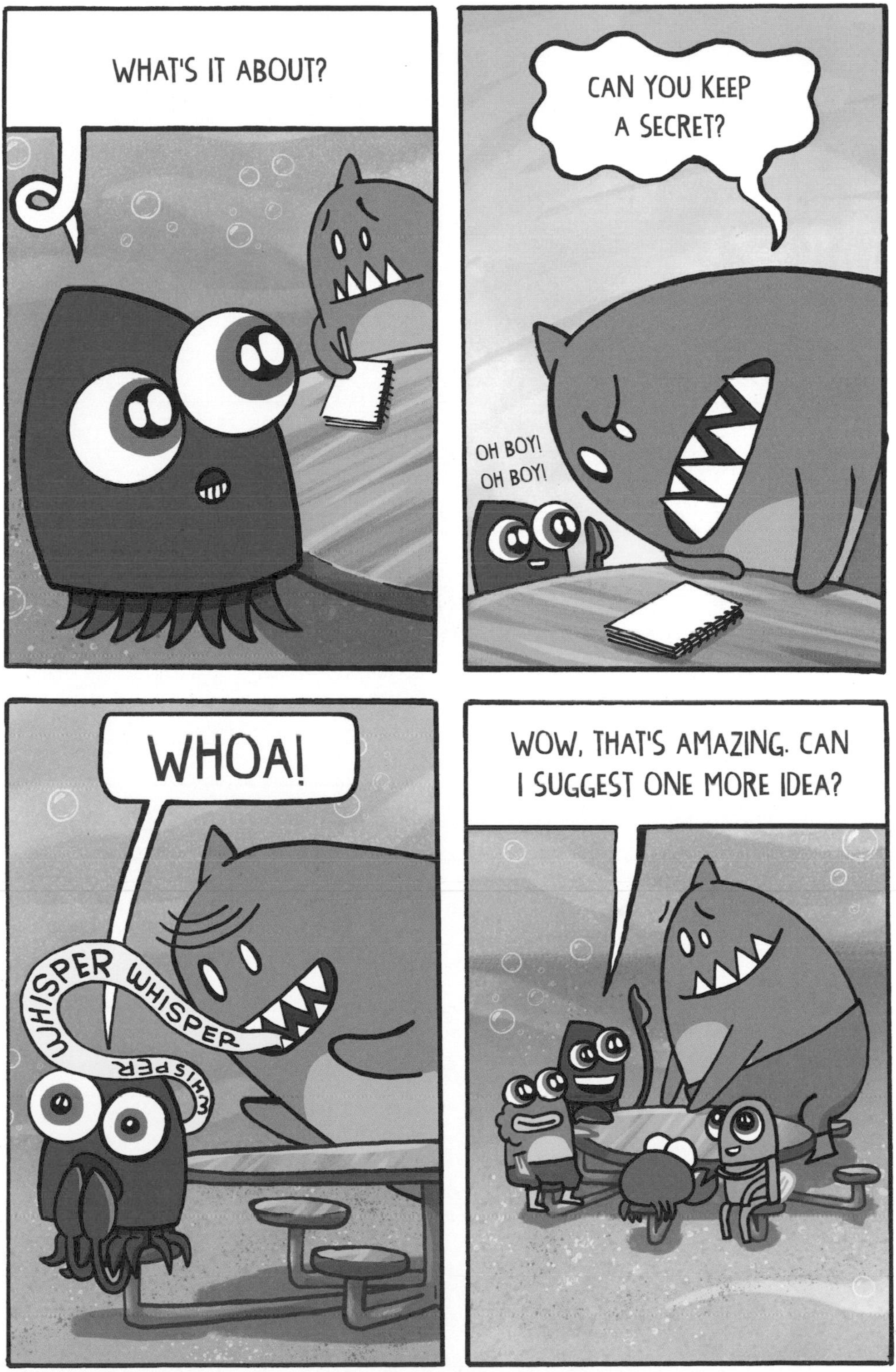
WHAT'S IT ABOUT?
CAN YOU KEEP A SECRET?
OH BOY! OH BOY!
WHOA!
WHISPER WHISPER WHISPER WHISPER
WOW, THAT'S AMAZING. CAN I SUGGEST ONE MORE IDEA?

CHAPTER 5

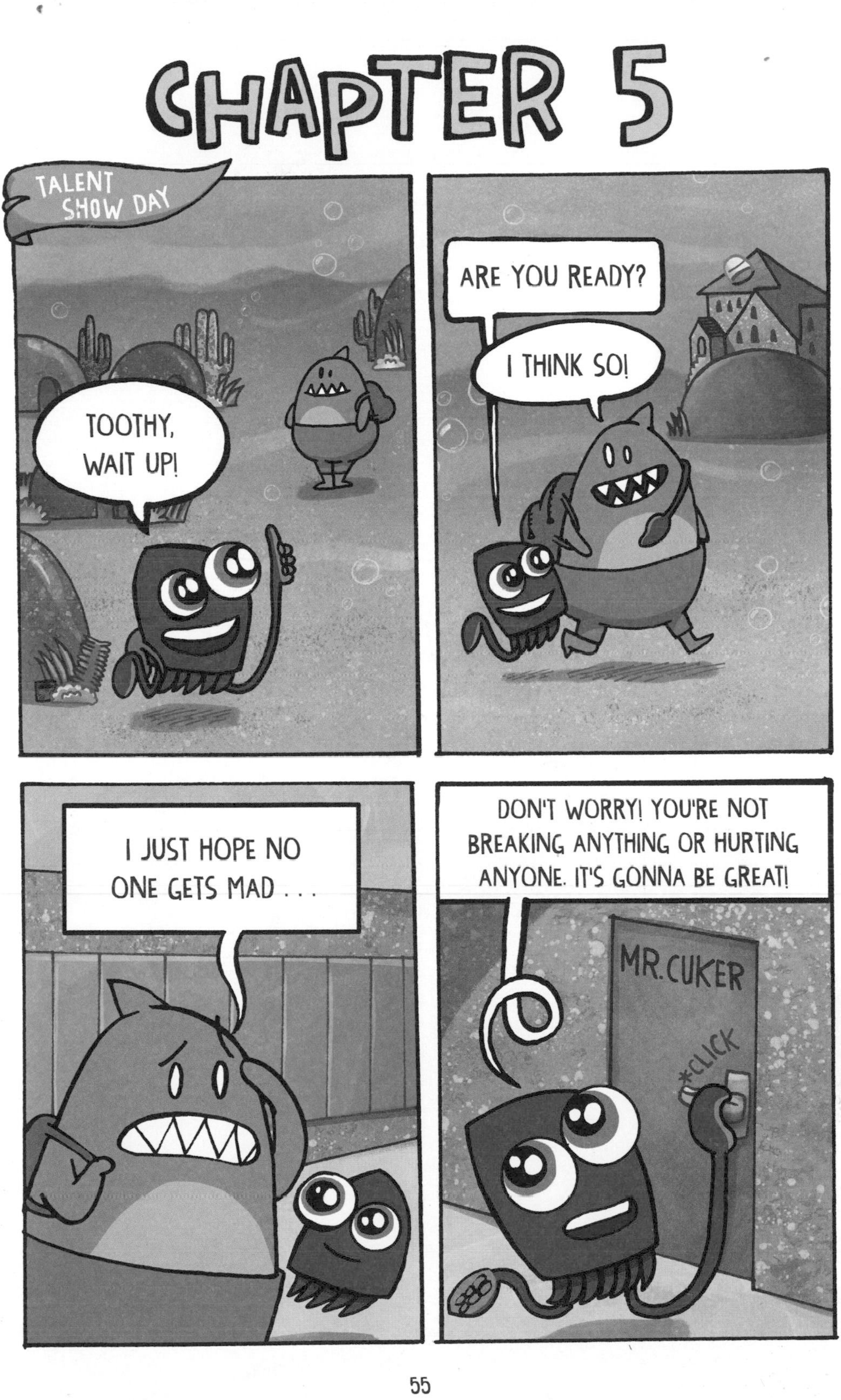
TALENT SHOW DAY
TOOTHY, WAIT UP!
ARE YOU READY?
I THINK SO!
I JUST HOPE NO ONE GETS MAD . . .
DON'T WORRY! YOU'RE NOT BREAKING ANYTHING OR HURTING ANYONE. IT'S GONNA BE GREAT!
MR. CUKER
*CLICK

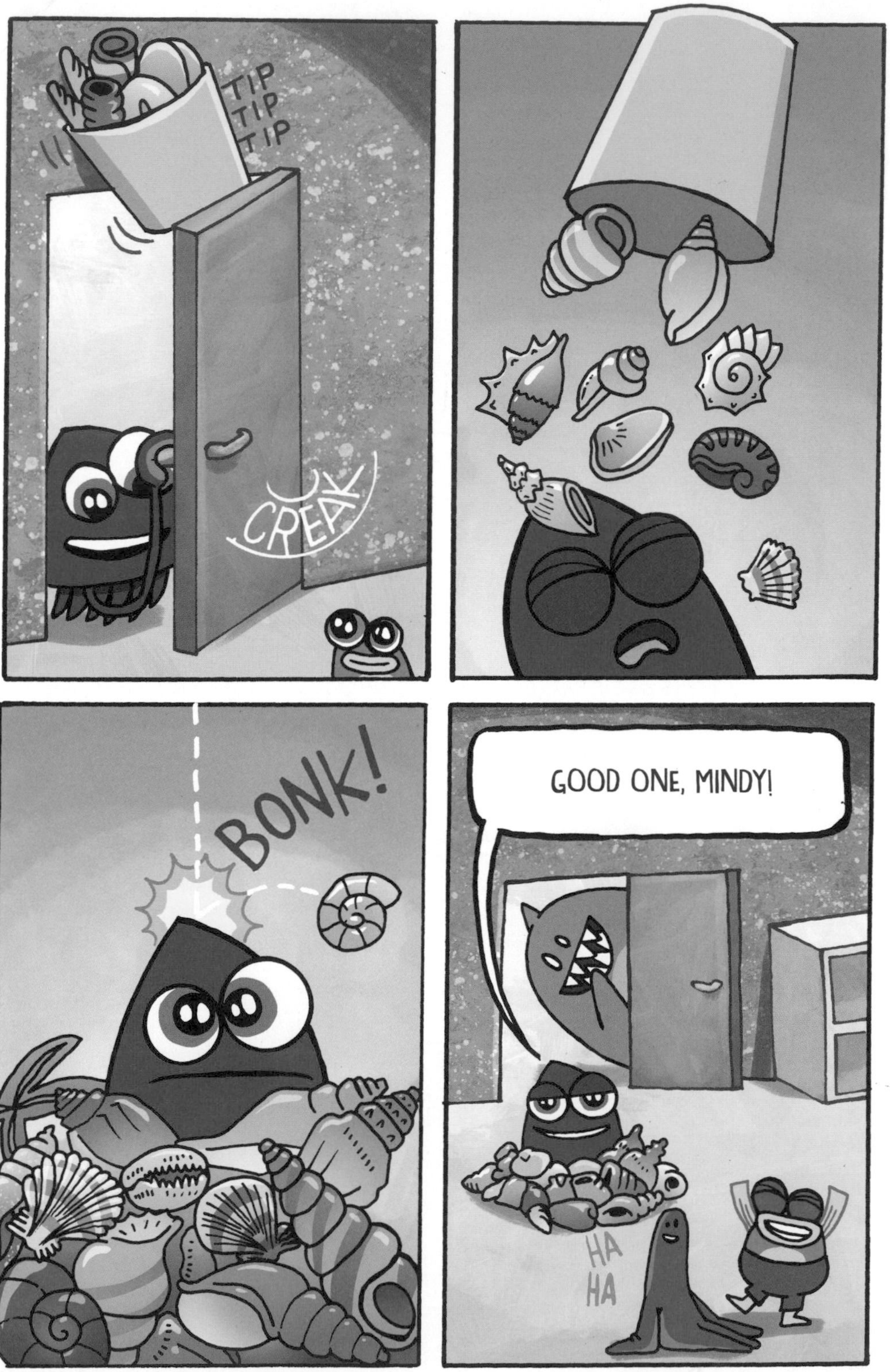
TIP
TIP
TIP
CREAK
BONK!
GOOD ONE, MINDY!
HA
HA

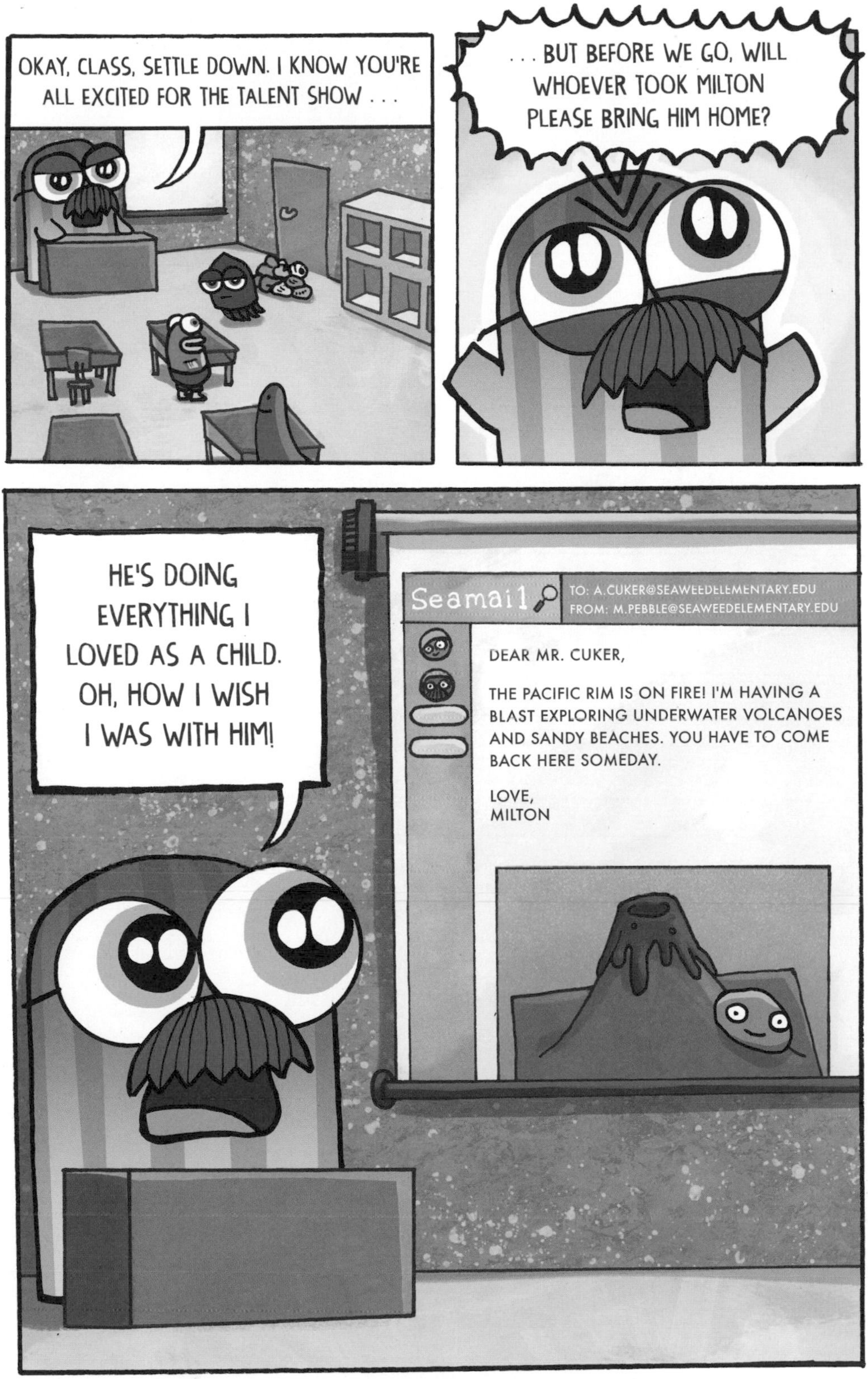
OKAY, CLASS, SETTLE DOWN. I KNOW YOU'RE ALL EXCITED FOR THE TALENT SHOW . . .
. . . BUT BEFORE WE GO, WILL WHOEVER TOOK MILTON PLEASE BRING HIM HOME?
HE'S DOING EVERYTHING I LOVED AS A CHILD. OH, HOW I WISH I WAS WITH HIM!
Seamail
TO: A.CUKER@SEAWEEDELEMENTARY.EDU
FROM: M.PEBBLE@SEAWEEDELEMENTARY.EDU
DEAR MR. CUKER,
THE PACIFIC RIM IS ON FIRE! I'M HAVING A BLAST EXPLORING UNDERWATER VOLCANOES AND SANDY BEACHES. YOU HAVE TO COME BACK HERE SOMEDAY.
LOVE,
MILTON

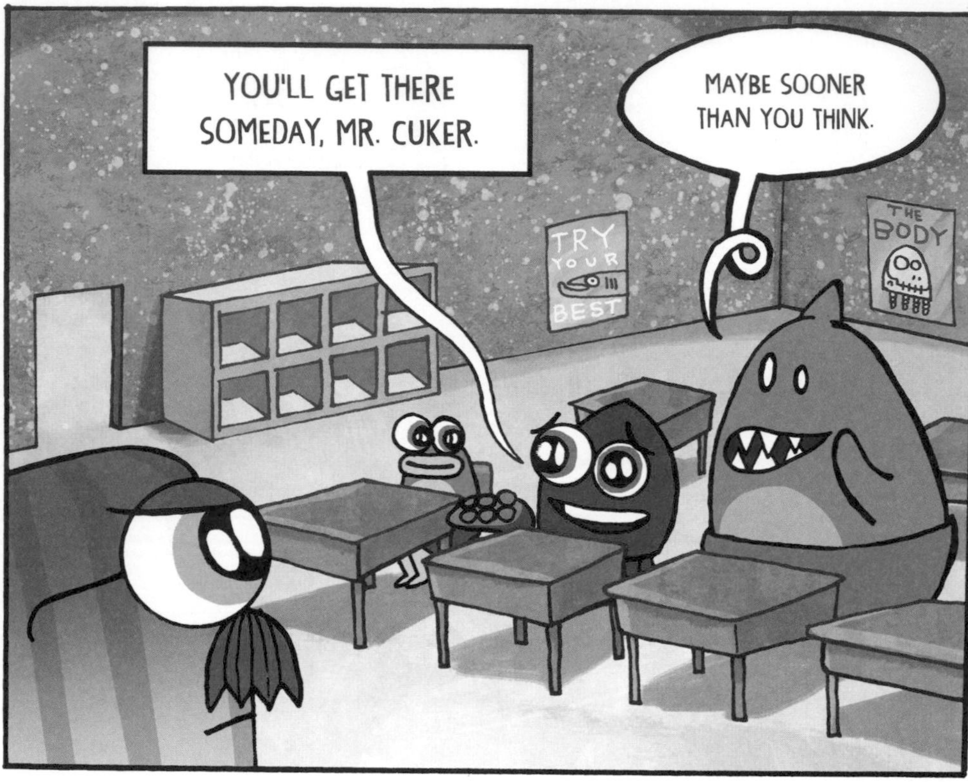
YOU'LL GET THERE SOMEDAY, MR. CUKER.
MAYBE SOONER THAN YOU THINK.
TRY YOUR BEST
THE BODY

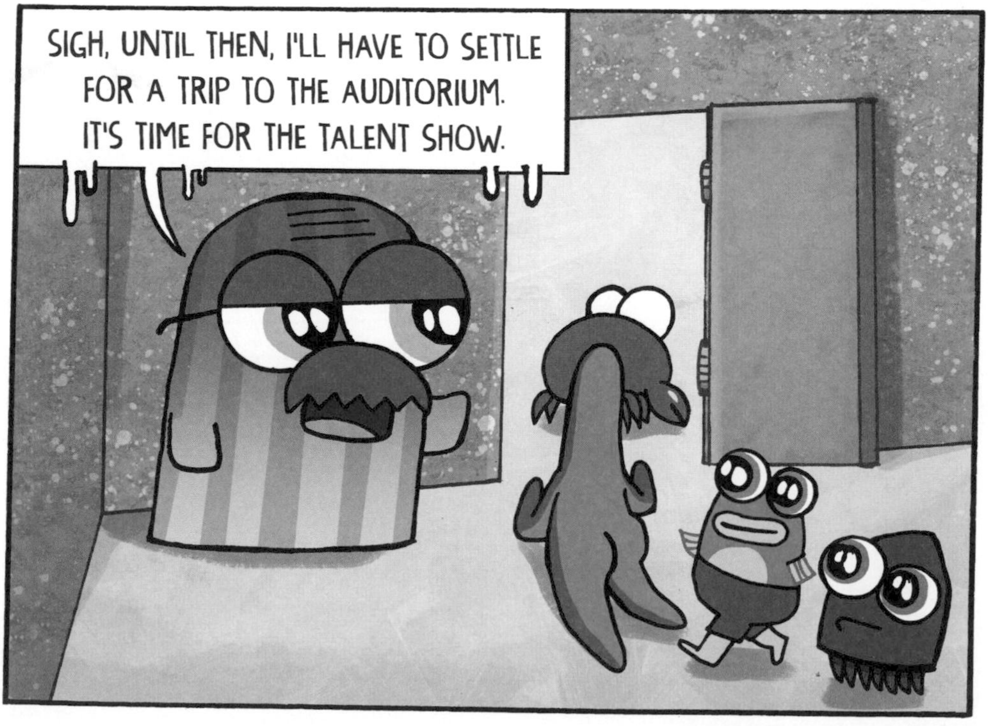
SIGH, UNTIL THEN, I'LL HAVE TO SETTLE FOR A TRIP TO THE AUDITORIUM. IT'S TIME FOR THE TALENT SHOW.

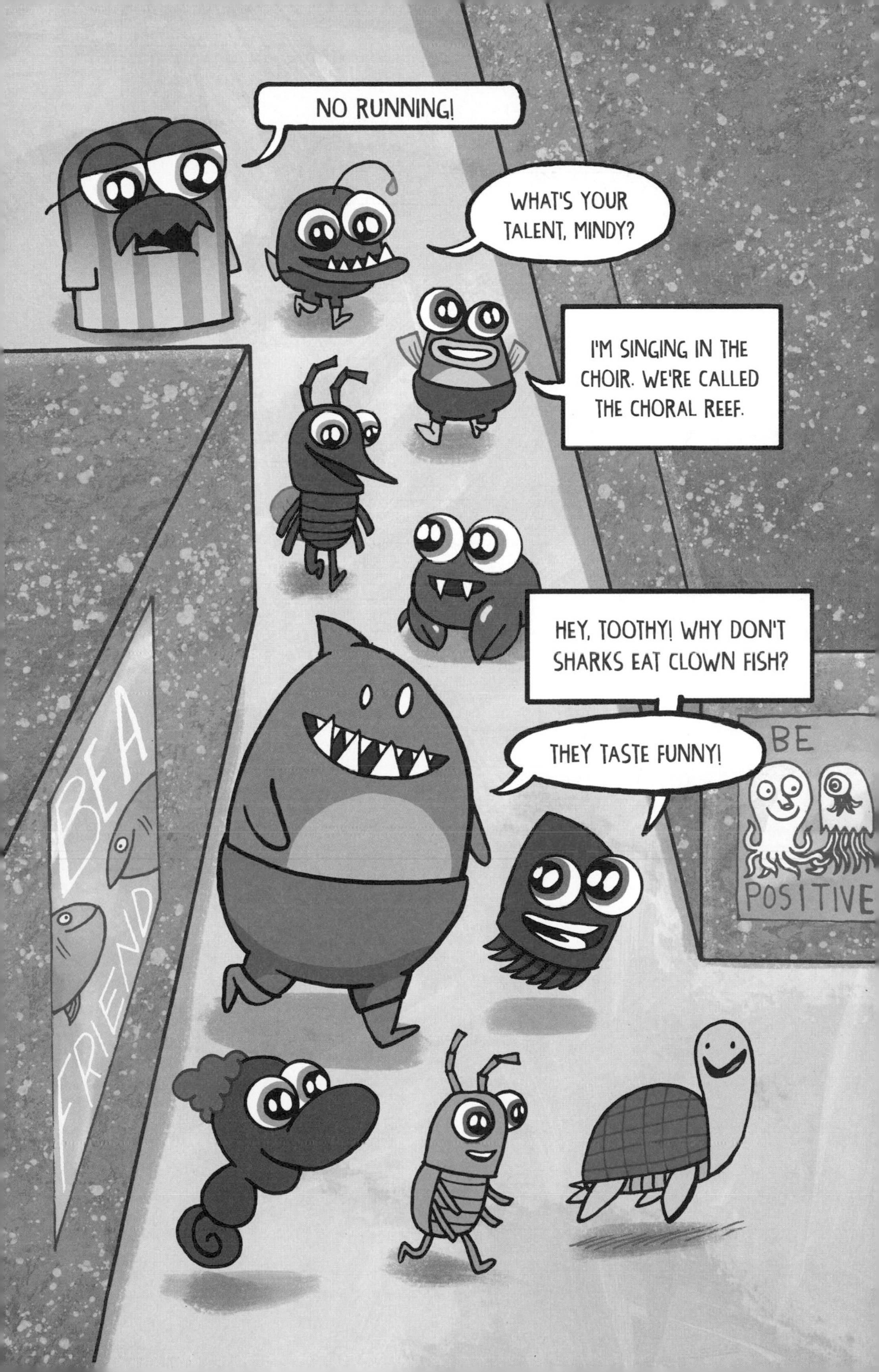
NO RUNNING!
WHAT'S YOUR TALENT, MINDY?
I'M SINGING IN THE CHOIR. WE'RE CALLED THE CHORAL REEF.
HEY, TOOTHY! WHY DON'T SHARKS EAT CLOWN FISH?
THEY TASTE FUNNY!
BE A FRIEND
BE POSITIVE

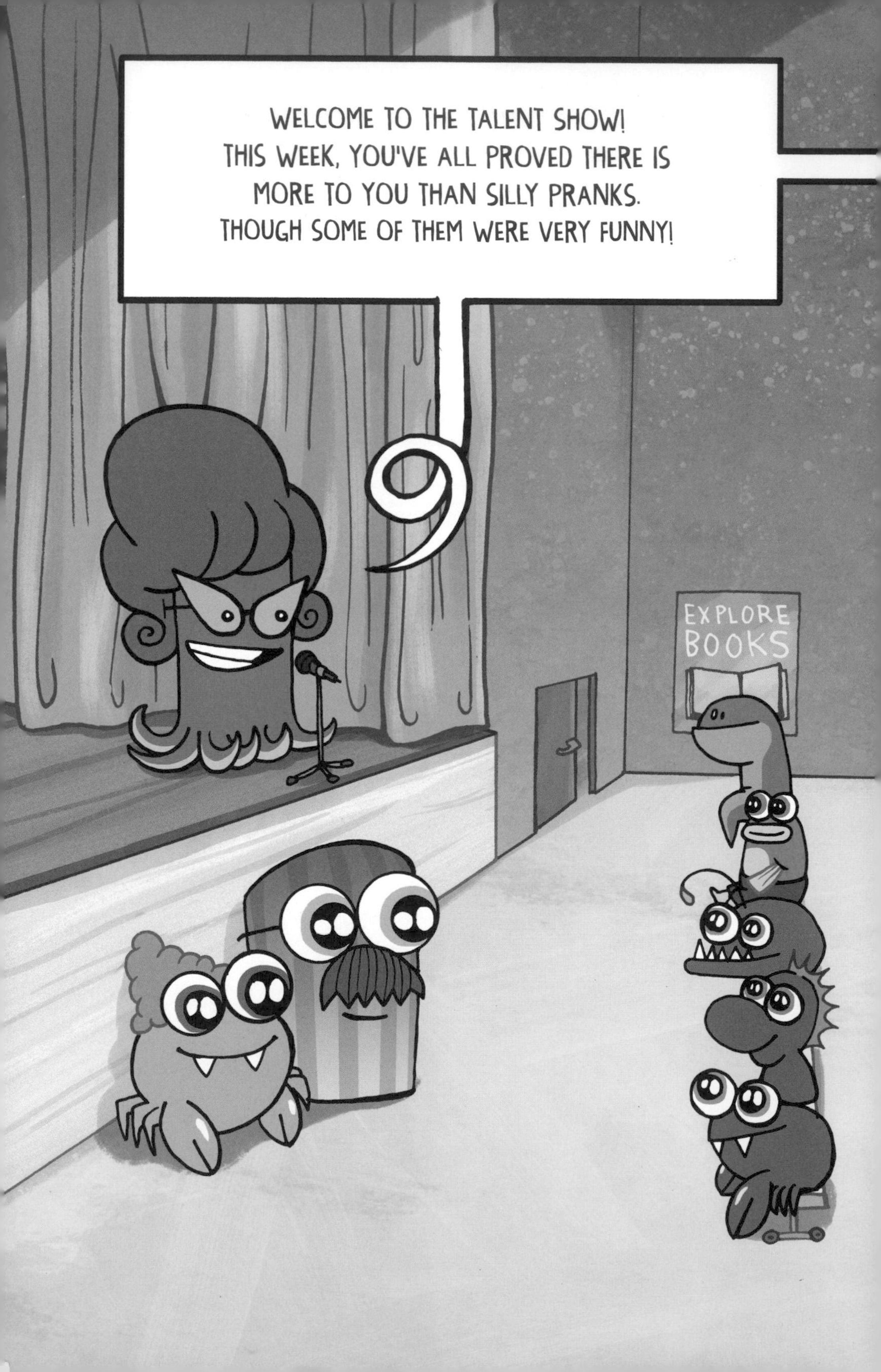
WELCOME TO THE TALENT SHOW! THIS WEEK, YOU'VE ALL PROVED THERE IS MORE TO YOU THAN SILLY PRANKS. THOUGH SOME OF THEM WERE VERY FUNNY!
EXPLORE BOOKS

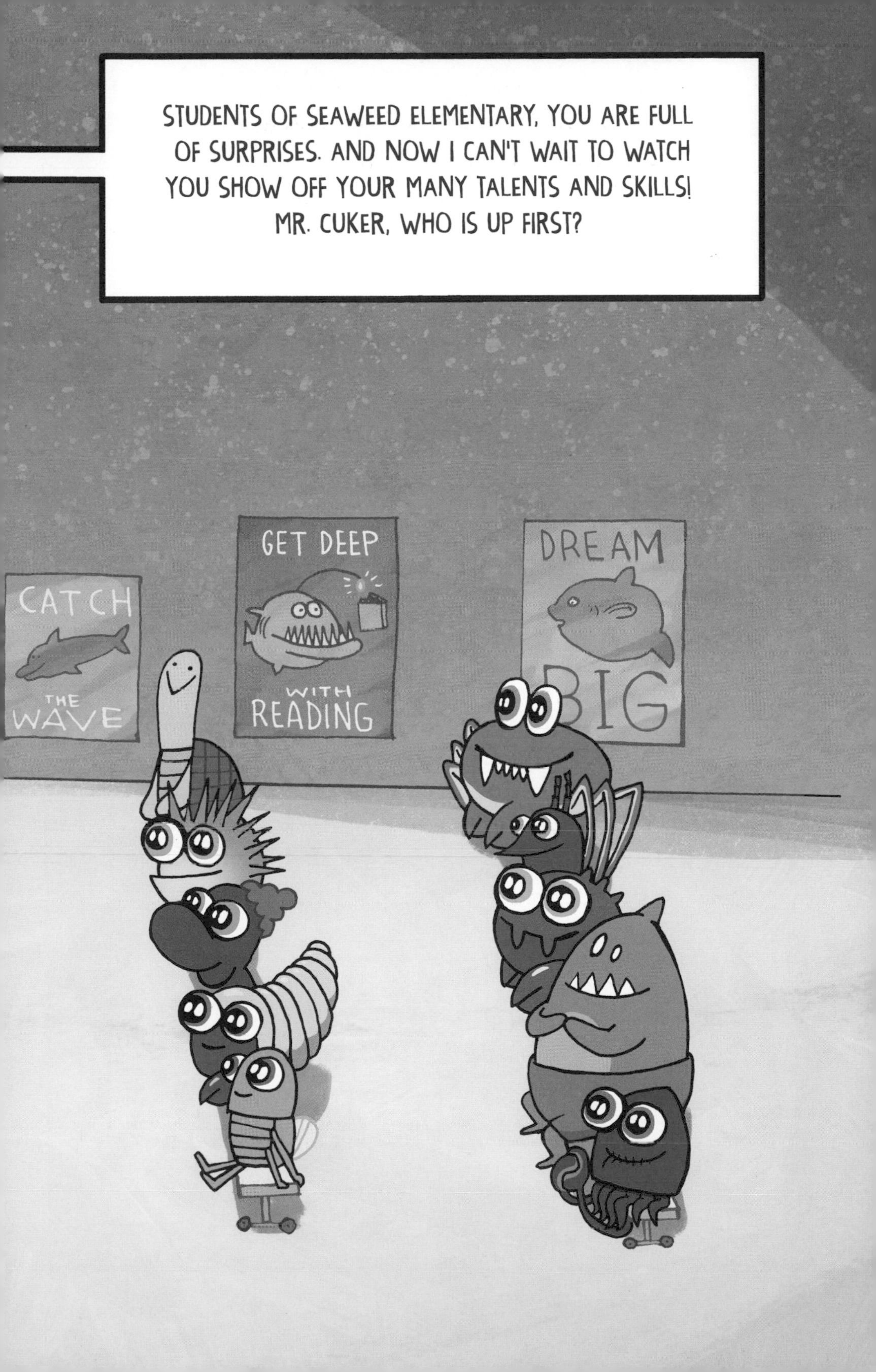
STUDENTS OF SEAWEED ELEMENTARY, YOU ARE FULL OF SURPRISES. AND NOW I CAN'T WAIT TO WATCH YOU SHOW OFF YOUR MANY TALENTS AND SKILLS! MR. CUKER, WHO IS UP FIRST?
CATCH THE WAVE
GET DEEP WITH READING
DREAM BIG

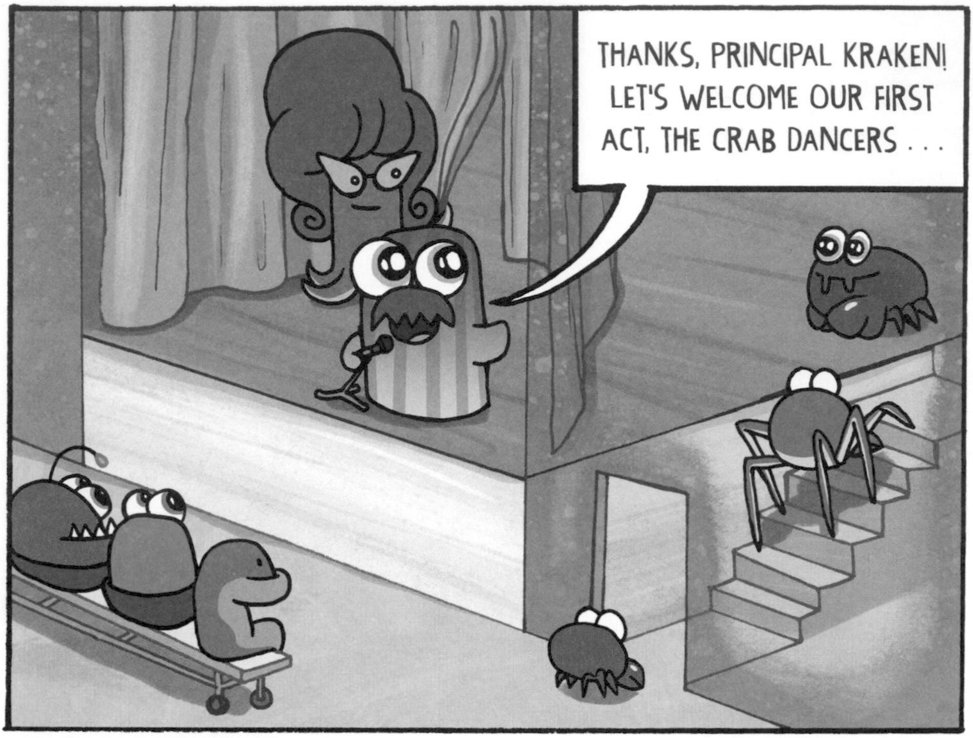
THANKS, PRINCIPAL KRAKEN! LET'S WELCOME OUR FIRST ACT, THE CRAB DANCERS . . .

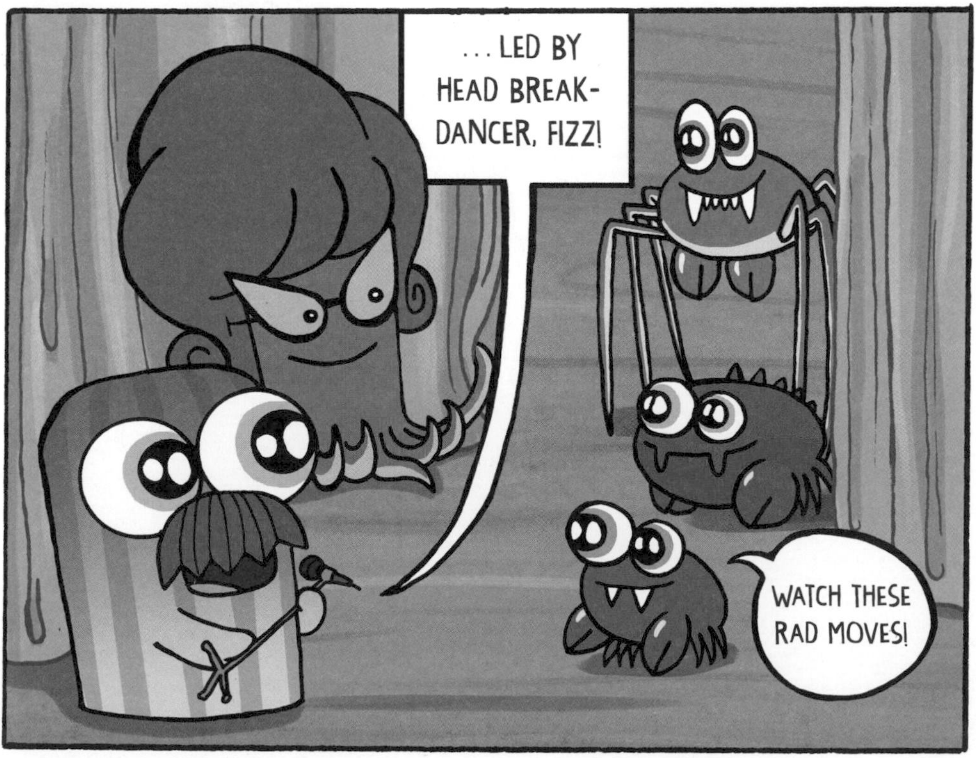
. . . LED BY HEAD BREAK-DANCER, FIZZ!
WATCH THESE RAD MOVES!

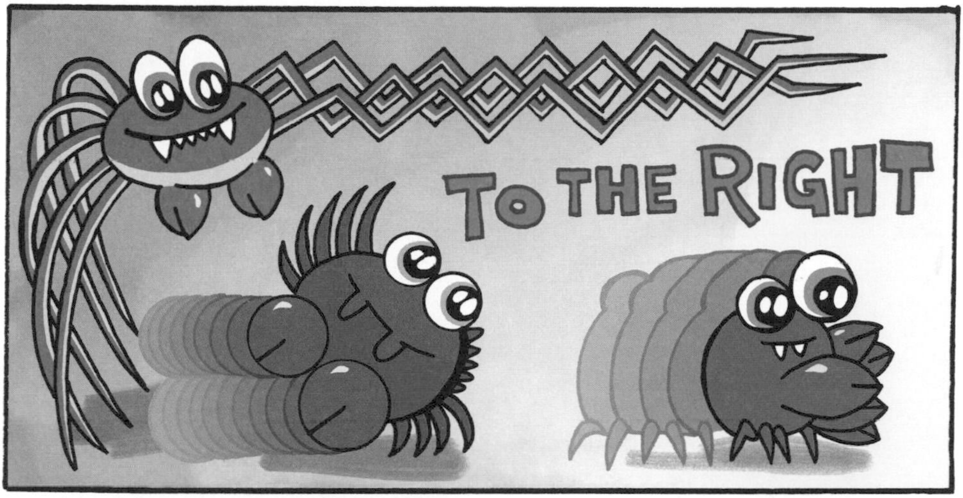
TO THE RIGHT

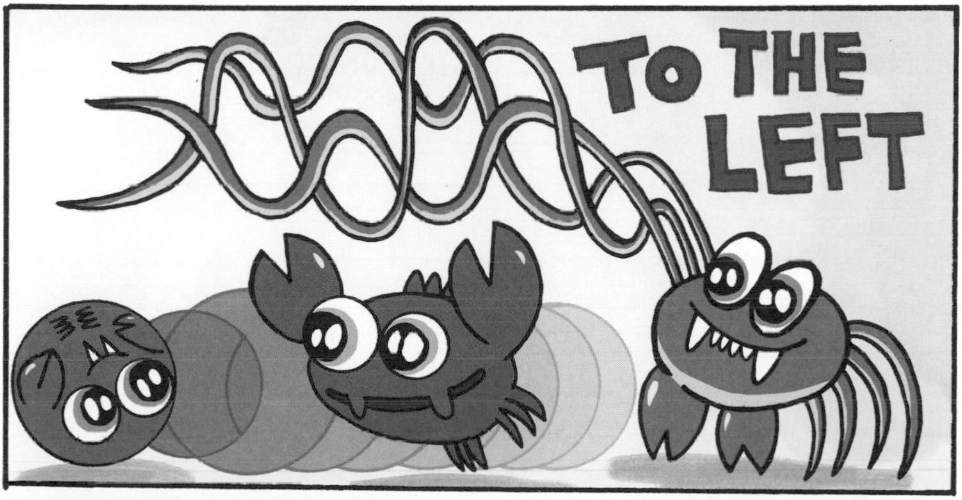
TO THE LEFT

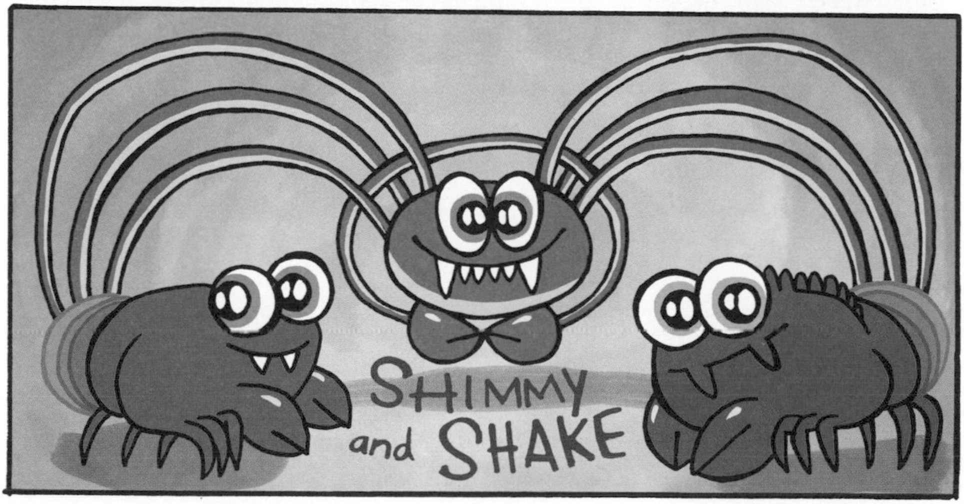
SHIMMY and SHAKE

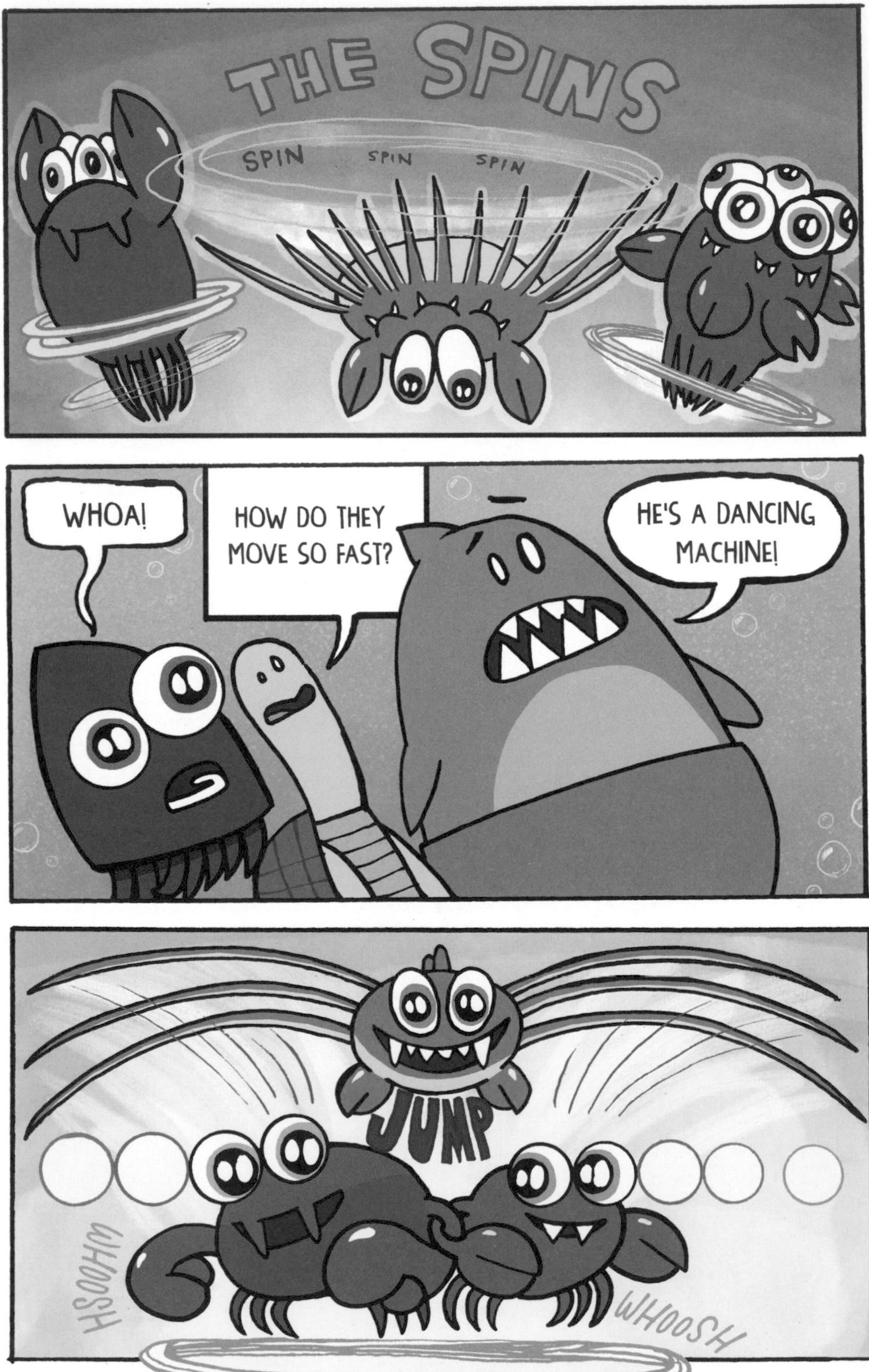
THE SPINS
SPIN
SPIN
SPIN
WHOA!
HOW DO THEY MOVE SO FAST?
HE'S A DANCING MACHINE!
JUMP
WHOOSH
WHOOSH

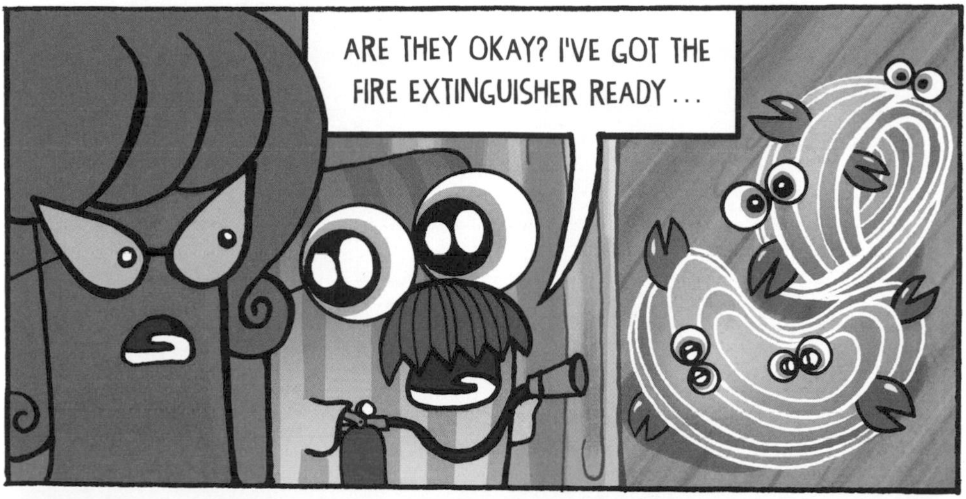
ARE THEY OKAY? I'VE GOT THE FIRE EXTINGUISHER READY . . .

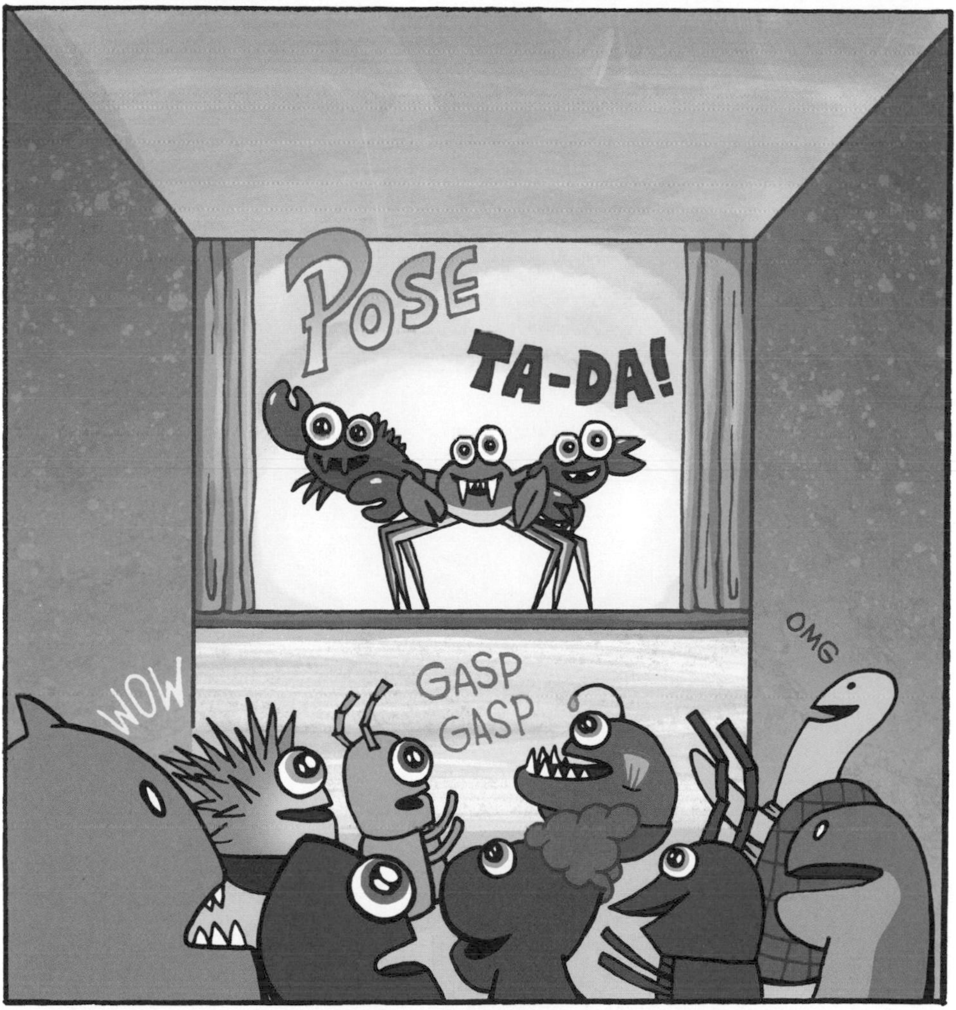
POSE
TA-DA!
OMG
WOW
GASP
GASP

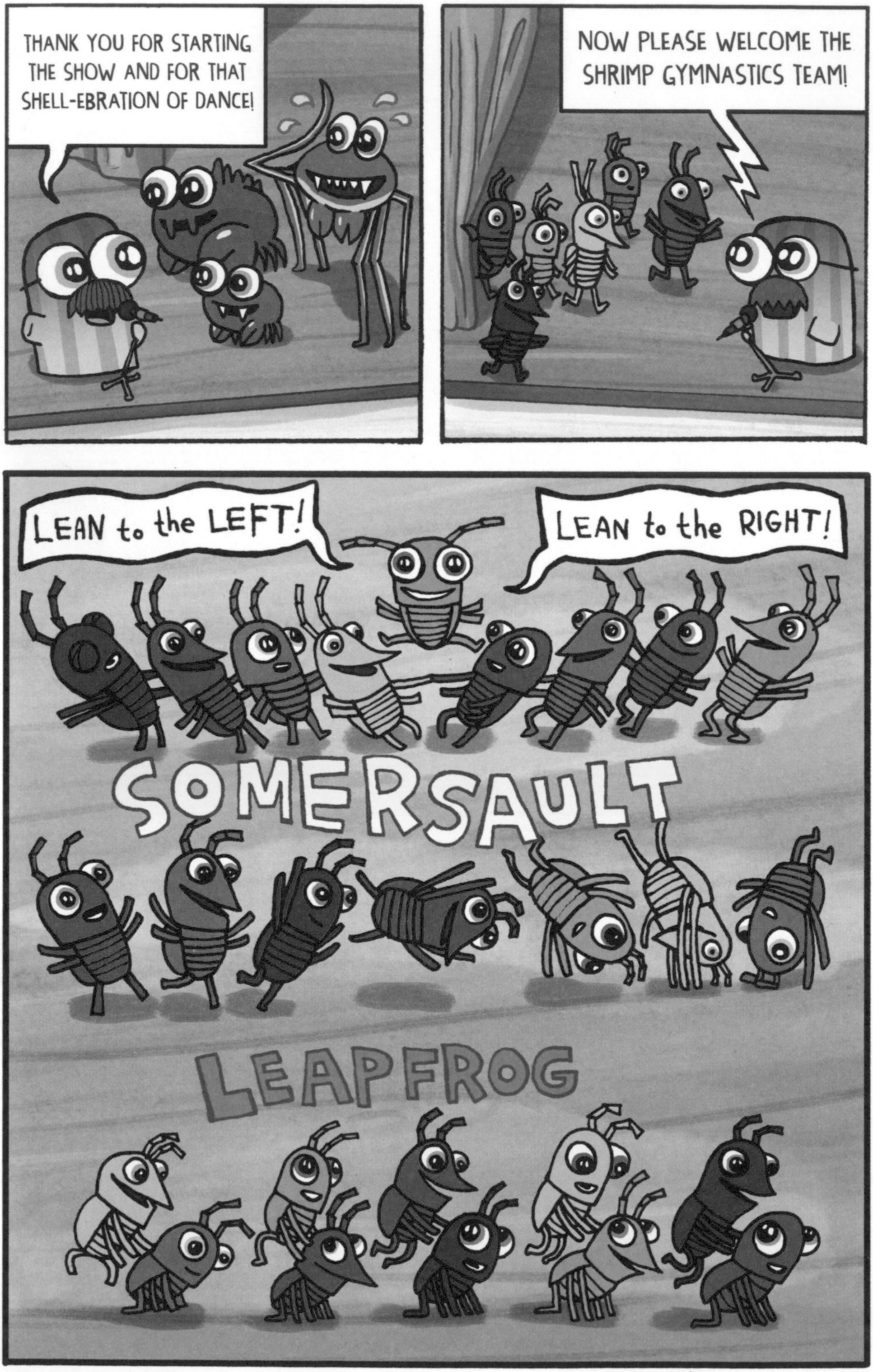
THANK YOU FOR STARTING THE SHOW AND FOR THAT SHELL-EBRATION OF DANCE!
NOW PLEASE WELCOME THE SHRIMP GYMNASTICS TEAM!
LEAN to the LEFT!
LEAN to the RIGHT!
SOMERSAULT
LEAPFROG

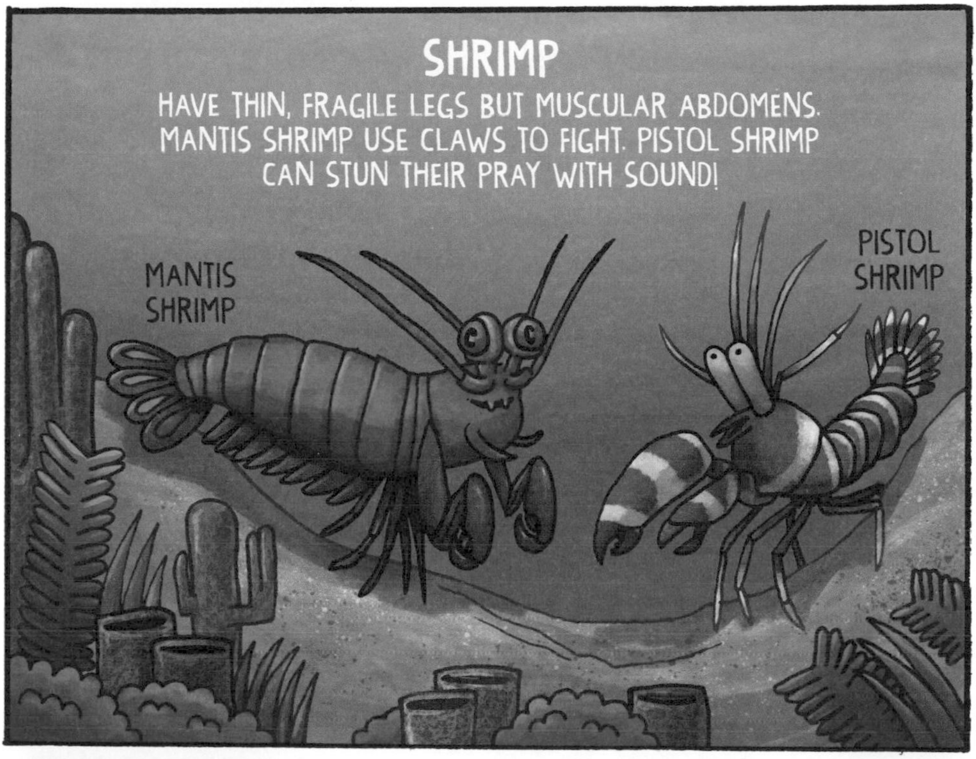
SHRIMP
HAVE THIN, FRAGILE LEGS BUT MUSCULAR ABDOMENS. MANTIS SHRIMP USE CLAWS TO FIGHT. PISTOL SHRIMP CAN STUN THEIR PRAY WITH SOUND!
MANTIS SHRIMP
PISTOL SHRIMP

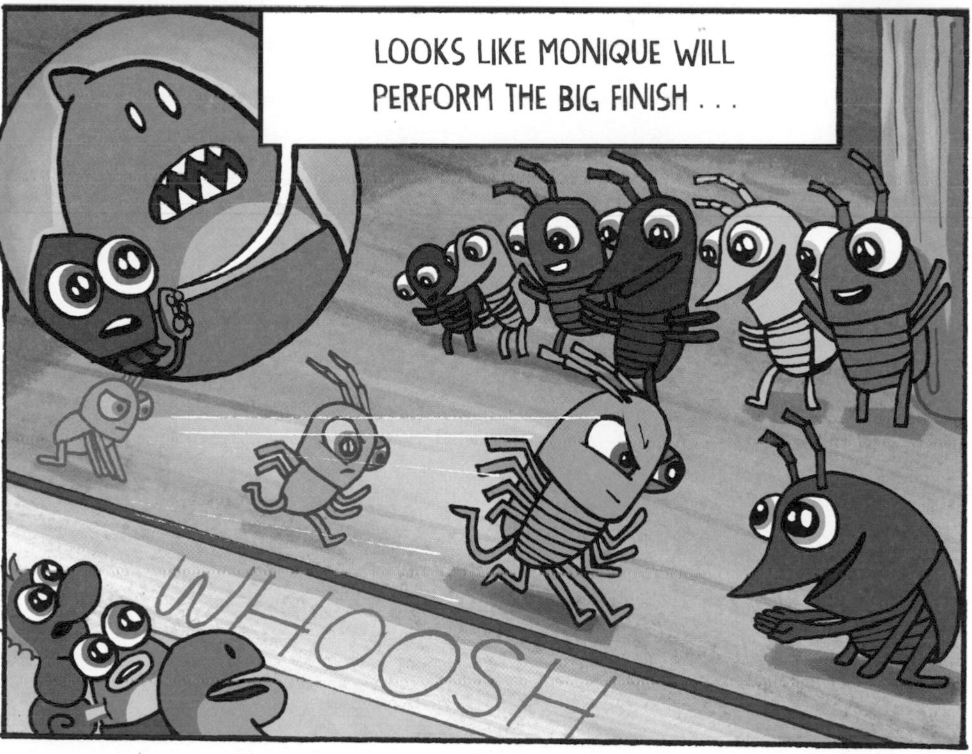
LOOKS LIKE MONIQUE WILL PERFORM THE BIG FINISH . . .
WHOOSH

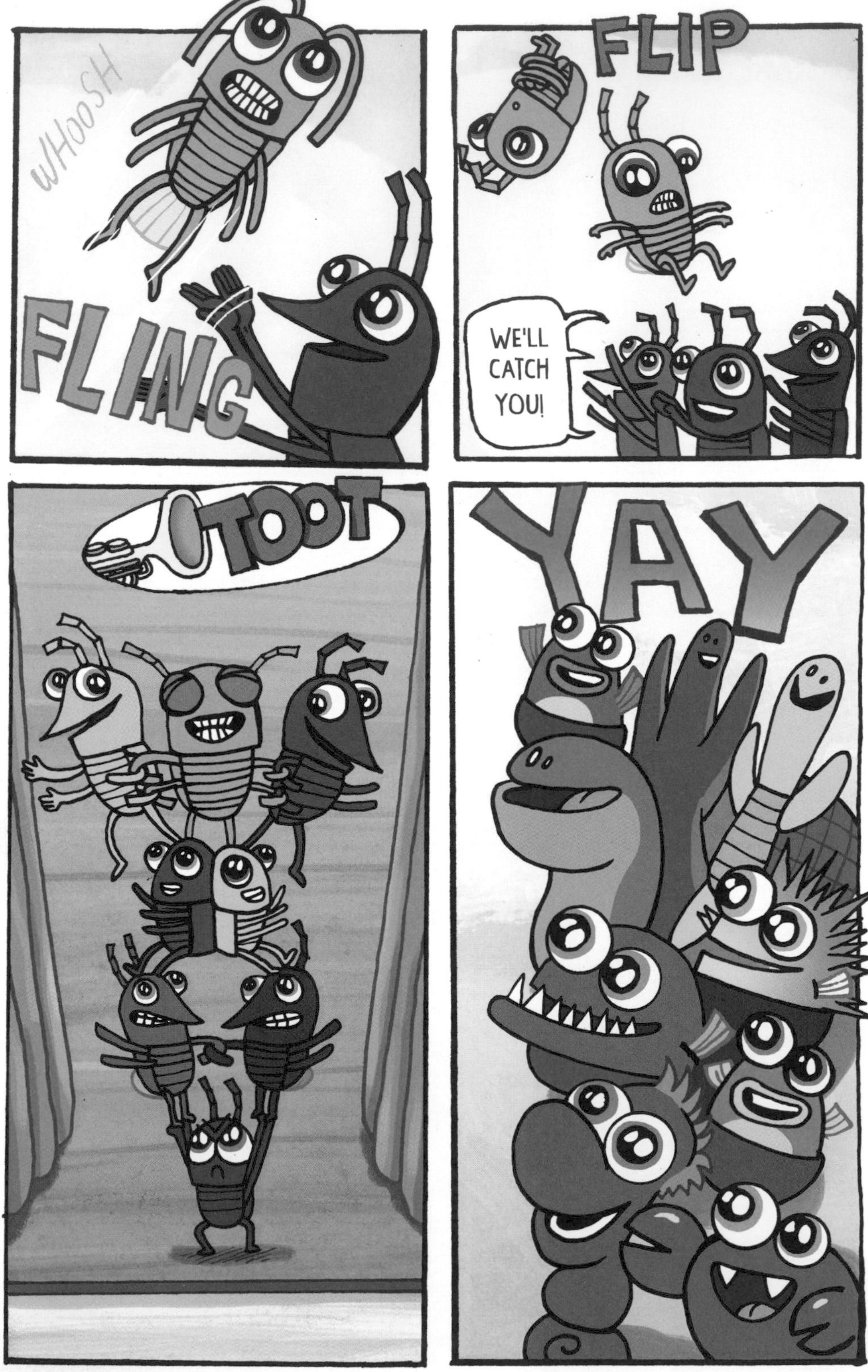
WHOOSH
FLING
FLIP
WE'LL CATCH YOU!
TOOT
YAY

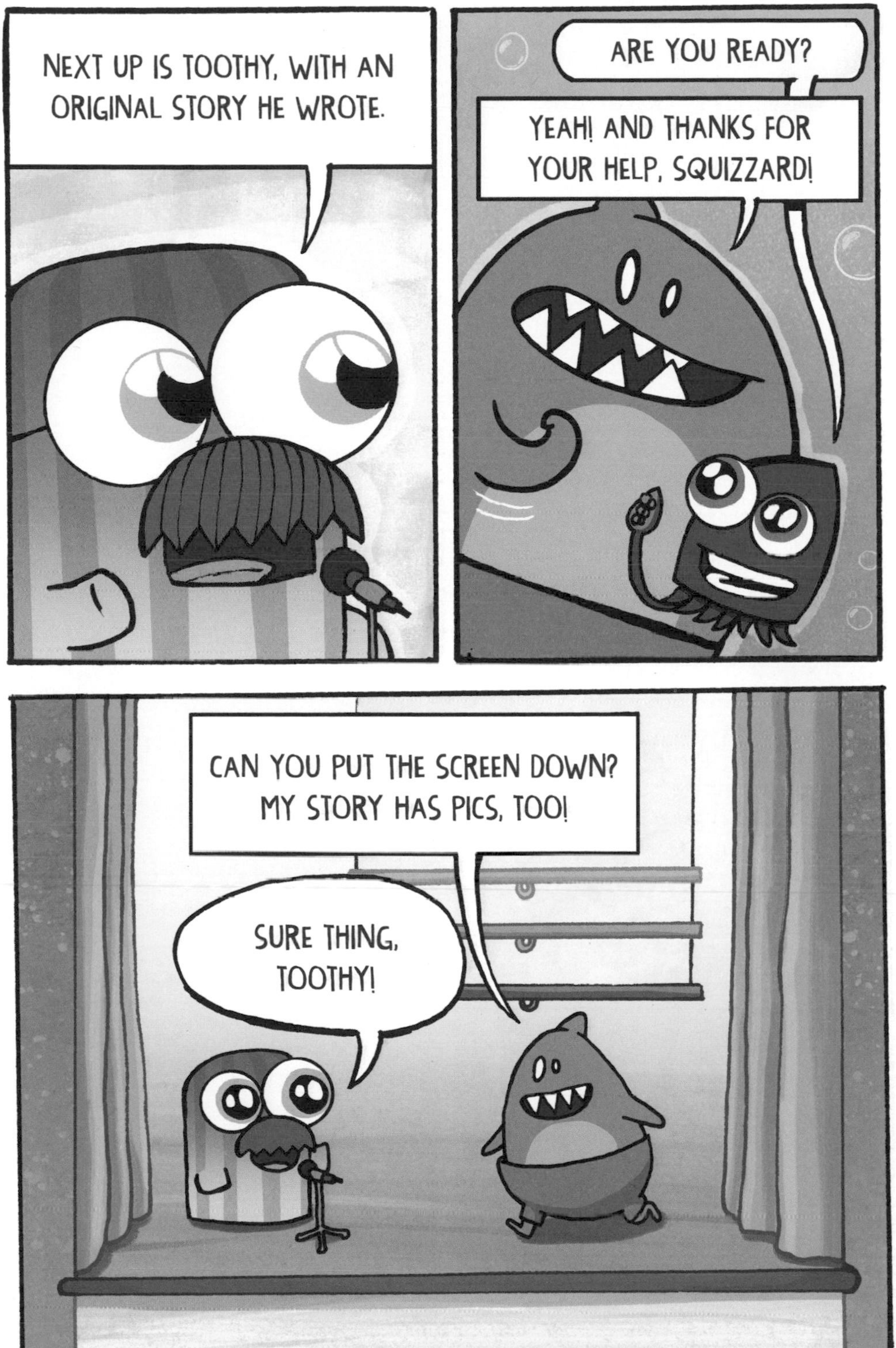
NEXT UP IS TOOTHY, WITH AN ORIGINAL STORY HE WROTE.
ARE YOU READY?
YEAH! AND THANKS FOR YOUR HELP, SQUIZZARD!
CAN YOU PUT THE SCREEN DOWN? MY STORY HAS PICS, TOO!
SURE THING, TOOTHY!

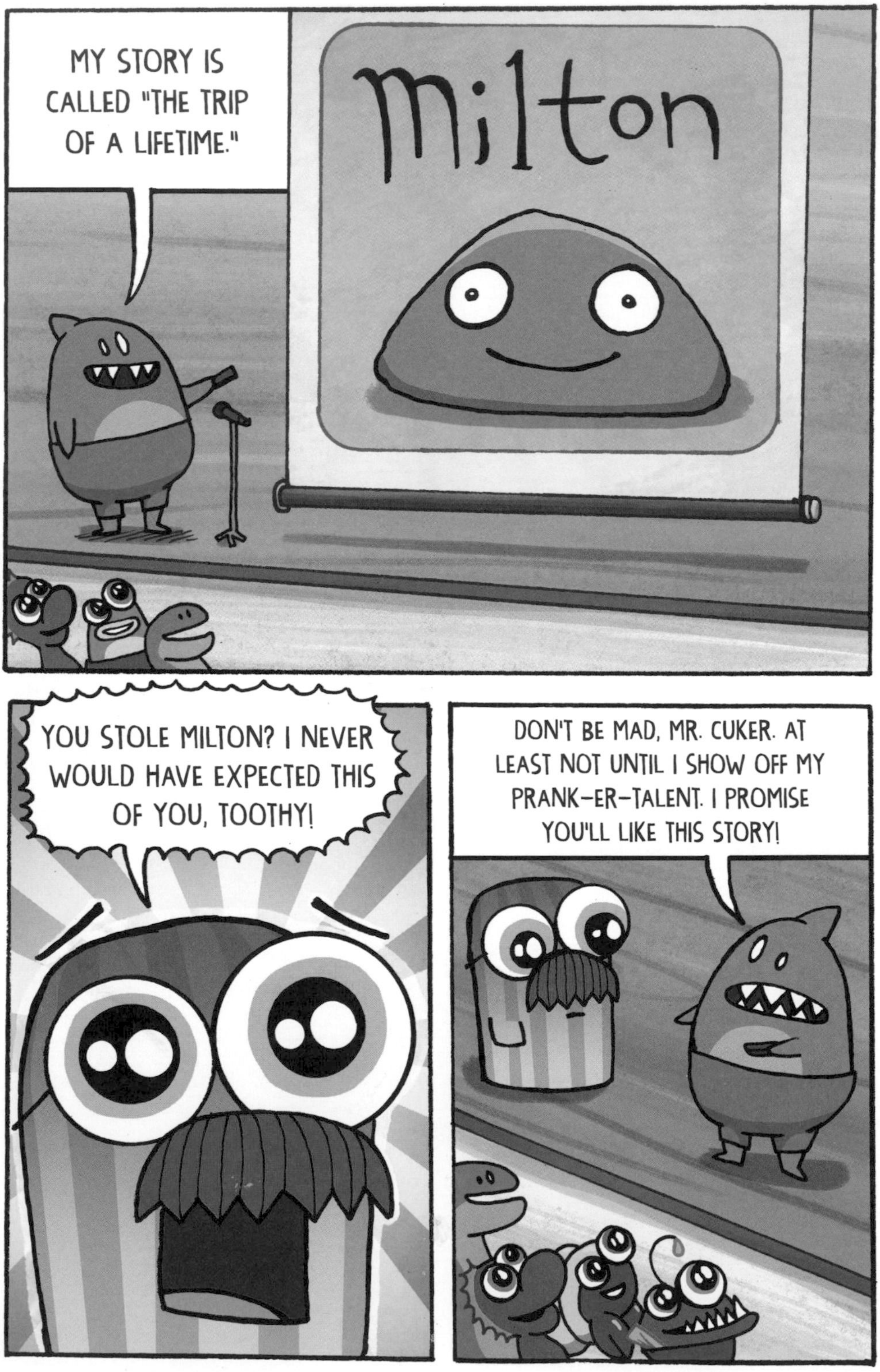
MY STORY IS CALLED "THE TRIP OF A LIFETIME."
Milton
YOU STOLE MILTON? I NEVER WOULD HAVE EXPECTED THIS OF YOU, TOOTHY!
DON'T BE MAD, MR. CUKER. AT LEAST NOT UNTIL I SHOW OFF MY PRANK-ER-TALENT. I PROMISE YOU'LL LIKE THIS STORY!

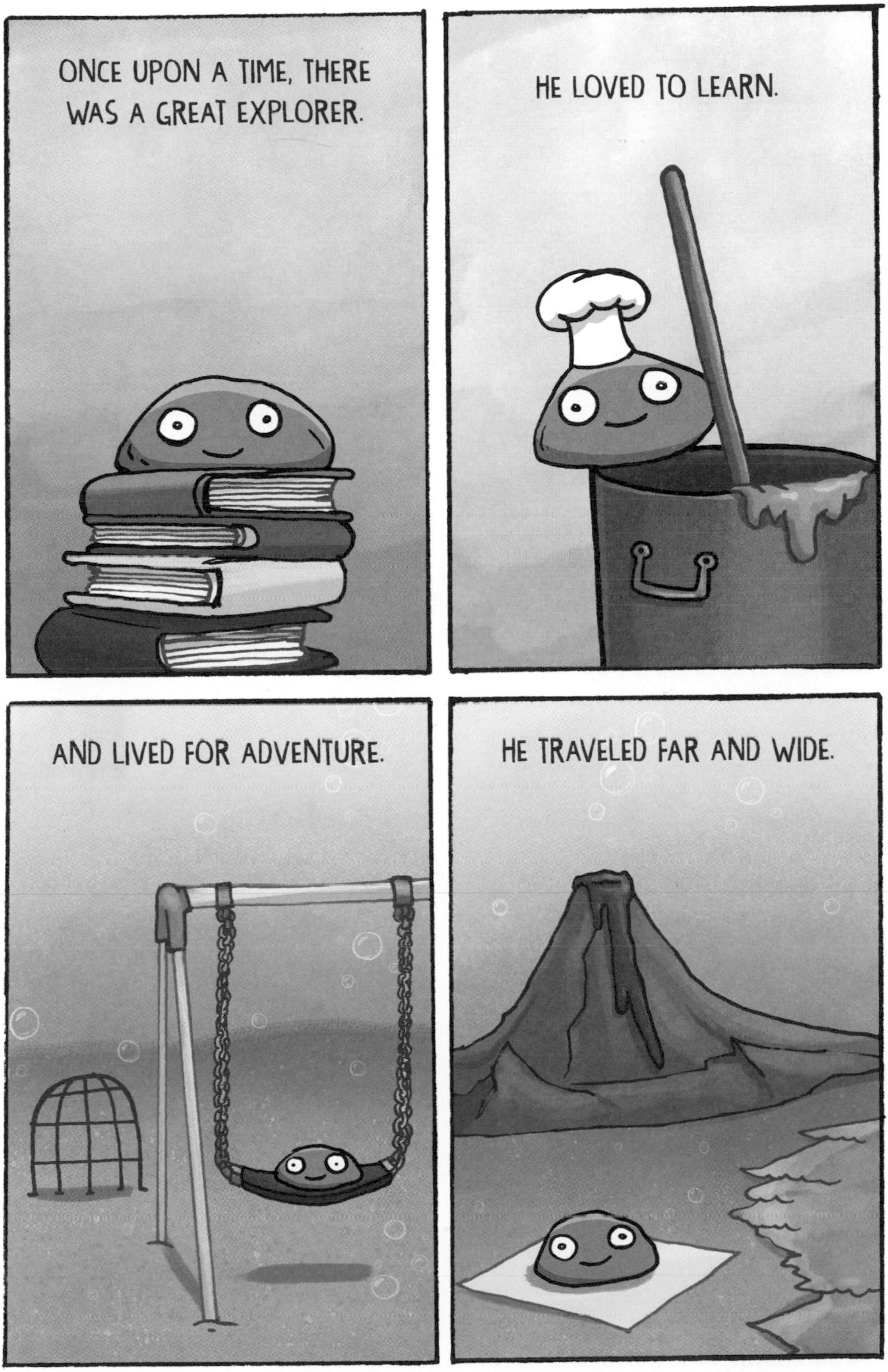
ONCE UPON A TIME, THERE WAS A GREAT EXPLORER.
HE LOVED TO LEARN.
AND LIVED FOR ADVENTURE.
HE TRAVELED FAR AND WIDE.

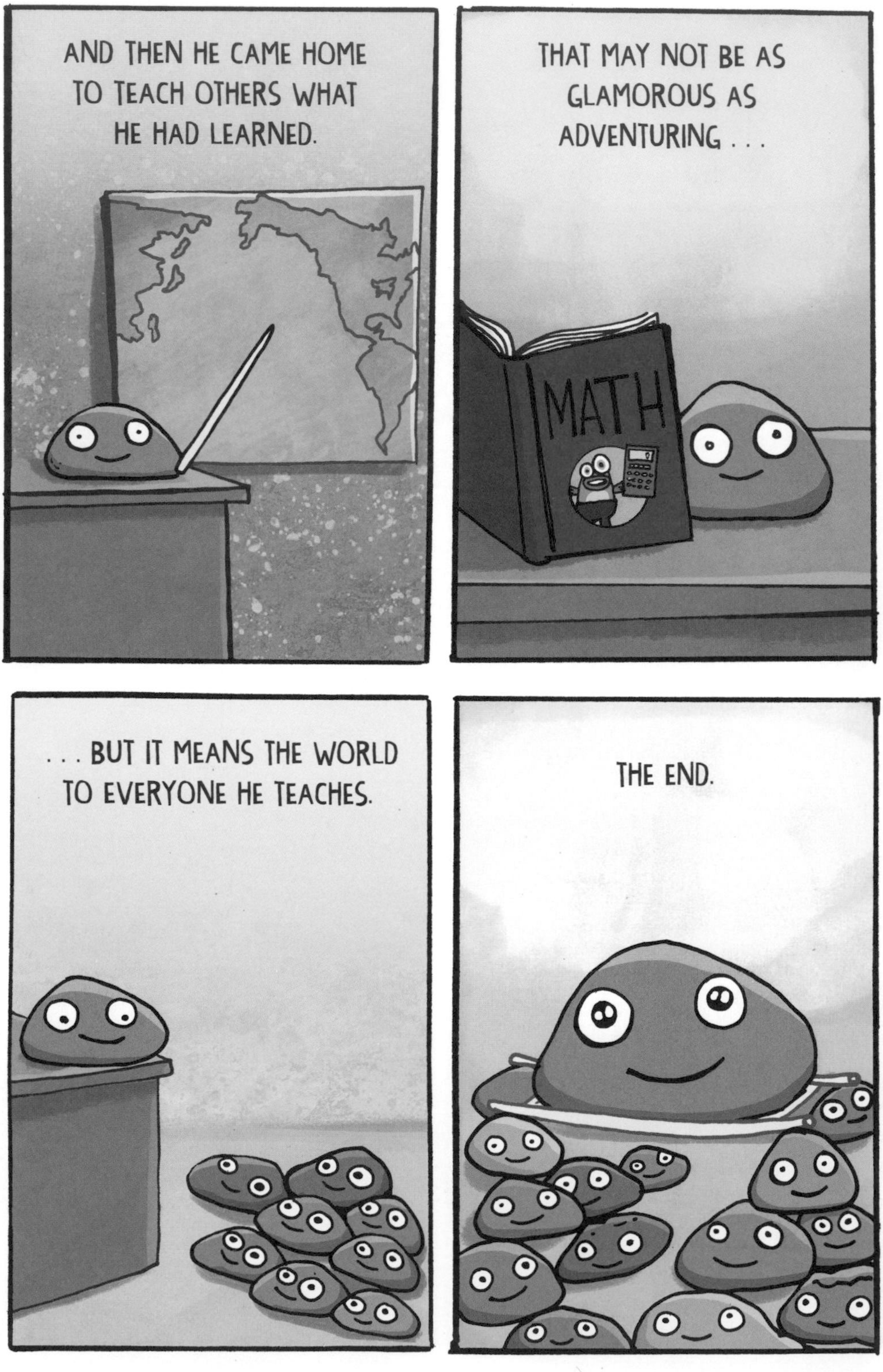
AND THEN HE CAME HOME TO TEACH OTHERS WHAT HE HAD LEARNED.
THAT MAY NOT BE AS GLAMOROUS AS ADVENTURING . . .
MATH
. . . BUT IT MEANS THE WORLD TO EVERYONE HE TEACHES.
THE END.

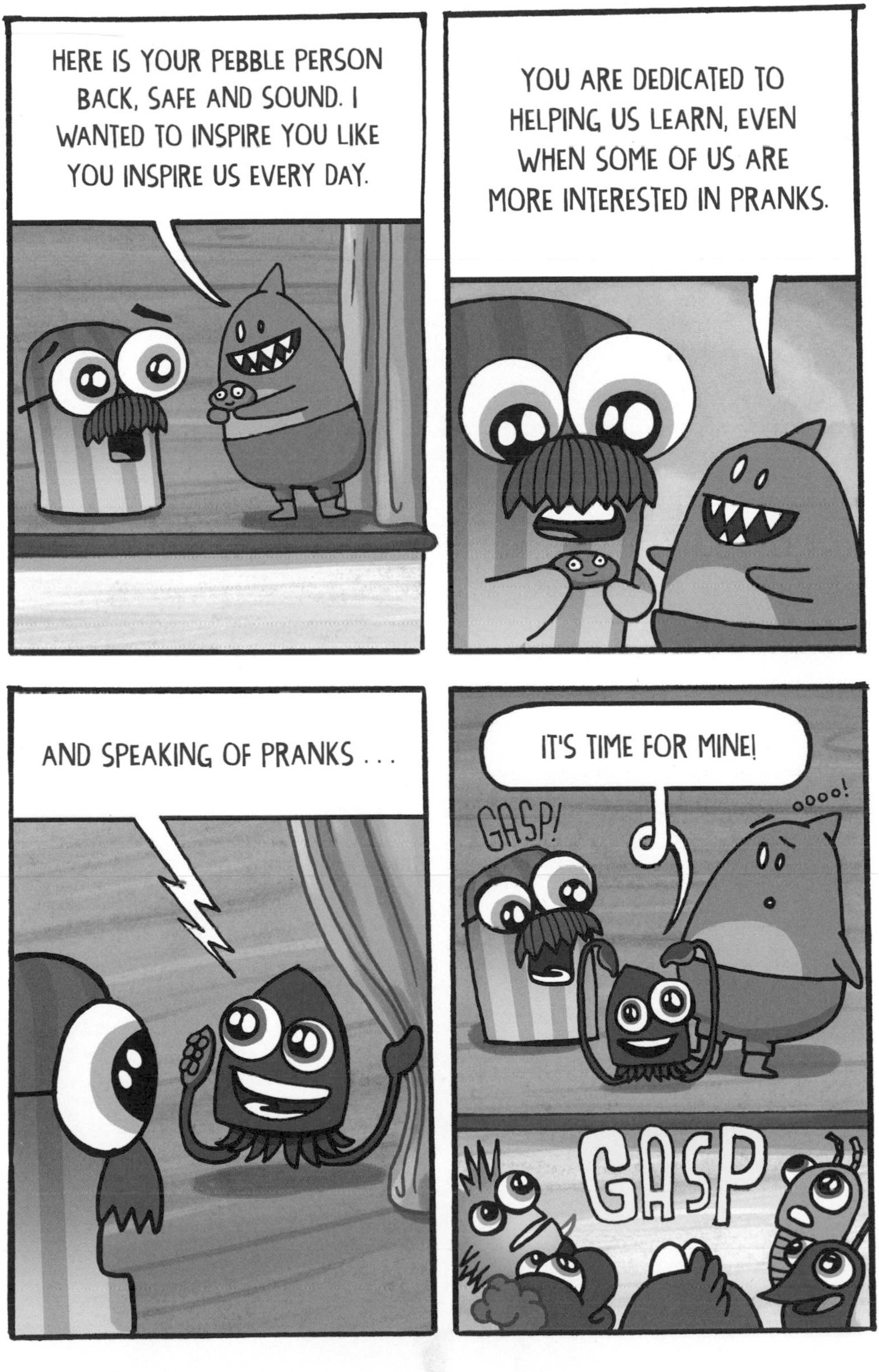
HERE IS YOUR PEBBLE PERSON BACK, SAFE AND SOUND. I WANTED TO INSPIRE YOU LIKE YOU INSPIRE US EVERY DAY.
YOU ARE DEDICATED TO HELPING US LEARN, EVEN WHEN SOME OF US ARE MORE INTERESTED IN PRANKS.
AND SPEAKING OF PRANKS . . .
IT'S TIME FOR MINE!
GASP!
oooo!
GASP

CHAPTER 6

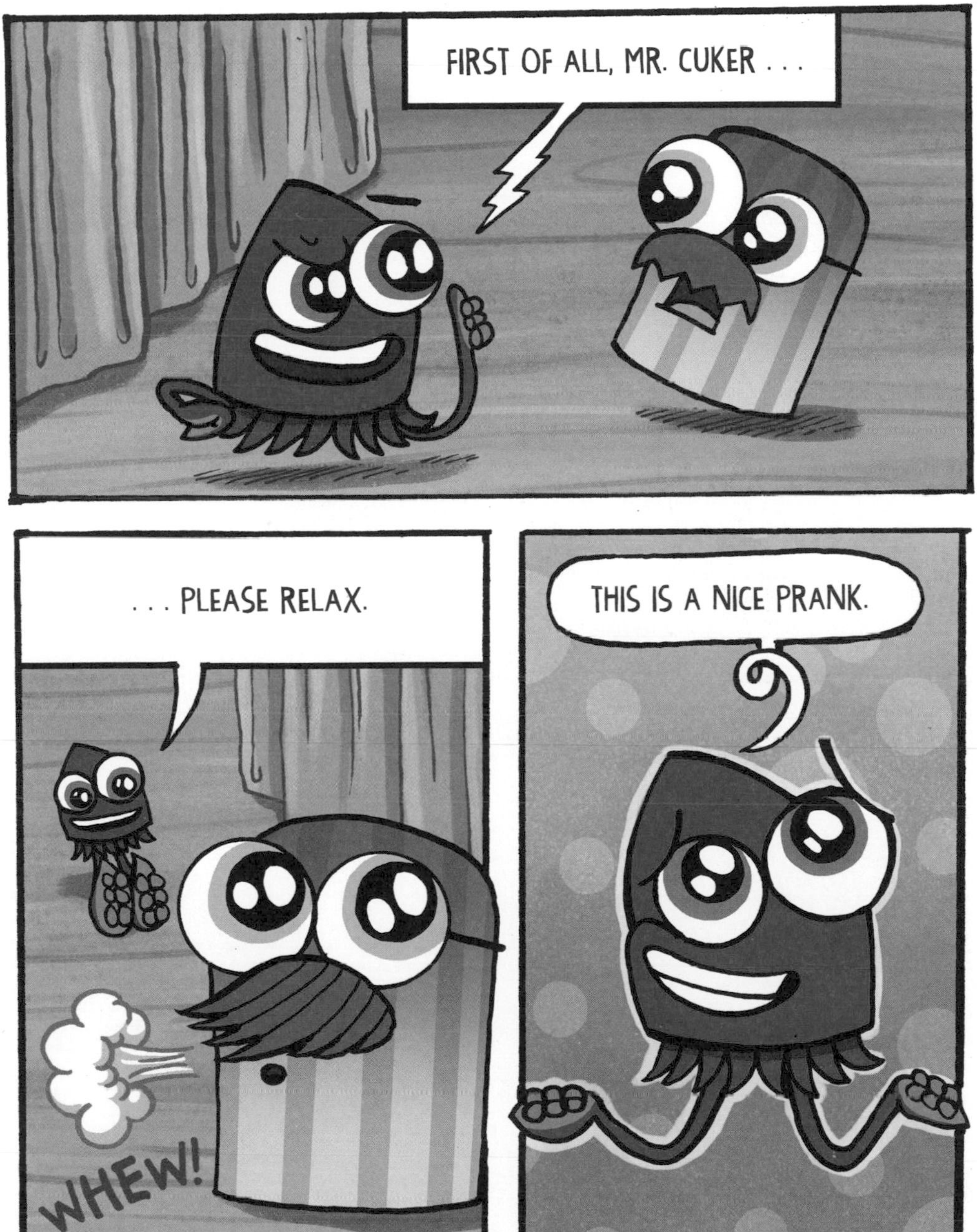
FIRST OF ALL, MR. CUKER . . .
. . . PLEASE RELAX.
WHEW!
THIS IS A NICE PRANK.

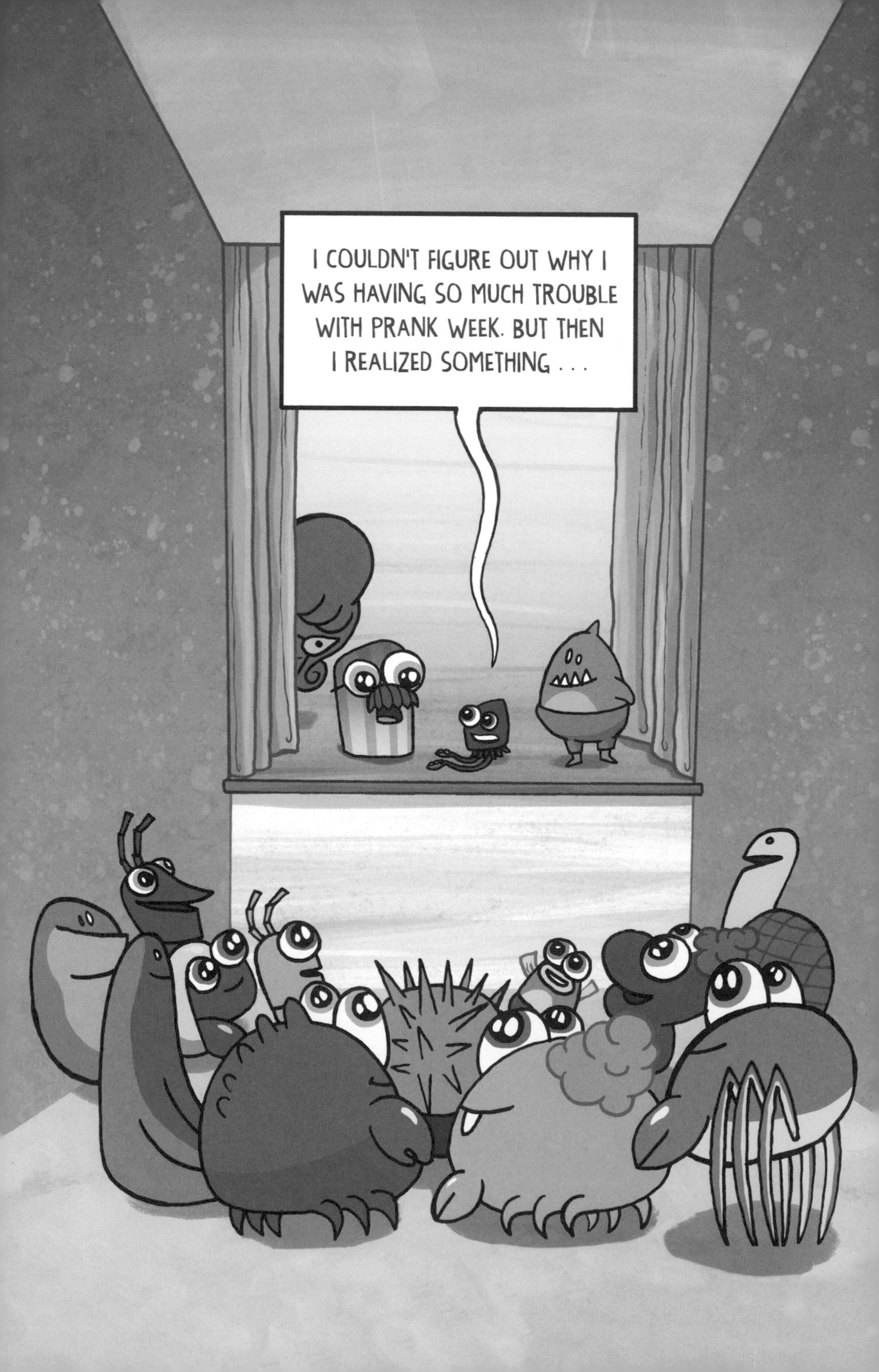
I COULDN'T FIGURE OUT WHY I WAS HAVING SO MUCH TROUBLE WITH PRANK WEEK. BUT THEN I REALIZED SOMETHING . . .

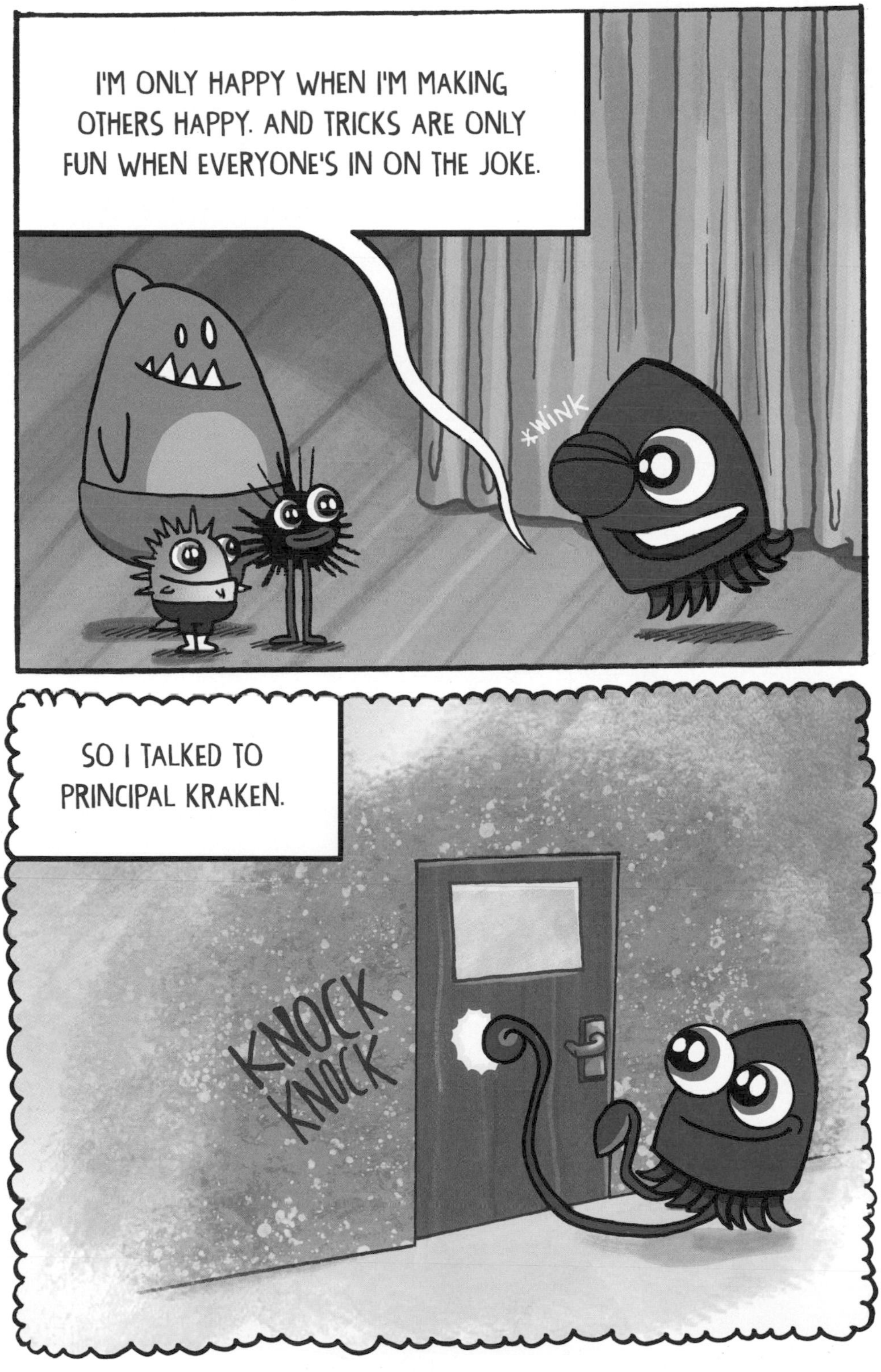
I'M ONLY HAPPY WHEN I'M MAKING OTHERS HAPPY. AND TRICKS ARE ONLY FUN WHEN EVERYONE'S IN ON THE JOKE.
*WINK
SO I TALKED TO PRINCIPAL KRAKEN.
KNOCK KNOCK

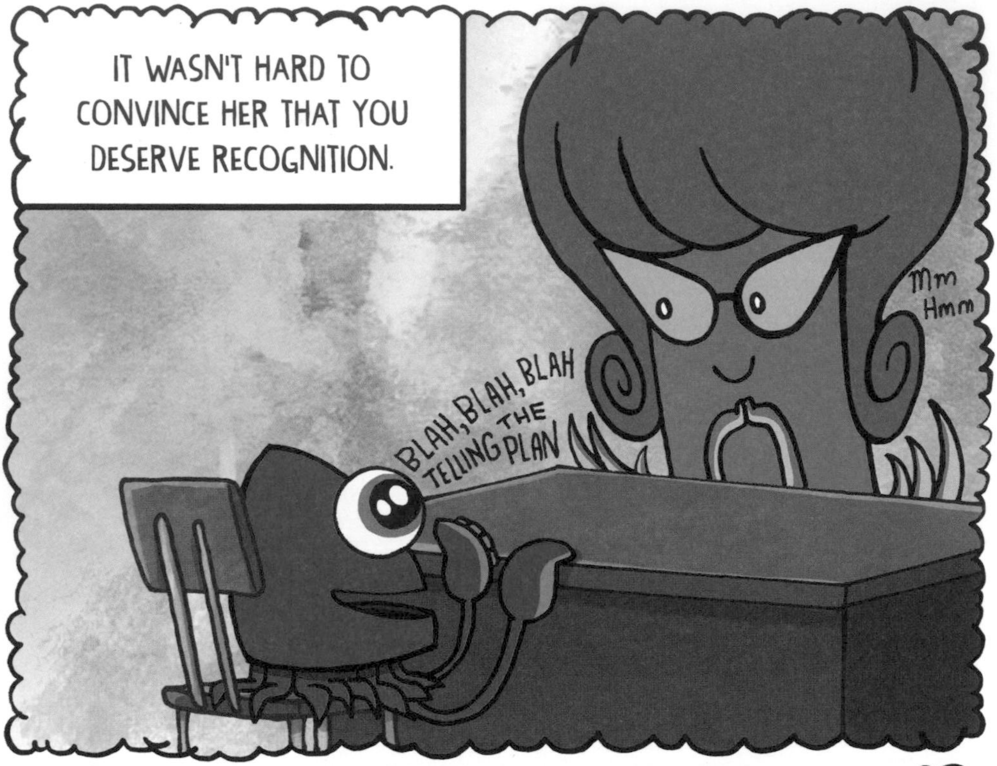
IT WASN'T HARD TO CONVINCE HER THAT YOU DESERVE RECOGNITION.
BLAH, BLAH, BLAH TELLING THE PLAN
Mm Hmm

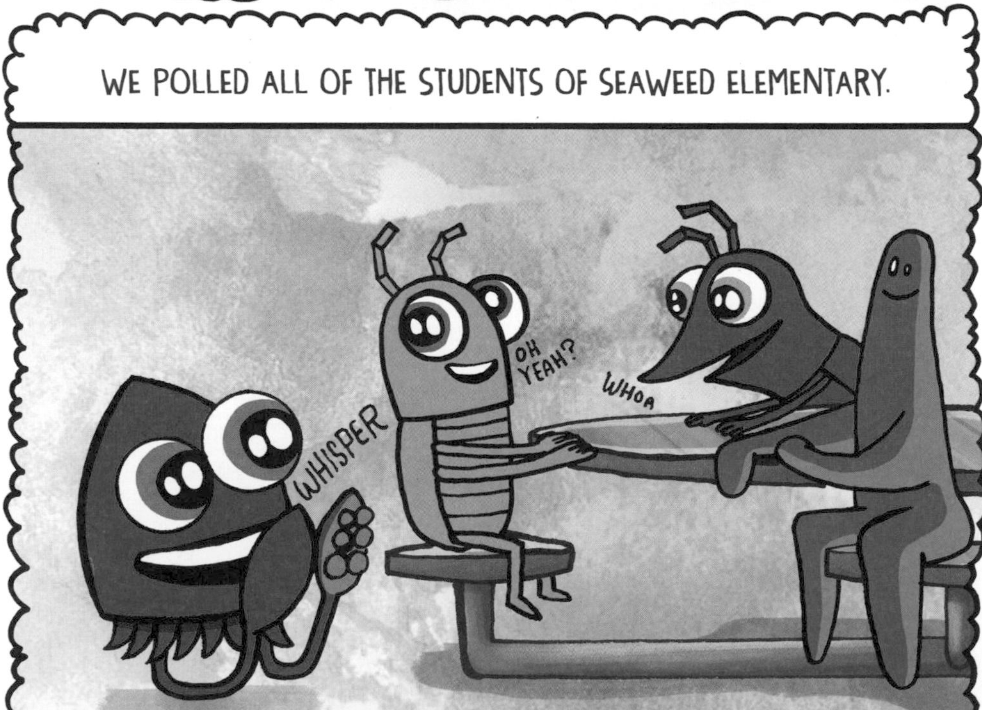
WE POLLED ALL OF THE STUDENTS OF SEAWEED ELEMENTARY.
WHISPER
OH YEAH?
WHOA

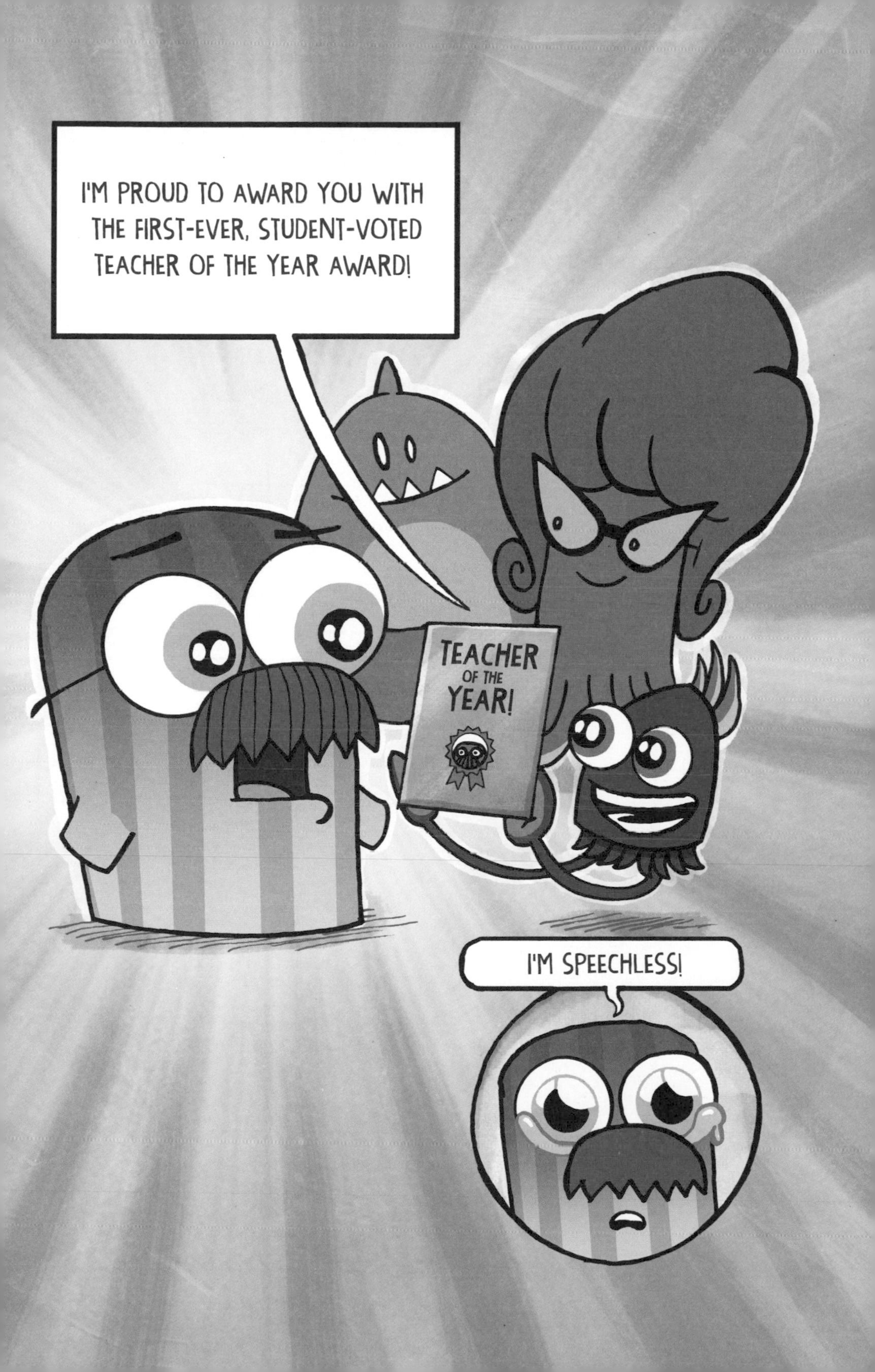
I'M PROUD TO AWARD YOU WITH THE FIRST-EVER, STUDENT-VOTED TEACHER OF THE YEAR AWARD!
TEACHER OF THE YEAR!
I'M SPEECHLESS!

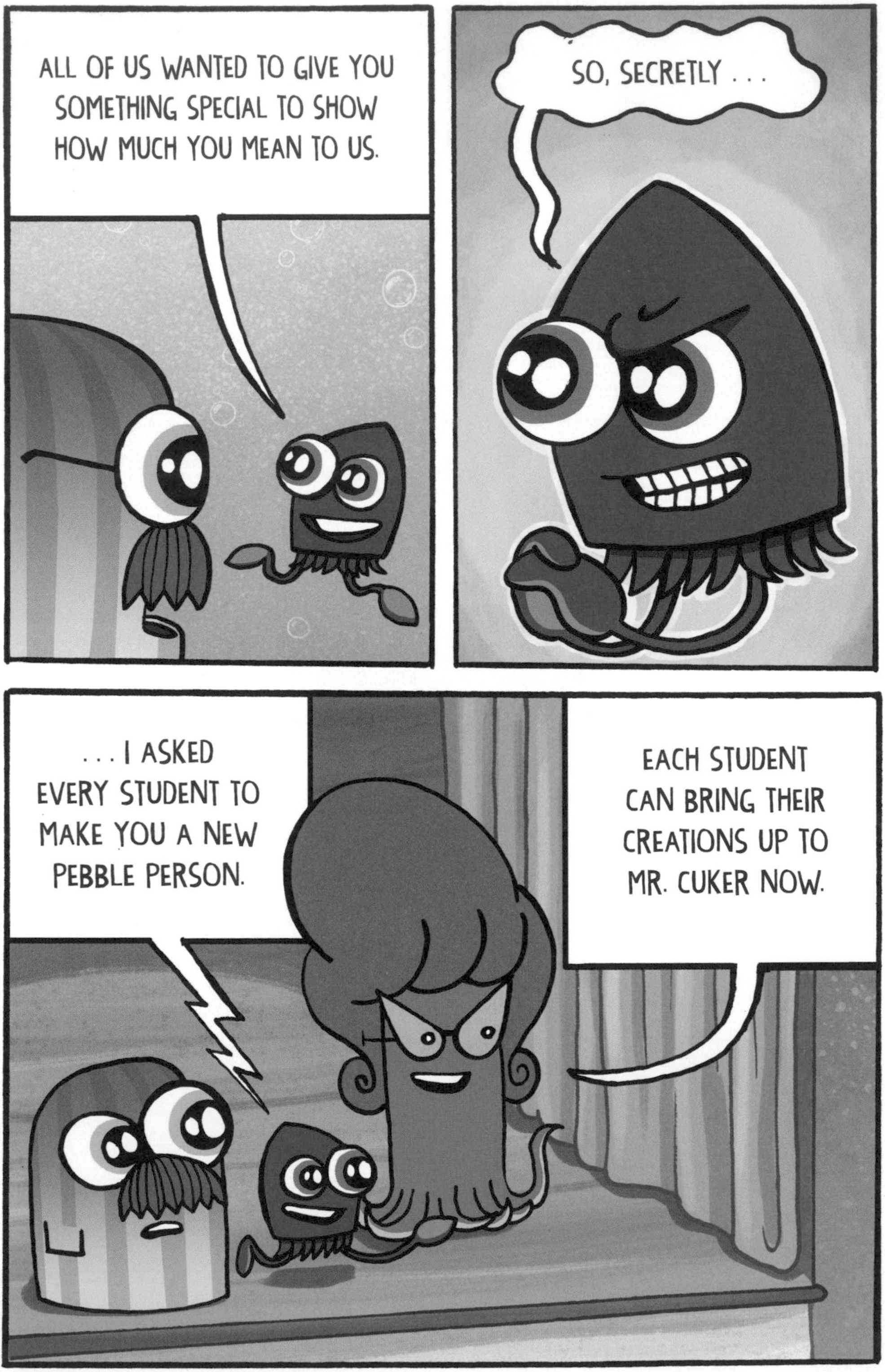
ALL OF US WANTED TO GIVE YOU SOMETHING SPECIAL TO SHOW HOW MUCH YOU MEAN TO US.
SO, SECRETLY . . .
. . . I ASKED EVERY STUDENT TO MAKE YOU A NEW PEBBLE PERSON.
EACH STUDENT CAN BRING THEIR CREATIONS UP TO MR. CUKER NOW.

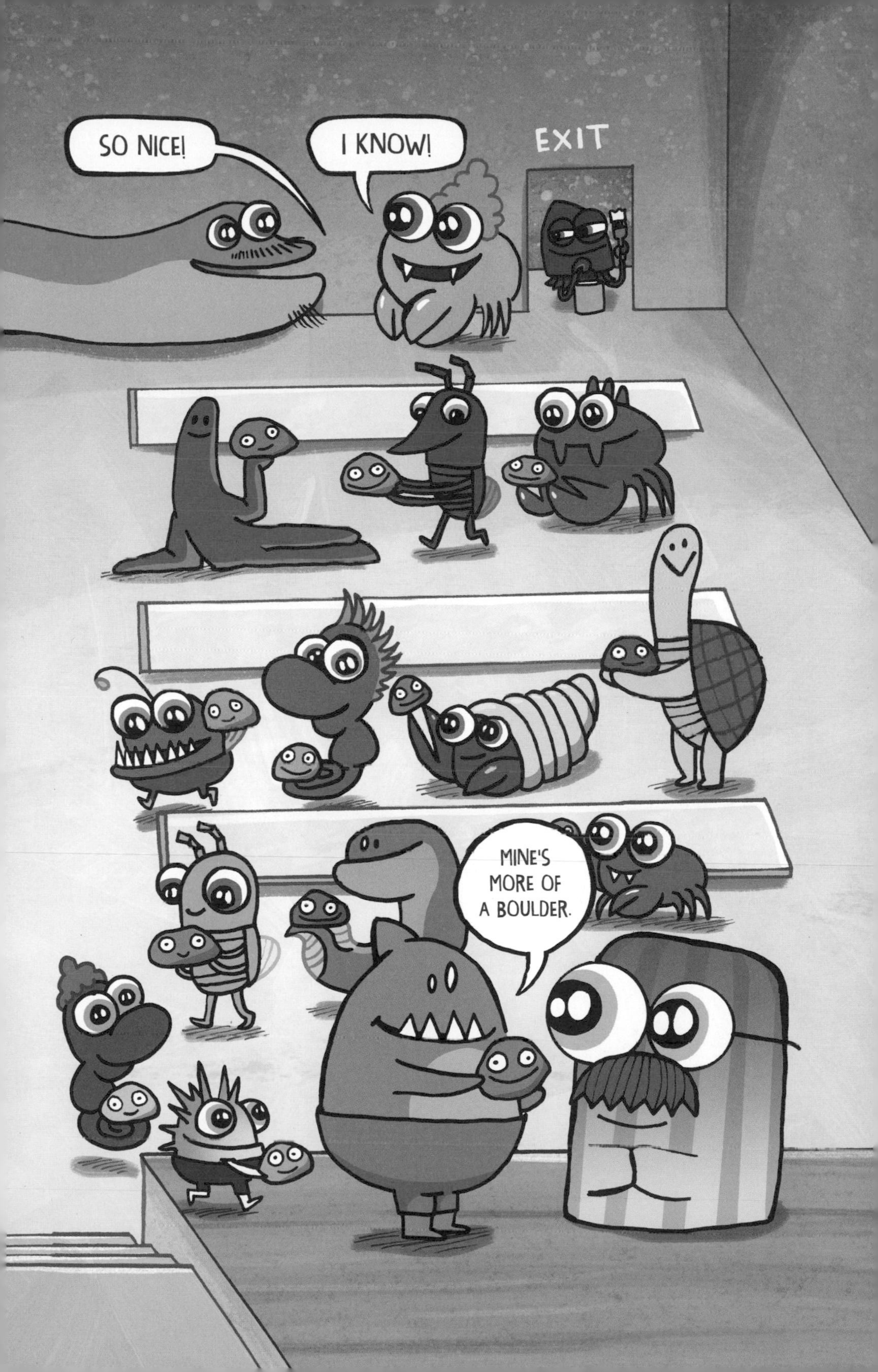
SO NICE!
I KNOW!
EXIT
MINE'S MORE OF A BOULDER.

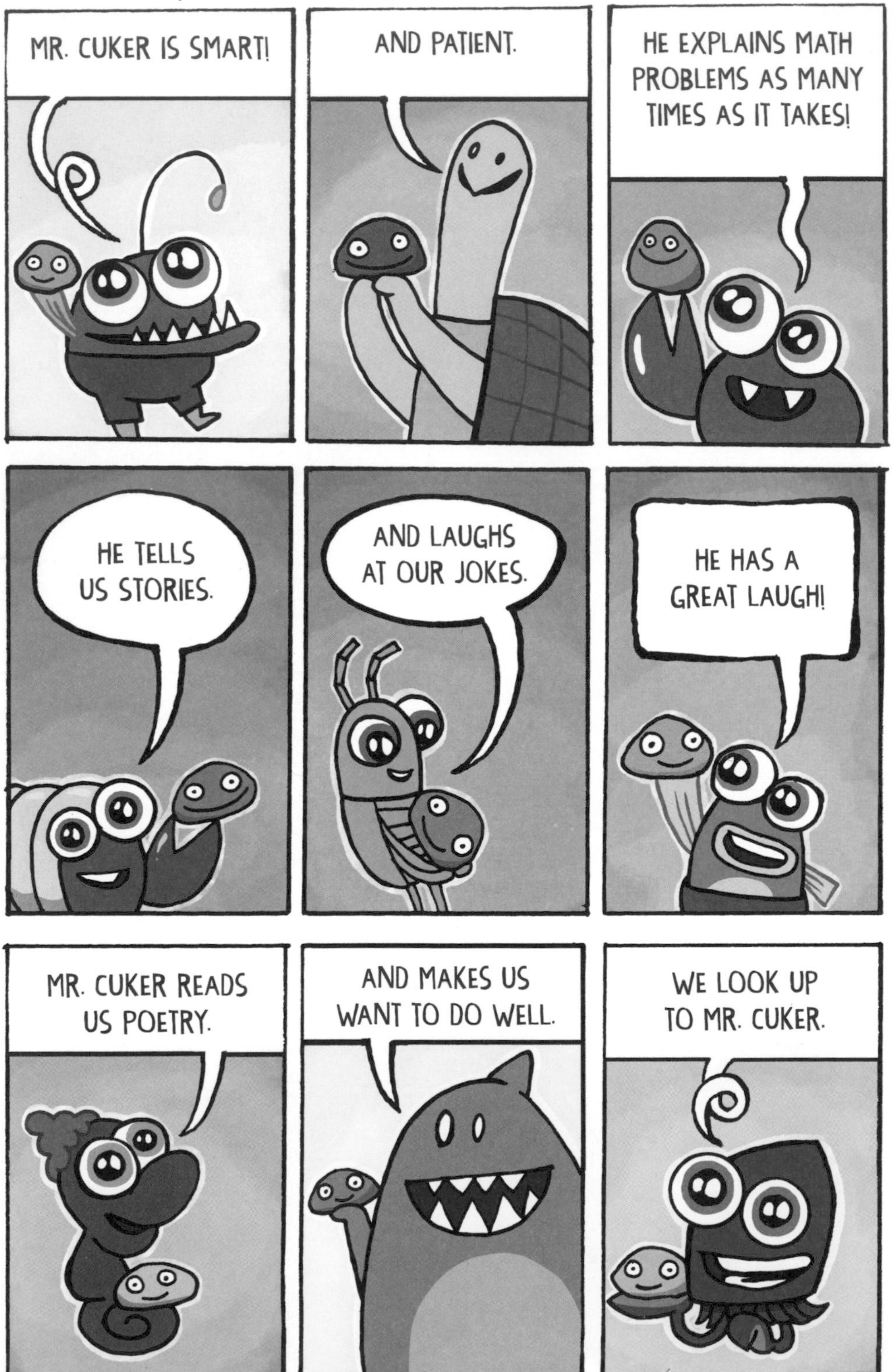
MR. CUKER IS SMART!
AND PATIENT.
HE EXPLAINS MATH PROBLEMS AS MANY TIMES AS IT TAKES!
HE TELLS US STORIES.
AND LAUGHS AT OUR JOKES.
HE HAS A GREAT LAUGH!
MR. CUKER READS US POETRY.
AND MAKES US WANT TO DO WELL.
WE LOOK UP TO MR. CUKER.

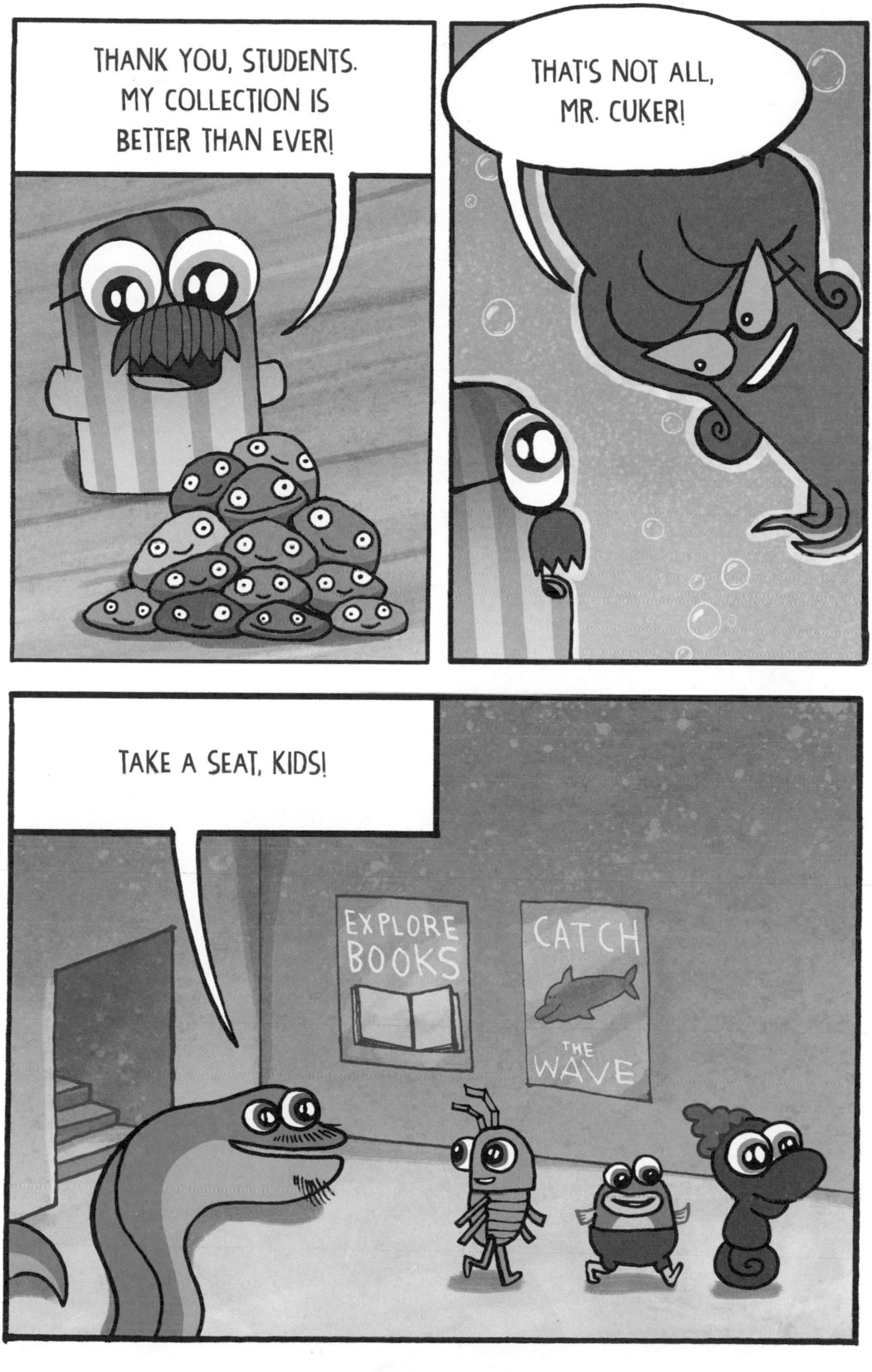
THANK YOU, STUDENTS. MY COLLECTION IS BETTER THAN EVER!
THAT'S NOT ALL, MR. CUKER!
TAKE A SEAT, KIDS!
EXPLORE BOOKS
CATCH THE WAVE

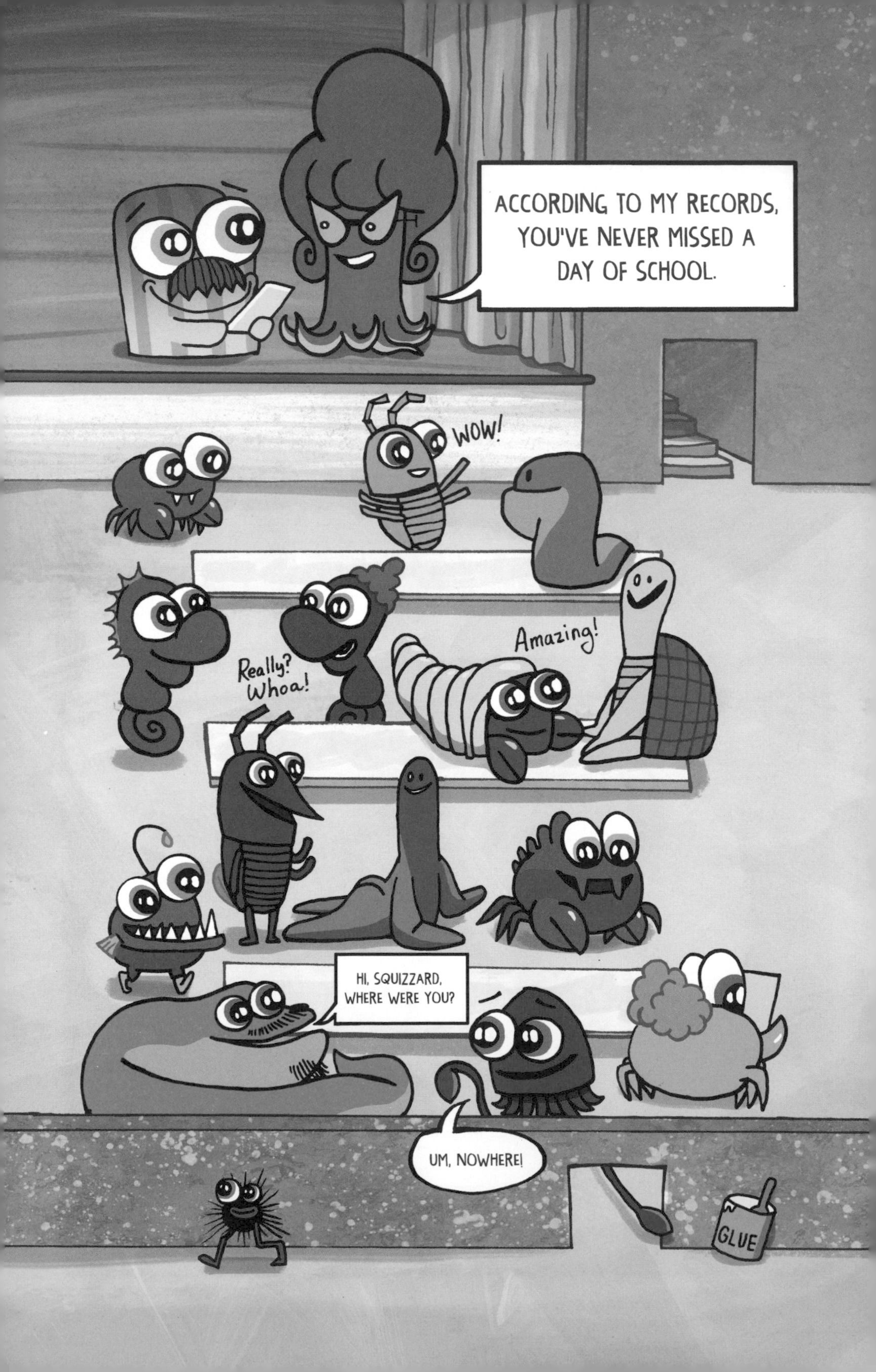
ACCORDING TO MY RECORDS, YOU'VE NEVER MISSED A DAY OF SCHOOL.
WOW!
Really? Whoa!
Amazing!
HI, SQUIZZARD, WHERE WERE YOU?
UM, NOWHERE!
GLUE

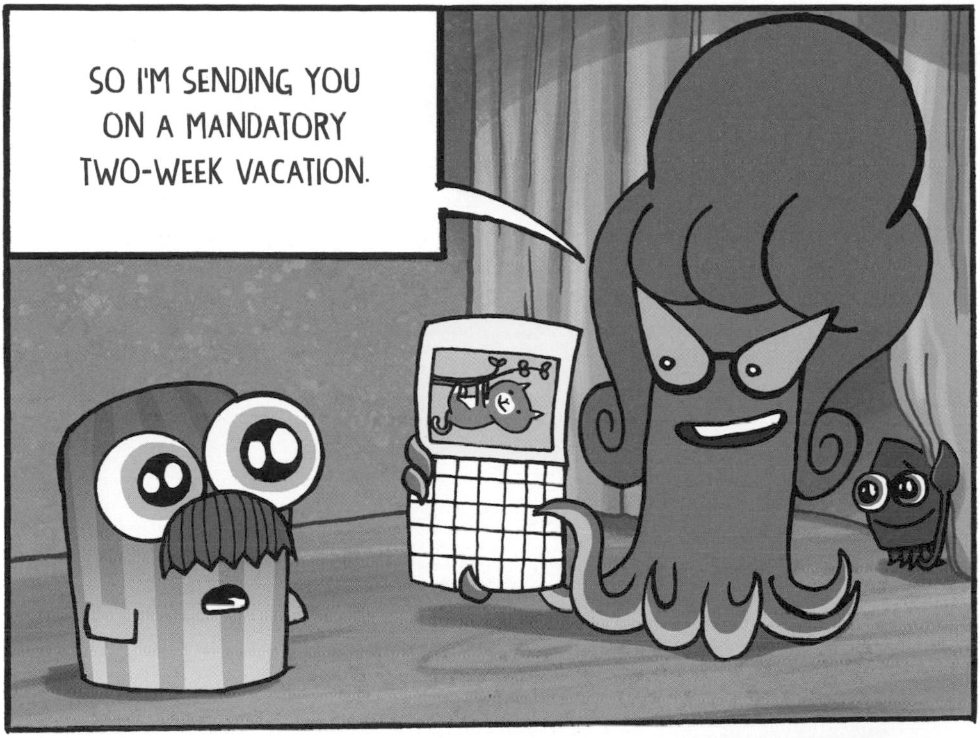
SO I'M SENDING YOU ON A MANDATORY TWO-WEEK VACATION.

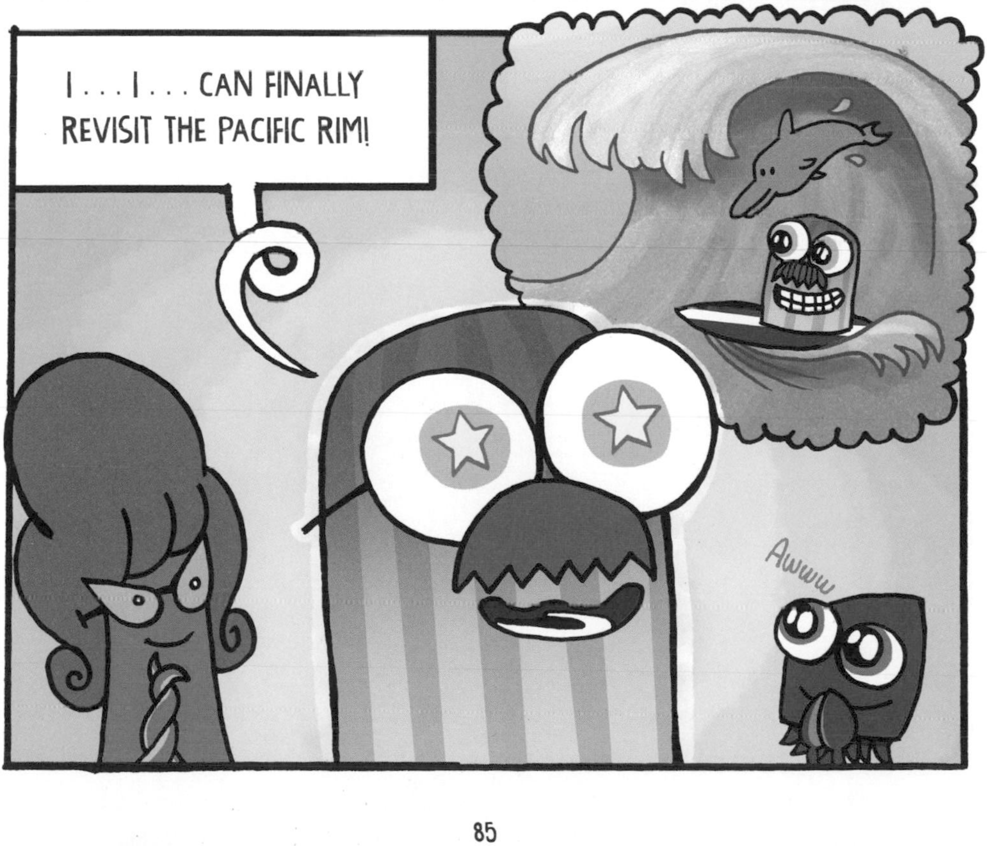
I . . . I . . . CAN FINALLY REVISIT THE PACIFIC RIM!
Awww

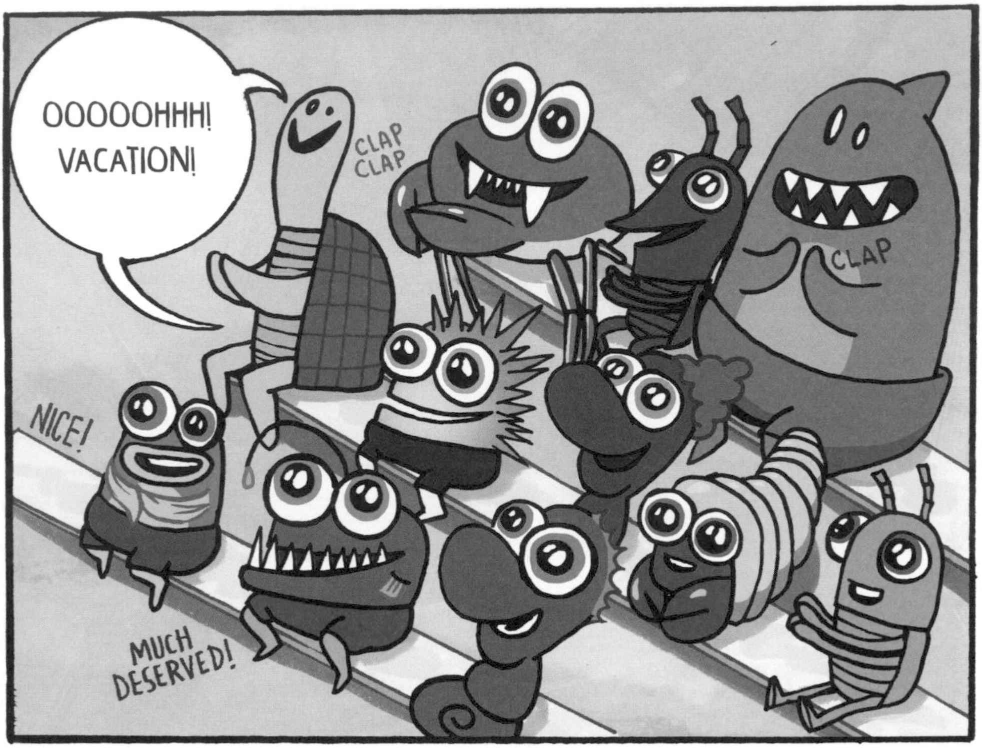
OOOOOHHH! VACATION!
CLAP CLAP
CLAP
NICE!
MUCH DESERVED!

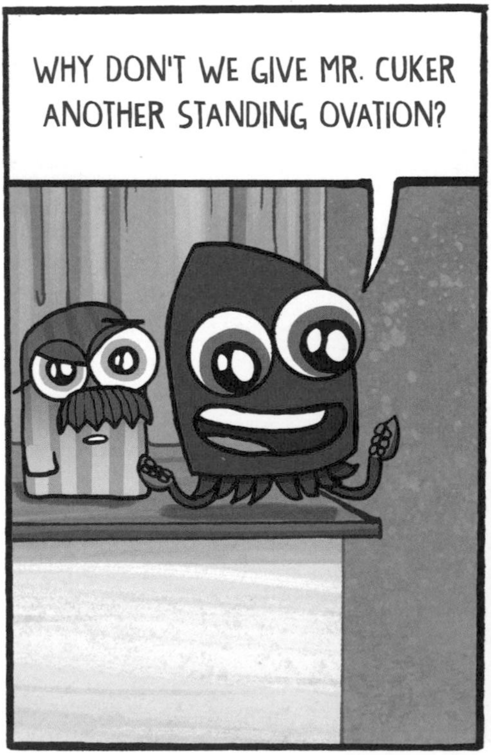
WHY DON'T WE GIVE MR. CUKER ANOTHER STANDING OVATION?

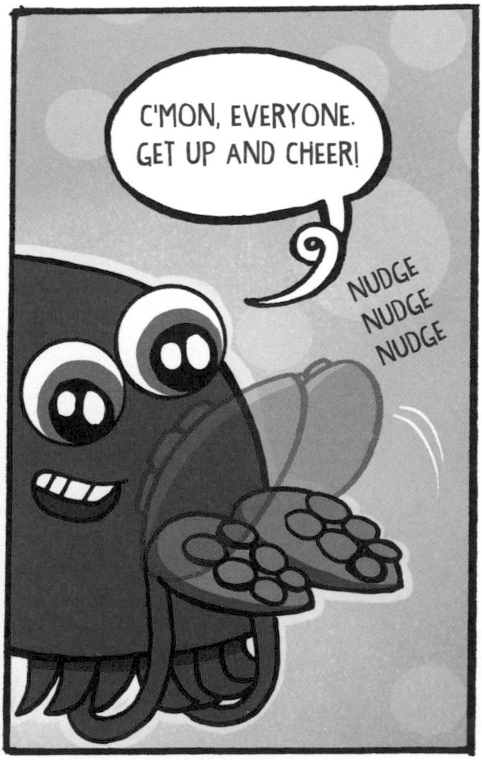
C'MON, EVERYONE. GET UP AND CHEER!
NUDGE NUDGE NUDGE

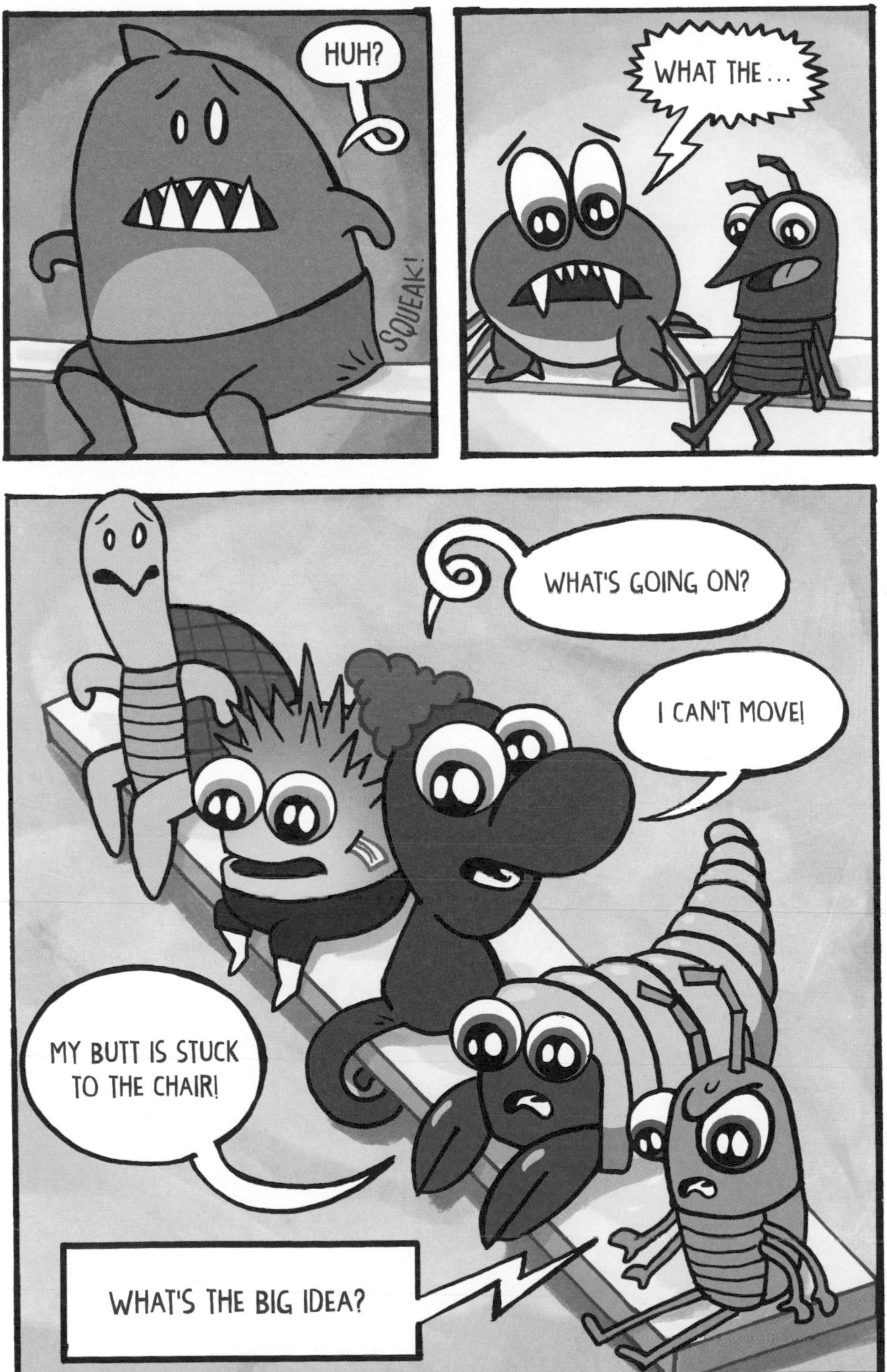
HUH?
SQUEAK!
WHAT THE...
WHAT'S GOING ON?
I CAN'T MOVE!
MY BUTT IS STUCK TO THE CHAIR!
WHAT'S THE BIG IDEA?

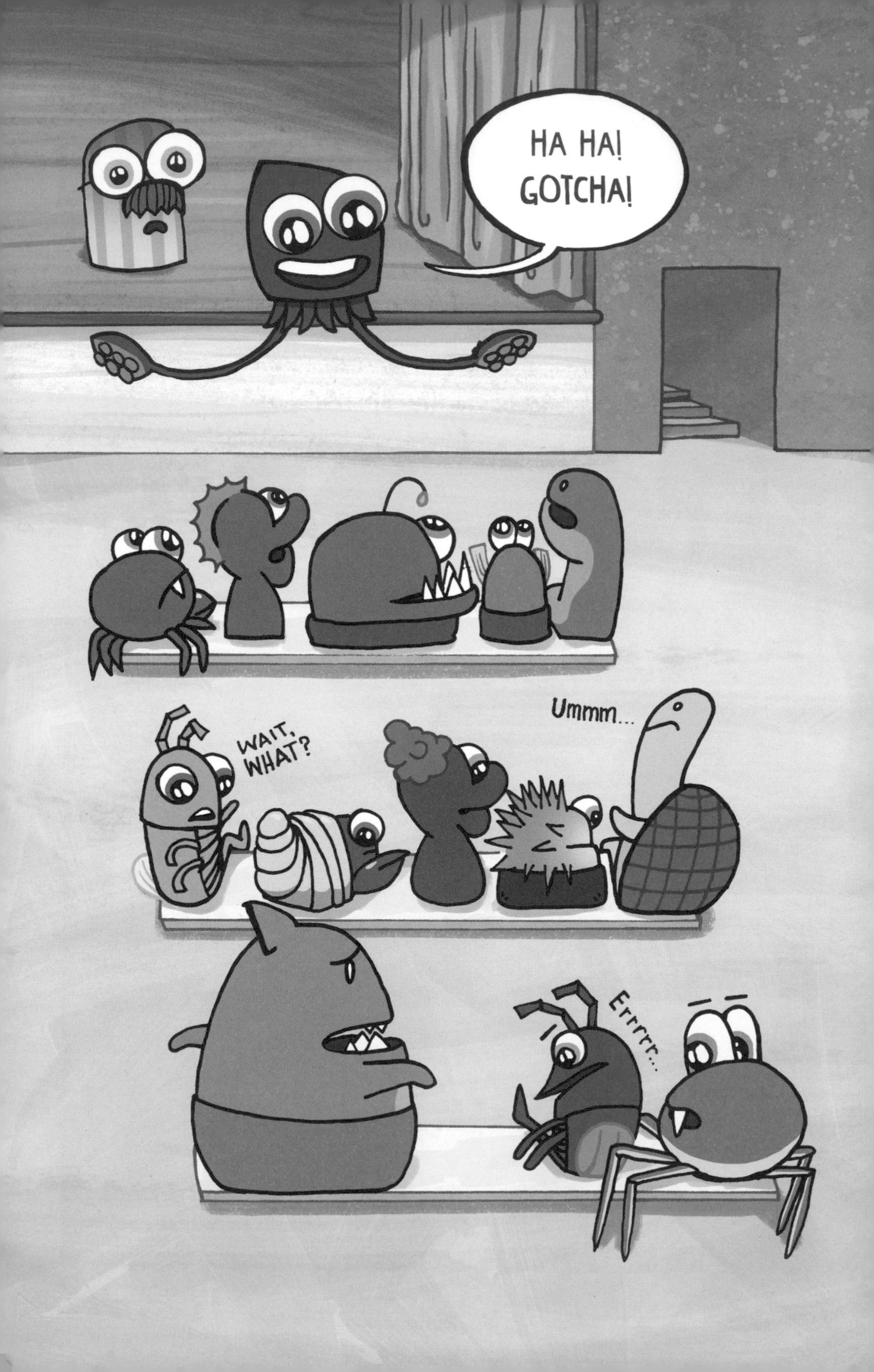
HA HA! GOTCHA!
WAIT, WHAT?
Ummm...
Errrrr...

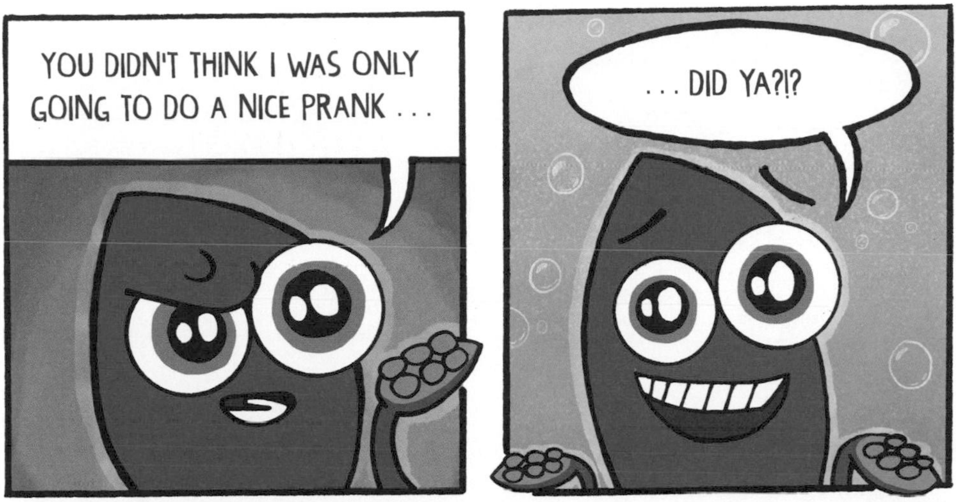
YOU DIDN'T THINK I WAS ONLY GOING TO DO A NICE PRANK . . .
. . . DID YA?!?

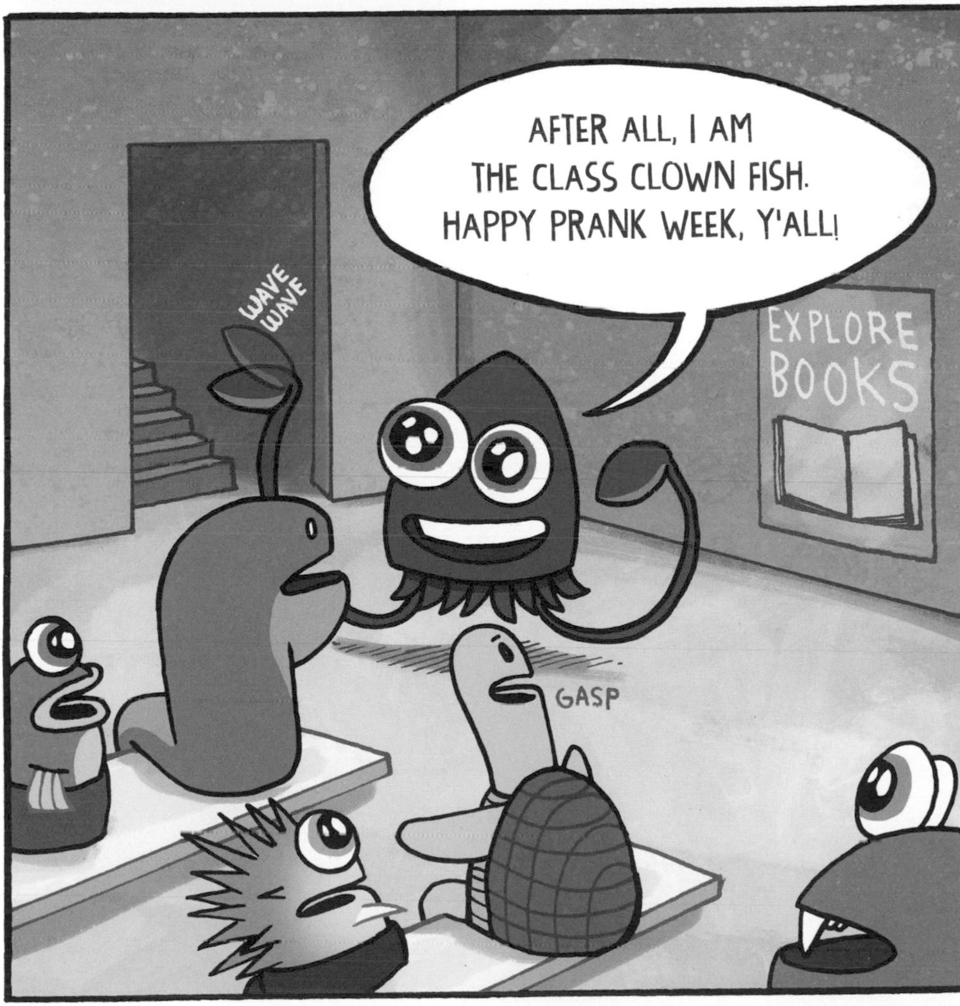
AFTER ALL, I AM THE CLASS CLOWN FISH. HAPPY PRANK WEEK, Y'ALL!
WAVE WAVE
EXPLORE BOOKS
GASP

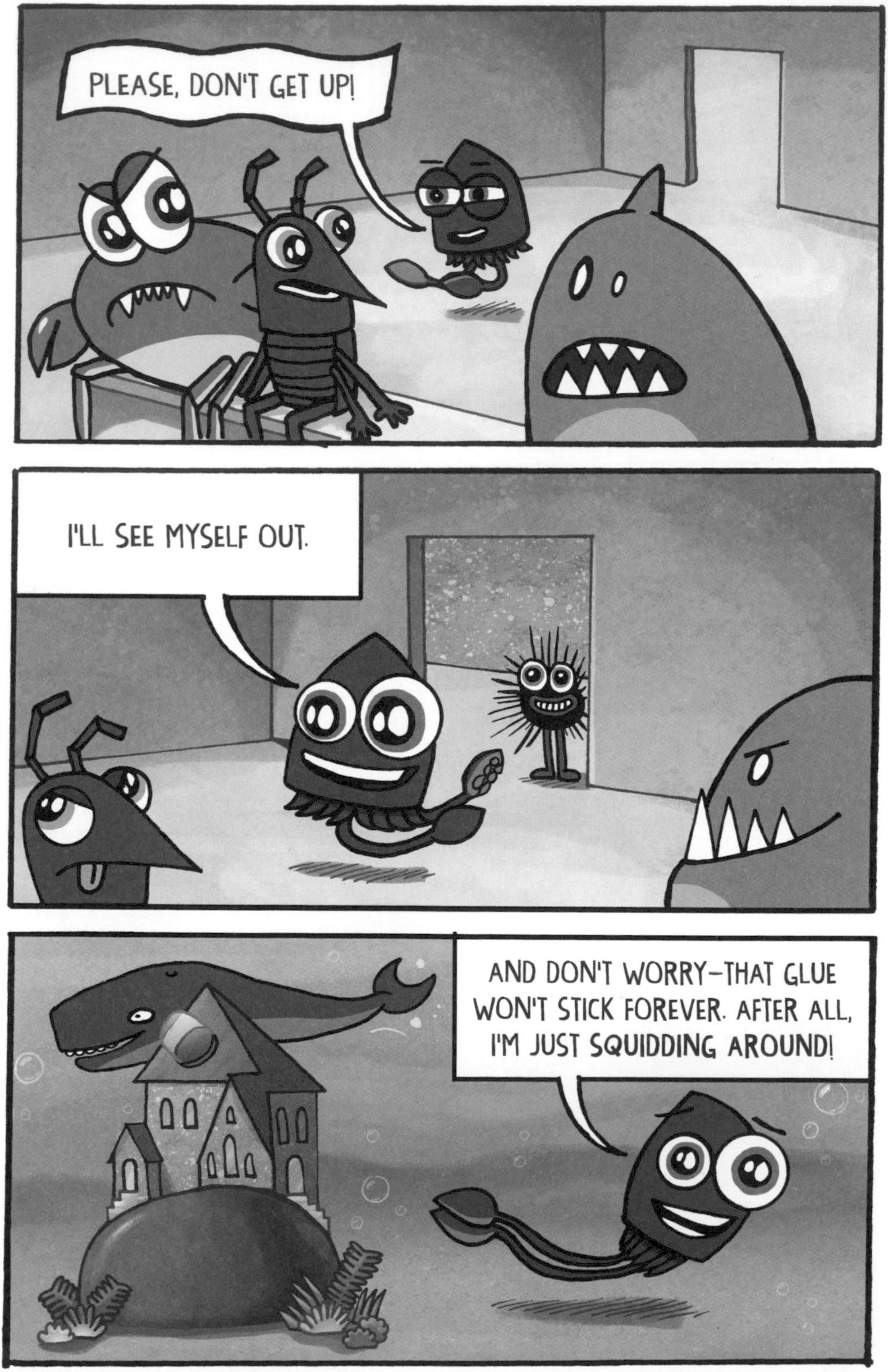
PLEASE, DON'T GET UP!
I'LL SEE MYSELF OUT.
AND DON'T WORRY—THAT GLUE WON'T STICK FOREVER. AFTER ALL, I'M JUST SQUIDDING AROUND!

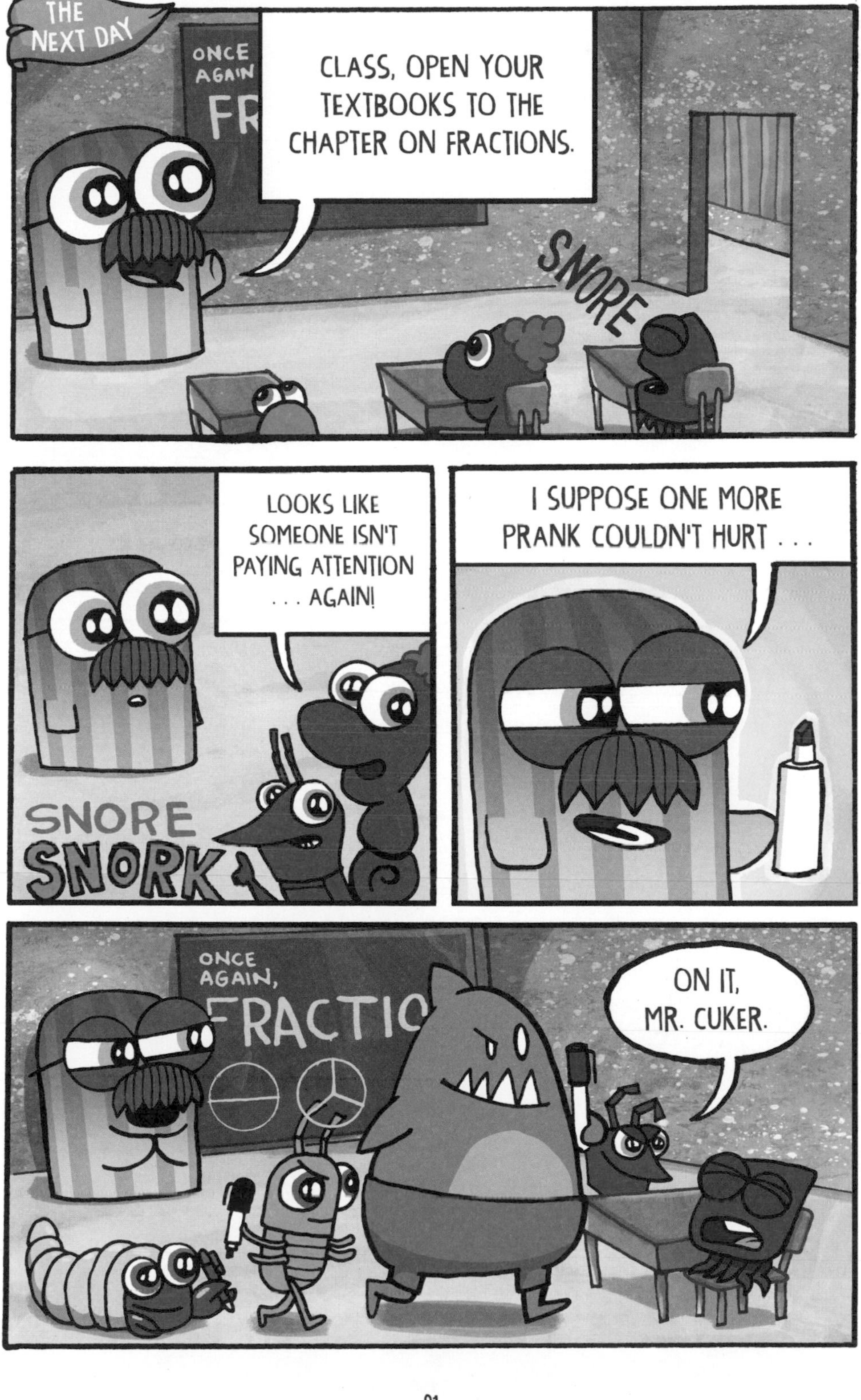
THE NEXT DAY
ONCE AGAIN FR
CLASS, OPEN YOUR TEXTBOOKS TO THE CHAPTER ON FRACTIONS.
SNORE
LOOKS LIKE SOMEONE ISN'T PAYING ATTENTION . . . AGAIN!
SNORE
SNORK
I SUPPOSE ONE MORE PRANK COULDN'T HURT . . .
ONCE AGAIN, FRACTIO
ON IT, MR. CUKER.

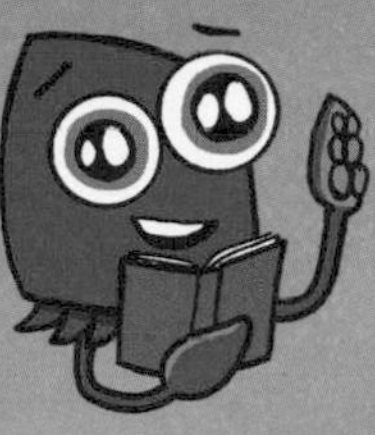

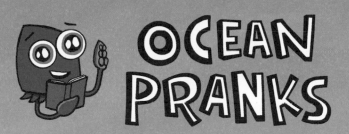

OCEAN PRANKS

To survive under the sea, some animals play tricks to hide from predators. They camouflage (KA-muh-flahj) themselves, changing their appearance to hide in plain sight by blending into their surroundings. Here are a few of their best tricks:

Decorator crabs have tiny hooks all over their bodies that act like Velcro for the rocks, coral, seaweed, and even other small animals they use to disguise themselves.

Some flounders, cuttlefish, squid, and octopi can change the color of their skin to match the seafloor.

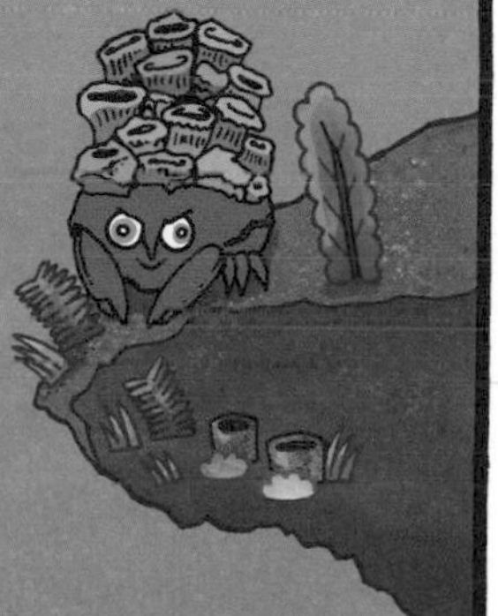

The leafy sea dragon has limbs that look like algae, making it hard to spot.

It's no wonder Squizzard and his friends are such pranksters!

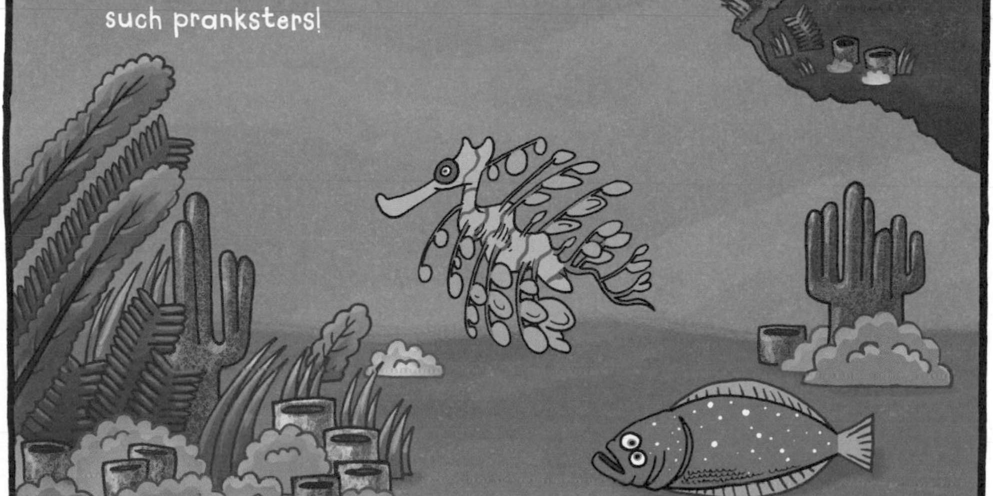

KEVIN SHERRY is the author and illustrator of many children's picture books, most notably The Yeti Files and Remy Sneakers series and the picture book I'M THE BIGGEST THING IN THE OCEAN, which received starred reviews and won an original artwork award from the Society of Illustrators. He's a man of many interests: a chef, an avid cyclist and screen printer, and a performer of hilarious puppet shows for kids and adults. Kevin lives in Baltimore, Maryland.

ACKNOWLEDGMENTS

Thanks to my wife Erin for her encouragement, to Rachel Orr for her expertise, and to Mom, Dad, Brian, Margie, Amelia, and Aidrian. And a very special thanks to Dan Deacon, a person who pulled off one of the biggest pranks of all time, and who I have also pranked many times. Huge thanks to Wes Dzioba for the lush vaporwave colors throughout our books.

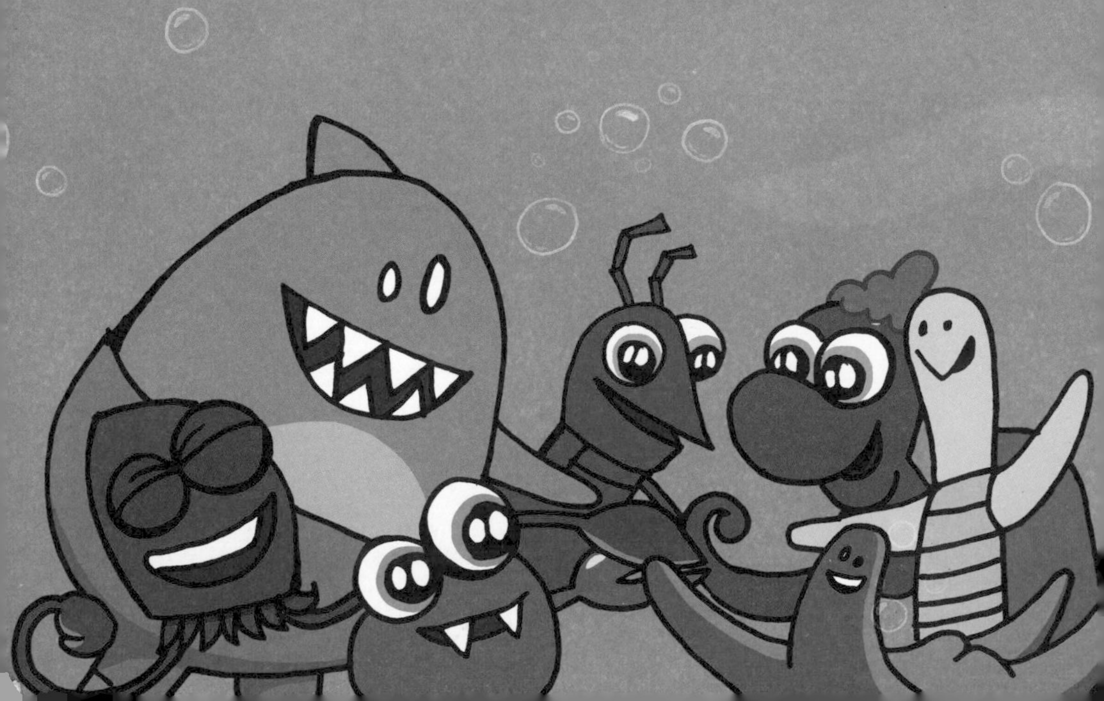